LAY THIS BODY DOWN

A GIDEON STOLTZ MYSTERY

CHARLES FERGUS

ARCADE
CRIMEWISE

An Arcade CrimeWise Book

Other books in the series:

A Stranger Here Below: A Gideon Stoltz Mystery
Nighthawk's Wing: A Gideon Stoltz Mystery

First Arcade CrimeWise Edition

This is a work of fiction. Names, places, characters, and incidents are either the products of the author's imagination or are used fictitiously.

Arcade Publishing books may be purchased in bulk at special discounts for sales promotion, corporate gifts, fund-raising, or educational purposes. Special editions can also be created to specifications. For details, contact the Special Sales Department, Arcade Publishing, 307 West 36th Street, 11th Floor, New York, NY 10018 or arcade@skyhorsepublishing.com.

Arcade Publishing® and CrimeWise® are registered trademarks of Skyhorse Publishing, Inc.®, a Delaware corporation.

Visit our website at www.arcadepub.com.

10 9 8 7 6 5 4 3 2 1

Library of Congress Cataloging-in-Publication Data is available on file.

Cover design by Erin Seaward-Hiatt
Cover artwork: Slava Gerj/Shutterstock
Map created by Claire Van Vliet

ISBN: 978-1-956763-44-7
Ebook ISBN: 978-1-956763-45-4

Printed in the United States of America

This novel is dedicated to James Pembrook, David Walton, Mehlon Hopewell, George Stewart, James Myers, Sophia Gordon, and all the other people who risked their lives fleeing to Pennsylvania to escape slavery.

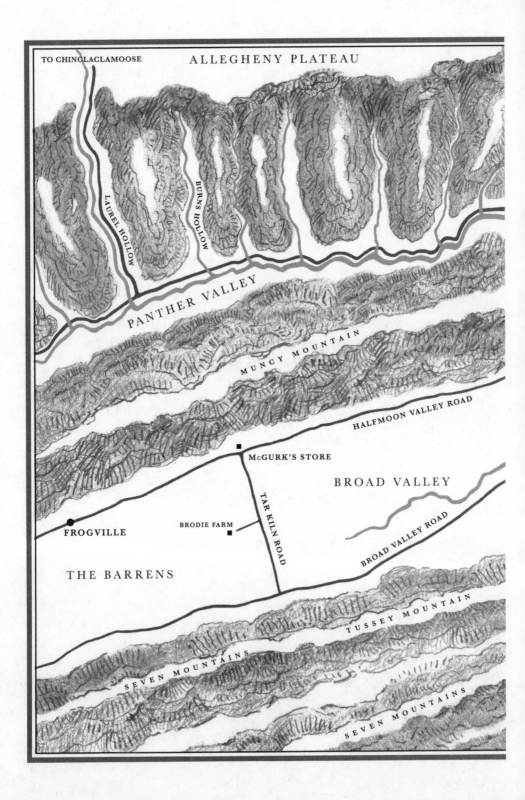

TO CHINGLACLAMOOSE

ALLEGHENY PLATEAU

LAUREL HOLLOW

BURNS HOLLOW

PANTHER VALLEY

MUNCY MOUNTAIN

HALFMOON VALLEY ROAD

McGURK'S STORE

BROAD VALLEY

TAR KILN ROAD

FROGVILLE

BRODIE FARM

BROAD VALLEY ROAD

THE BARRENS

TUSSEY MOUNTAIN

SEVEN MOUNTAINS

SEVEN MOUNTAINS

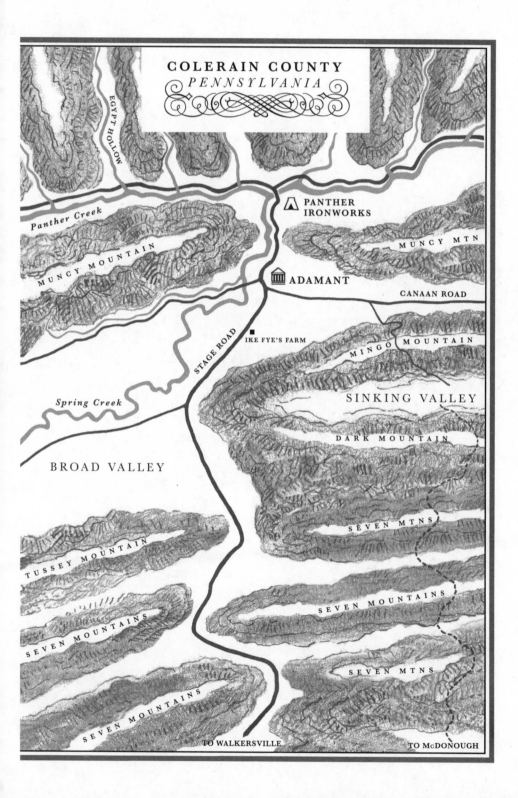

One cold freezing morning
I lay this body down

African American spiritual

Author's Note

———✦———

A HISTORICAL NOVEL SHOULD BE TRUE TO THE TIME AND PLACE IT depicts: in this case, central Pennsylvania in 1837. Fifty-seven years earlier, in 1780, Pennsylvania had passed a law abolishing slavery. In their quest to be free, enslaved African Americans from Maryland, Virginia, and other Southern states made their way into Pennsylvania and might have passed through or taken up residence in a backwoods town like my fictional Adamant, some eighty miles north of the Maryland border.

I have begun the book's chapters with short passages from actual newspaper advertisements and printed notices placing bounties on the heads of people who fled slavery.

In these ads, and in day-to-day speech, the words used to describe African Americans in the early nineteenth century included "black," "negro," "colored," and others, including some I've chosen not to use.

Black generally meant a person of full or almost-full African descent.

Negro, from the Spanish or Portuguese word for the color black, meant a dark-skinned person. Its use in print with a capital *N* did not become general until the early twentieth century.

Colored referred to a person with both black and white ancestors. David Walker, a prominent African American anti-slavery activist in Boston, used it in the title of his 1829 manifesto, *Walker's Appeal in Four Articles: Together with a Preamble to the Colored Citizens of the World, but in Particular, and Very Expressly, to Those of the United States of America.*

A *mulatto* had one white and one black parent; a *quadroon* was the child of a mulatto and a white; and an *octoroon* was the child of a quadroon and a white. Such people were all considered to be "colored" and not white.

The fugitive ads are shocking reminders of the cruelty and brutality toward African Americans that was widely accepted in the United States in the 1830s. As well as being desperate, the people who fled must have been courageous beyond reckoning to have faced the hardships that awaited them when they embarked on their journeys into an unknown and often hostile terrain. We can only hope that they ultimately found freedom.

TWO HUNDRED DOLLARS REWARD. My servant David, who calls himself David Walton, had permission to visit his wife, belonging to Arthur West, Esq. near the Wood Yard; since then he has been absent, and I have every reason to believe he has made for Pennsylvania.

Chapter 1

———— ❧ ————

GIDEON STOLTZ, THE COLERAIN COUNTY SHERIFF, LOOKED OUT over the crowded church pews. He spotted his deputy across the sanctuary doing the same.

The speaker that evening was a young white man clad in a suit whose sleeves and pant legs were too short for his gangling limbs. Brown hair hung in ringlets to his shoulders, and a reddish-brown beard came halfway down his chest.

His voice, deeper and more powerful than his reedy body suggested, filled the church:

"I have sworn to God! I have sworn to THE GREAT GOD ALMIGHTY that I will not cut one lock of my hair, nor a strand of my beard, until the ABOMINATION THAT IS SLAVERY has ended!"

As if to emphasize the point, he gave his hirsute head a shake.

He aimed a finger at his audience. "TWO MILLION SEVEN HUNDRED THOUSAND SLAVES IN THE LAND!" He strode from one side of the platform to the other, then spun about to face his audience again. "YOU! AND I! Here in the North, ALL OF US benefit from slavery as much as do the slaveholders in the South! Our banks loan their lucre to investors in the South. Those same banks accept slaves—ENSLAVED HUMAN BEINGS!—as collateral for loans. We sell our goods and products in the South, letting slaveholders expand their wicked empire westward, planting more cotton and rice and cane—all worked by slaves toiling under an overseer's lash. We eat rice from the South! We sweeten our coffee with sugar from the South! Our mills weave THEIR COTTON, SOUTHERN COTTON, into cloth!"

"Adamant has no cotton mill!" someone shouted from the audience.

"Just as we enjoy the fruits of slavery, so will their bitterness choke us! Slavery is a sin foul as the crater pool of hell. It must end, I tell you. And if we do not end it, SLAVERY WILL TEAR THIS NATION APART!"

Earlier Gideon had been hurriedly introduced to the speaker, one Charles C. Burleigh, of Brooklyn, Connecticut, on a lecture tour of Pennsylvania towns. Burleigh had identified himself as one of "the Seventy," a cadre of young men dispatched across the country by the famed abolitionist orator Theodore Dwight Weld. Gideon had read about Weld in the newspaper: the man had spoken out against slavery so often and so vociferously that he had ruined his vocal cords.

Burleigh might be on the way to losing his voice, too, Gideon thought.

"They say the negroes are HAPPY in the South, HAPPY in their enslavement!" Burleigh thundered. "That they are CONTENT! I ask you, then, WHY DO SO MANY OF THEM RUN? Do you read the fugitive notices? Do you consider the brutality they convey? 'MUCH SCARRED WITH THE WHIP!' 'LEFT EAR CROPPED!' 'BRANDED ON THE RIGHT BREAST!'"

Another cry from the audience: "There are no slaves in Adamant!"

"Do you read the notices? Or do you look away? YOU CANNOT LOOK AWAY! THERE CAN BE NO LOOKING AWAY! There can be no neutrality toward slavery, no indifference! Each and every one of us is guilty—GUILTY!—if we fail to demand its immediate abolition!"

A man in the audience stood and called out: "Why do you come here and agitate?" Gideon recognized him as the owner of one of the town's banks: his belly like a stuffed grain sack, a red face with pouchy cheeks and a habitual frown. "You're nothing but a reckless fool!"

Another man rose, pulled back his arm, and whipped it forward. Something sailed through the air and hit Burleigh in the chest. A corncob.

Burleigh smiled and raised his hands.

More men in the audience jumped up. Corncobs flew, some finding their mark. A din of shouted objections. Women hissed— whether at the throwers or the abolitionist, Gideon couldn't tell.

When a rotten apple struck Burleigh in the shoulder, splattering his coat and making him stagger backward, Gideon strode to the platform. His deputy, Alonzo Bell, joined him.

"Enough!" Gideon shouted. "That's enough." He and Alonzo stood flanking the abolitionist. A man from the audience came down the aisle and joined them: tall lanky Hack Latimer, a member of the Colerain County Anti-Slavery Society, the group that had invited Burleigh to speak. Two sturdy black men also came forward: Melchior Dorfman, who owned a tin shop in town, and a young wagoner who drove freight.

Men in the audience hesitated, then lowered their arms. The banker sat down; others remained standing. A general grumbling, but no more missiles flew.

Burleigh resumed his speech: "We claim that we live in an honorable country. But THERE CAN BE NO HONOR in a republic founded on slavery! BUILT ON SLAVERY! No honor in a nation determined to perpetuate this MONSTROSITY, this disease that is ROTTING THE HEART AND SOUL OF THESE UNITED STATES!"

Gideon reckoned that well over a hundred people had packed the Episcopal church, Adamant's finest house of worship. The pews were full, and listeners stood along the sides and in back. Gideon saw men and women from his own church, Methodist, smaller and humbler, a low log building. He spotted his brother-in-law Jesse

Burns, whose face wore the smirk that was Jesse's version of a smile. He saw his friend Horatio Foote, the white-haired headmaster of the Adamant Academy. Phineas Potter, publisher of the *Adamant Argus*, scribbled in a notebook; Hosea Belknap, who owned the competing *Colerain Democrat*, did the same. Gideon recognized shopkeepers, craftsmen, the man who ran the hotel. Several dozen women were present: he glimpsed his own wife True standing in back. Most of Adamant's adult black residents were in attendance, around thirty men.

"Slavery must be abolished!" Burleigh exclaimed. "NOT NEXT YEAR! NOT NEXT WEEK! NOT TOMORROW! NOW!"

Gideon's eyes settled on two strangers seated beside each other near the back of the church. One looked to be about fifty. He was bull-necked and bald-headed. The other was younger, in his thirties, with a pale moustache and a chin beard. Over the last few days, Gideon had seen the two around town. He had noted the good leather boots they wore and the weathered slouch hats. Now, bareheaded in the church, they sat silently as the abolitionist tried to continue while members of the audience shouted him down.

"Humanity cries out against this FOUL STAIN!"

"You horse's ass!"

"Prating fool!"

"In the sight of God, SLAVERY IS A GROTESQUE SIN—"

"Wake up, you dough-faced dreamer!"

"We'll cut your hair for you, and that beard, too!"

And, piercing Gideon's awareness, a slur that perhaps came from his brother-in-law Jesse and was surely directed at himself: "You goddamned Dutch blockhead!"

An egg whizzed past Gideon's head and went *crump* behind him. Then a fresh barrage of corncobs, apples, and small rocks.

Gideon grabbed Burleigh by the arm and hustled him out a side door, Alonzo following. "Where are you staying?" Gideon asked. The abolitionist told him. "See that he gets there," Gideon ordered his deputy. Off they went, Burleigh protesting that he must finish his speech while Alonzo hurried him along in the darkness.

Gideon went back inside. Hoots and guffaws, although the hubbub was lessening. Jesse, his brother-in-law, had vanished. Others filed out through the narthex, taking their laughter with them. Gideon didn't see the two strangers who'd been seated in back.

Adamant's black citizens stood in small knots at the front of the church, talking among themselves. All except Mel Dorfman, the tinner, who was caught up in an argument with the newspaperman Phineas Potter. Dorfman jutted his dark face close to Potter's pale one. He held Potter's lapel with one hand and jabbed him in the chest with the fingers of his other hand. Potter recoiled, blinking. Gideon moved to separate them, but before he could get there, Dorfman let go. Potter brushed himself off and walked away.

"What was that about?" Gideon asked.

"Nothing worth mentioning," Dorfman growled. He was a barrel-chested man in his middle years with a bit of a paunch, gray frosting the black hair at his temples. He turned and stalked off.

★★★

True strolled toward home in the dirt street. She glanced up at the stars, floating in a hazy sky. Late April, a warm breeze from the south. Whip-poor-wills chanted from the brushy hills. Toads trilled in the mill ponds strung out along Spring Creek, the stream that gushed forth from the Big Spring, around which the town of Adamant had grown.

She heard someone coming up from behind. She turned and saw her husband.

Gideon put out his arm.

True hesitated, then linked her arm through his.

She was trying. Trying to be a good wife. To embrace life. A year and a half had passed since they'd lost their baby boy, David. True still grieved for her son, but the ache had lessened, sunk deep like an old burn.

She was trying to overcome the melancholia that had visited her off and on for as long as she could remember. Her grandmother, Arabella Burns, was also subject to bouts of depression, which the old woman called "the black wolf." Gram Burns had shown True how to use certain plants, rattleweed and skullcap and bee balm, to push back the despair. True had also inherited from her grandmother an uncanny sense that the old woman called the "second sight": like her gram, True sometimes had visions and prescient dreams. She'd had one before her baby had died.

"Things got pretty tense in that church," Gideon said.

"I'm glad you and Alonzo were there," True replied. "Otherwise they might have cut that fellow's hair, or tarred and feathered him."

"People don't like talking about slavery."

"Or thinking about it."

"At the jail we get plenty of advertisements for runaways."

Her husband's Pennsylvania Dutch accent made True smile. She wasn't Dutch, nor were many others in Colerain County, inhabited mainly by Scotch-Irish.

"Do you and Alonzo watch out for fugitives?" she asked.

"Not really. We're eighty miles from the Maryland line. But I suppose some of them could pass through here on their way north."

"What would you do if a person caught one and brought him to the jail?"

Gideon hesitated. "I'm not sure. I should look into the law, or ask the state's attorney, just in case."

True gave his arm a squeeze. "I hope you would do the right thing."

"What if the right thing—whatever it is—and what the law requires turn out to be two different things?" Gideon said.

True stopped and turned her face upward. "Listen."

From far above came a faint twittering, like old voices whispering secrets: birds calling to one another as their flocks streamed north through the night.

★★★

At the house they were greeted with barks and tail-wagging by Old Dick, the red setter who was Gideon's hunting dog and True's companion and friend. The dog was on a chain in their yard. True ran her hands through the setter's fur. She went inside and brought out scraps from the evening meal. Old Dick wolfed them down.

It was early for bedtime when she went back inside, but True easily read the look on Gideon's face. She slipped out of her clothes and lay down with him in their bed.

After David's death, they had drifted apart. True had not let him touch her for almost a year.

Now, under the quilt, she let her husband enfold her. He kissed her eyes and cheeks and lips, her neck and shoulders and breasts. And, at last, gently entered her. True liked having Gideon hold her close. She was willing to give him pleasure. But she stayed in a part of her mind separate from this joining. She was not ready to conceive another child, even though Gideon wanted one. Too much to lose, tying up so much love in a new soul that could flit away as quickly as a bird on the wing.

Thanks to Gram Burns, True knew how to keep that from happening.

Ran away from the subscriber, a NEGRO BOY, named GEORGE STEWART, a slave for life. About 20 years of age, five feet in height, of a bright mulatto color. Had on a pair of blue pants, black frock coat, black hat, and coarse shoes.

Chapter 2

———— ∞∞ ————

MORNING SUNLIGHT SPARKLED AND MIST CLUNG TO THE HILLS. On his way to the jail, Gideon thought about the anger that the abolitionist's speech had provoked last evening. And his *dummkop* brother-in-law, yelling out that he was a Dutch blockhead. Or maybe it was someone else. Lots of folks in Colerain County scorned him because he was Pennsylvania Dutch—the word came from *Deutsch*, which meant German—as well as an outsider and the sheriff. That he was also only twenty-four years old didn't help.

He told himself he didn't care. It was unsurprising for people to resent someone who held authority over them, especially if he wasn't a longtime resident. Someone who could make them confront the fact that things they did might be wrong, against the law, even downright wicked. He hadn't set out to be a sheriff, but the job suited him. Because laws needed to be upheld, and justice needed to be served.

Almost four years had passed since Gideon had first come to this place. He had left his family's farm in settled southeastern Pennsylvania and ridden west on his mare Maude—swum her across the broad Susquehanna to avoid the bridge toll, then taken rough roads into the mountains.

A dark memory had driven his flight: the persistent recall of an event that had happened when he was ten years old. It had changed the way he looked at the world, and at people, ever since.

It happened on a bright midsummer day: they'd been making hay in the fair weather, he had stolen away from the work and gone inside the house all hot and sweaty. The picture of what he had seen there began to form in his mind yet again. He shook his head. As if that motion could eject the vision that was always ready to appear, always ready to trigger grief and fear anew.

He had never told True what happened back then. Many times he had wanted to unburden himself, but something always held him back. Joy, mostly. They had fallen deeply in love soon after they met. They married right away, and True got pregnant and gave birth to a baby boy. For seven months they had loved their little son dearly—until the influenza swept through Adamant, ending David's life before it really began.

Gideon kept plodding along in the street, trying to let go of the bad memories. He adjusted his hat so the brim shielded his eyes from the sun. His fine new hat, made for him by the town's hatter, of brown beaver felt and with its low crown banded by a brown ribbon.

A sheriff needed to look professional, like he knew what he was doing.

At the jail, he checked in with Alonzo and made sure his deputy had gotten the abolitionist speaker home safely. Then he went back out again.

Typical for a Monday, Adamant hummed with activity. People from town and the surrounding countryside entered stores and shops. They called out greetings and stood conversing. Carts and wagons threaded through the streets, horse hooves thudding, axles squealing, harness bells jingling. The scents of burning wood and charcoal mingled with the aromas of meat cooking and bread baking.

Gideon went into George Watkins's barbershop. Watkins sat on a bench reading the *Adamant Argus*. "Sheriff Stoltz," he said. He rose and set the paper aside. "Shave and a haircut?"

"Just a shave, please."

Gideon hung up his jacket and hat and sat on the stool. Watkins draped a towel over his shoulders and lathered soap onto his face. A person looking in the window would have seen a broad-shouldered white man with even features and sandy hair attended to by a short, wiry black man wielding a bone-handled razor, his pinky finger upraised as he bladed off beard stubble.

"I came past your shop on Saturday," Gideon said. "You were shaving one man while another man sat waiting. I had never seen them before." Gideon described the man sitting on the stool: white, around fifty years of age, solidly built, with a horseshoe of dark hair ringing the back of his head. The other man had a blond mustache and a chin beard.

Watkins cleared soap and whiskers from the razor against the heel of his hand. "Southerners," he said.

"Where from?" Gideon asked.

"Virginia."

"Is that where you are from?"

"No, sir. I'm from Maryland. Bought my freedom in 'twenty-seven. Got the papers to prove it."

"Any idea why those men are in town?"

"They are looking for a boy." Watkins drew back, appraised his work. "A runaway."

"His name?"

Watkins stared at Gideon for a moment, as if weighing whether or not to answer. Finally: "The boy is called Leo Waller."

"Did they say what he looks like?"

Watkins resumed shaving Gideon's face. "Medium brown in color. Thirteen years old, small for his age. They said he knows how to handle livestock, especially horses."

Gideon had met a boy like that. Last summer, in Greer County, the next county south. The lad had stuck out like a sore thumb in a shabby backwoods settlement. But the youngster had given a different name. Gideon searched his memory until he recalled it: Otis. No last name, at least none that Gideon remembered. The boy had helped him out of a dangerous situation when he had been investigating a murder. The lad had asked about Adamant, its colored residents, whether work could be found there. He had claimed to be good with horses.

"Those Virginians are staying at the American," Watkins said. "They asked me to put out the word. Anyone who catches that boy, they can get a reward." He paused. "Two hundred dollars."

Gideon's eyebrows rose. Most notices of runaways that came to the jail advertised rewards of twenty-five dollars, fifty dollars, rarely as much as one hundred.

"Do you know of any boy around here who answers to that description?" he asked. Knowing already what the barber's answer would be.

"No, sir. Don't know of any boy like that."

Watkins set the razor aside. He got a towel from the rack and dabbed the remaining soap off Gideon's face. "That'll be a dime."

When Gideon left the barbershop, his shaved face felt cold in the breeze.

The American Hotel was new, and it was Adamant's best house of lodging: three stories, fancy brickwork, a street-level dining room that did a brisk trade. The manager, Curran, stood behind the desk.

"I saw you at the speech last night," Gideon said.

Curran wagged his head. He spoke with a brogue: "A donkey of a man, that abolitionist."

"You didn't agree with what he said?"

"Not at all. To accuse us of enabling slavery—an amazingly insulting performance. If you ask me, he got the reception he deserved."

Gideon described the two strangers he was seeking: one of them stocky, the other lean. From Virginia. "I'm told they are staying here."

The hotelier pointed to two names in the register. "Mr. Tazewell Waller, of Harpers Ferry, Virginia, and Mr. Franklin Blaine of Alexandria. In adjacent rooms on the second floor. Mr. Waller paid for their stay."

"Are they in the hotel now?"

"They are not. Took an early breakfast, and out they went."

"How long are they staying?"

"Paid ahead for the week."

Gideon asked Curran to tell the men that if they wished to talk to him, they should come to the jail. Wondering, as he spoke, why they hadn't done so already.

He continued on several blocks to Melchior Dorfman's tin shop. Dorfman was Adamant's only tinsmith and a leader in the town's black community. His wife ran a school for children in their home.

Dorfman was at his bench using a hammer and punch to make a starburst design in a shiny rectangle of tin that looked like it would become a cylindrical lantern: several finished lanterns sat on a shelf, along with pans, cups, candle molds, wall sconces.

Dorfman laid his tools aside. "Good morning, Sheriff."

"Good morning, Mr. Dorfman. Are you aware that two men from Virginia are in town?" He described them briefly and gave their names. "They are offering a reward of two hundred dollars for a fugitive, a thirteen-year-old boy named Leo Waller."

The tinner's eyes narrowed and a dark line deepened at the bridge of his nose. "I heard that. And before you ask, I don't know of any such boy in Adamant. Sheriff Stoltz, I voted for you last fall. So did every other colored man I know. Maybe you heard what happened when we went to mark our ballots. A dozen of us walked over to the Diamond together. All of us honest citizens, taxpayers and church-going men. The man who was running the election told us we couldn't vote."

Dorfman glowered. "I was expecting that. I had a copy of the state constitution in my pocket. It says that every freeman of the age of twenty-one who has paid a state or county tax shall enjoy the rights of an elector. Doesn't say a thing about the color of the man's skin." The tinner's voice was tight. "You know why we voted for you? Because you have never mistreated us. And we have faith that you will enforce the law."

"Thanks for your vote." Gideon tried to keep the puzzlement off his face: he wasn't sure whether Dorfman was referring to a specific law or was making a general statement.

"I'm glad you came in here," the tinner said. "Saves me from having to go to the jail. There's something I need to tell you. Folks have gone missing lately. Colored folks."

"Who?"

"Do you know John Horne? He wears an old blue army coat. A shy soul. Maybe forty years old. John lives west of here, in a cabin on Muncie Mountain. He has a dog that looks like a wolf—a big gray bitch that follows him everywhere."

"I've seen them."

"John walks to Adamant every Sunday, rain or shine, barefoot most of the year to save shoe leather. He gets up before dawn and makes it here in time for church."

Gideon had heard that the town's black citizens had started their own church. African Methodist Episcopal, he thought it was. A circuit preacher once a month, and lay preachers on the other Sundays. The people met in folks' homes and were said to be looking to buy a lot and build a real church.

"After the service, John stays over with one of our families," Dorfman said. "Then on Monday he buys supplies and totes them back home. He wasn't in town yesterday. That's two Sundays in a row. Something must have happened to him."

Gideon nodded. "You said that 'colored *folks*' had gone missing."

"There's two more I heard about. A man and a woman. Both light-skinned, mixed race." Dorfman looked down, fiddled with the tools on his bench. "From that house owned by Annie Picard."

Annie Picard was a Frenchwoman who surreptitiously sold liquor out of a dilapidated house in Hammertown, as the seamy side of Adamant was known. The house was also a site of prostitution.

"Last week, the man and his girl disappeared," Dorfman said. "I heard they left their belongings behind. Sheriff, I'm a married man. You won't find me down in Hammertown. But there's a rumor going around that those two good-for-nothing folks got kidnapped. Maybe that happened to John Horne, too."

"Kidnapped? Why?"

Dorfman looked at Gideon as if he were stupid. "To take them south. Sell them into slavery."

$30 Reward. A Negro Man named JIM, who calls himself James Myers, he is about 5 feet 7 or 8 inches high, stout made, with one or two scars on his face, also one on his ancle occasioned by an axe. He is well acquainted with farming and wagoning.

Chapter 3

———∞∞∞———

I N THE SLANTING LATE-DAY LIGHT GIDEON TROTTED HIS BAY MARE Maude down the Halfmoon Valley road. Alonzo followed on his paint gelding, cantering in places to keep up.

The farmer had come to the jail almost bursting with his news: "I was headed in to town like I do every Monday. Just poking along, when I saw 'em. Black toes sticking up from under a pile of branches."

"Black toes" instantly made Gideon think of the barefoot walker John Horne, whom Melchior Dorfman had reported missing that morning.

The farmer, bulky and florid, seemed pleased to have the undivided attention of the sheriff and his deputy. "I can't tell you why I looked in that direction. It could be the Lord wanted me to see those toes. On the north side of the road, in that patch of woods between John Waite's place and Ezra Wheeler's lime kiln."

Gideon glanced at Alonzo, who nodded that he knew the location.

The farmer said, emphatically, although neither Gideon nor Alonzo had asked: "No, sir, I did *not* disturb the body. Got down off the wagon and locked the wheels and went over to that pile of limbs with the toes sticking up."

"Black toes? A colored person?"

"I couldn't say. The toes being inside of socks. Good, black store-bought socks." The farmer had shrugged. "I thought about taking the branches off, getting him up in the wagon and bringing him in to town. But I said to myself, no sir, the Dutch Sheriff will want to see him right where he's at."

In fact, the Dutch Sheriff did not *want* to see the corpse, did not *want* to look at a dead body at all. And not just look at it: scrutinize it, learn everything he could from it. Examining a body was Gideon's responsibility—one that he'd needed to carry out too many times already during his three years as sheriff.

★★★

"Whoa!" Alonzo yelled from behind.

Gideon closed his hands on the reins and sat deep. Beneath him, Maude slowed to a walk, then stopped.

Looking north, he saw a pile of branches fifty feet off the road. The farmer must have good eyes: It took Gideon a while to pick out what appeared to be black-stockinged toes jutting up at the pile's edge.

Alonzo pointed down at two broad swerving furrows in the road's surface. "Could be he got run down. A wagon, from the size of the tires. Not the farmer's, he said he was just poking along. This one was barreling."

Gideon let his eyes wander through the second-growth forest. He spotted a metallic glint in a patch of mountain laurel. Closer in, the raking light revealed a long linear scrape on the ground: grass and low plants flattened where something had been knocked or dragged down off the road.

He dismounted and looped Maude's reins over a bush. Alonzo did the same with his gelding. They clambered down the bank to the pile of branches.

They began lifting off limbs.

The body belonged to a man. A white man, lying on his back, his clothing, face, and hair strewn with brown shards of rotted leaves and bits of bark. He wore good-quality moleskin trousers, a bottle-green vest, and a dark broadcloth coat. His skin was pallid. His eyes, half open, appeared collapsed and dull. One cheekbone had been smashed in. On the left side of the skull near the crown was a deep indentation. Dried maroon-colored blood hazed the face and made the hair stick out stiffly from the man's head.

Recognition dawned. "It's Phineas Potter," Gideon said. Potter was the owner and publisher of the *Adamant Argus*.

The pockets in Potter's coat had been turned inside out. Gideon recalled that the newspaperman wore a leather wallet on his belt. He parted the coat. The wallet was missing.

Alonzo picked up a crumpled hat. "Much the worse for wear. This hat and Phineas both."

"Why was he on this road?" Gideon asked. "And how did he get here? If he rode, someone took his horse or it wandered off."

"Took his boots, too," Alonzo said.

Gideon squatted down. Potter's head tilted slightly to one side, as if the newspaperman listened to a far-off sound. The right arm looked dislocated or broken. Deep scuff marks on the trousers at the thighs, black blotches where blood had soaked through the fabric. Gideon looked again at the stockinged feet with their upright toes. With a sudden pang in his heart, he remembered how one of his *memmi*'s feet had turned in toward the other, touching it with the big toe. Her bare feet, so ordinary, so familiar, spattered with blood in the kitchen where she lay.

He lurched up, his heart thumping. Taking slow and even breaths, he stared off into the woods, trying to leave behind that *greislich* vision from his childhood.

"Wait here," he said to Alonzo. He began walking. Slowly he paced a circle around the body, moving outward. His eyes searching the ground. He had gone around three times when he came to a depression, a cavity in the earth slightly larger than his fist. Dirt showed in the bottom of the small pit. He started walking again. He found a fist-sized rock lying in the leaves. He noticed a dark stain and several dark hairs sticking to the rock. He picked up the rock carefully and handed it to Alonzo.

Gideon went to the mountain laurel thicket where he'd spotted the metallic glint. On the ground beneath the glossy green leaves and dark springy stems lay a lantern. It was badly dented. He picked it up by the bail. Inside, a candle rattled. The lantern was stippled with holes in ornate patterns to let out light. The kind of lantern Melchior Dorfman made in his tin shop.

He turned to Alonzo. "I think you're right. He must have been hit by the wagon. Then someone finished him off with that rock."

They climbed back onto the road. Set the rock and the lantern and Potter's hat along the verge.

Gideon started west down the road. As he walked, he looked off to one side, then the other. After a hundred paces he stopped, turned around, and did the same thing coming back. He passed the body and Alonzo and the horses and continued eastward. On the south side of the road he spotted a patch of trampled ground with curved indentations made by iron horseshoes, and blades of grass cropped low.

He went to the patch, bent over, and picked up the butt of a smoked-down cigar. It gave off a musty, acrid smell. Someone had stood here smoking, while holding the reins of one or more horses. Gideon pocketed the cigar butt and returned to where Alonzo stood.

"What can you tell me about Potter?"

Alonzo had lived in Colerain County all his life.

"I didn't know him all that well," Alonzo said. "I'd pass the time of day with him when I went in his shop to get notices printed, the ones we posted around town."

"Did he have any family?"

Alonzo nodded. "Phineas had a leg up in life. His parents owned a big farm and a gristmill east of town. They sent him to the Academy. Then on to college; Philadelphy, I think. He came back here five, six years ago. His ma and pa had both passed on. Phineas sold the farm and the mill. He had that printing press freighted in. Which that was when he started his newspaper."

"How old would you say he was? Around thirty?"

" 'Bout that."

"Is there a Mrs. Potter?"

"Phineas never married. Smart move on his part."

Alonzo was a bachelor.

"Do you know if he had any enemies?"

"Plenty of folks didn't like what he put in his paper. An opinionated cuss, he was."

Gideon knew very well that Potter was opinionated, and a thoroughgoing Whig. Before last fall's election, the *Adamant Argus* had supported Gideon's opponent for the office of sheriff, a longtime Colerain Countian who was also a Whig. Gideon had run as a Democrat—not because he had any particular leanings in that direction, it was just that *Pennsylfawnisch Deitsch* folks where he had grown up in southeastern Pennsylvania mostly voted Democrat. He was still quite surprised that he had won.

"What about Potter's friends?" Gideon asked.

"I've seen him with the Cold Fish."

The "Cold Fish" was Alonzo's nickname for Alvin Fish, the state's attorney for Colerain County, and, as the county's prosecutor, Gideon's supervisor. Gideon did not like the man, and the feeling was mutual.

"Now and then they took meals together at the American." Alonzo scratched at his chin with dirty fingernails. "The hotel serves a damned good beefsteak. Which I am so hungry right now, I could eat like all wrath. I could eat a horse and chase the jockey down."

"Gaither should be here soon." Gideon had instructed Gaither Brown, a part-time deputy, to bring a wagon. Brown was a leather worker with a shop near the jail; neither a likable nor a completely dependable fellow, and something of a tippler, but Gideon was fairly sure he'd show up with the conveyance before long.

"Good thing," Alonzo said. "Leave poor Phineas out here another night, and the wolves might eat him down to his backbone."

Gideon looked at the body again. Why had it been left so close to the road? Why not drag it another hundred yards into the woods? Where it lay, the chances were good that animals would uncover it. Or that the stench, after a few days, would alert a passerby. They hadn't done a competent job of hiding the body: the sharp-eyed farmer had noticed the upthrust toes.

Well, people didn't always think straight in the moments after committing a crime. Especially a crime as heinous as murder.

"Last night at the church," Gideon said to Alonzo, "after you took that abolitionist speaker away, I saw Melchior Dorfman arguing with Potter. Dorfman looked furious. We need to talk to him."

★★★

Muncie Mountain rose on the left, the long wooded ridge shaded a deep purple. Above the broad valley a snipe circled, catching the day's last light. The bird plummeted toward the ground, disappearing into shadow, its tail feathers sounding a hollow ascendant *huhuhuhuhu* as it rose out of its dive.

Gideon and Alonzo rode behind the wagon.

Pounding hooves came up from behind. Someone called out: "Sheriff Stoltz!"

It was Melchior Dorfman on a dun horse.

"Thank God it's you!" the tinner said. "I've just come from John Horne's place. The door was open, a chair tipped over, a table broken. No sign of him anywhere."

Gaither Brown stopped the team. He turned his head, a sour look on his face.

Dorfman stood in his stirrups and looked into the wagon bed. "Don't tell me he's dead."

"It's someone else," Gideon said.

He watched Dorfman's face in the murky light.

The tinner's horse started to dance. Didn't like the wagon or didn't like what was in it.

"Do you recognize him?" Gideon asked.

"I don't think so."

Alonzo ranged up beside the tinner and took hold of his horse's reins. "It's Phineas Potter."

"What the devil—?" Dorfman blurted.

Gideon motioned for Alonzo to let go.

"Last night in the church, after the abolitionist's speech," Gideon said, "I saw you and Potter arguing. What was that about?"

Dorfman's mouth fell open. "You think I killed this man?"

"I just want to know what you were discussing."

"Of course, blame the colored man." Dorfman's tone was cutting. "What about John Horne? You haven't said a word about him, how you're going to find him. He may be dead like this man here. Or kidnapped, in chains and headed south."

"We don't know any of that yet, Mr. Dorfman. Please tell me what you and Mr. Potter were arguing about."

"Start talking, tin man," Alonzo said.

"Alonzo," Gideon warned.

Dorfman scowled. "If you must know, I was taking him to task over the tripe he puts in his paper, about how to solve what he calls 'the negro problem.' He claims—well, he claimed—to be an abolitionist. But he was always pushing for colonization, sending us back to Africa, to our 'native land.'"

"You don't agree with that?"

"No! Not in any way. A bunch of mealymouthed whites would like to see it happen, though. I tell you, my people have been Americans for generations—a lot longer than some of the white trash they're letting into the country these days. How long have your folks been here, Stoltz?"

Gideon took a deep breath. "Mr. Dorfman, where were you last night after the speech?"

"I went home. To my wife and children. I told Sarah what happened in that church, how so many of our good neighbors pelted that abolitionist with corncobs and rotten apples and wouldn't let him speak. I was with my wife all night. You don't believe me, ask her."

"That lantern, on the blanket next to Potter's corpse. Is it one of yours?"

Dorfman stared into the wagon's bed. "Looks like it. Potter came into the shop and bought one a few weeks back."

"All right," Gideon said. "Now tell me what you think should be done about John Horne."

The tinner's shoulders slumped. "I don't know. You need to find out what happened to him."

"Of course I will try to do that."

"I'll ask around," Dorfman said. "See if anyone has seen or heard anything. Maybe get folks to put up a reward."

Gideon called to Brown to start driving again and motioned for Alonzo to ride on ahead. He walked Maude next to Dorfman's horse. "You say you found a chair overturned and a table damaged at his cabin. Did you notice anything else? Bloodstains?"

"No. But I didn't search around much."

"What about his dog?"

"I didn't see it."

"Was anything missing?"

"Sheriff, I've only been to John's place once. Last fall. He had a lot of things to carry home from town, so I borrowed a wagon and helped him. I don't know much about him. Like I told you, he doesn't say much." The tinner bit off his words: "He was afraid, though. He was always afraid." Dorfman looked aside. As if wondering whether he'd said too much.

Gideon kept quiet and waited.

"Sometimes he'd stare off into the distance and start trembling all over, like a leaf in a storm," Dorfman said. "Like he was remembering awful things that he had seen or had done to him." The tinner added forcefully: "I'm sure he's been kidnapped. Those two slave catchers, the ones from Virginia. You need to arrest them."

"I'll talk with them," Gideon said.

$50 Reward for a girl, Maria. She is of a copper color, between 13 and 14 years of age—*bare headed* and *bare footed*, small for her age, very sprightly and very likely. She stated she was *going to see her mother* at Maysville.

Chapter 4

⸺◦∞∞◦⸺

D ORFMAN SPURRED HIS HORSE PAST THE WAGON AND RODE ON
ahead. Gideon reckoned he didn't want to keep company with
the other men, the living and the dead. Not surprising, since the
tinner clearly thought he was being accused of murder.

It was almost dark when the wagon rolled through Adamant and
stopped at the house of Dr. Dexter Beecham, the county coroner.
Beecham lit lamps as Gideon, Alonzo, and Gaither Brown carried
Potter's corpse into an anteroom off the parlor. Gideon explained
where the body had been found, and that ruts in the road and Potter's
injuries suggested he had been run down by a wagon. He gave
Beecham the rock he had recovered. He asked Alonzo to take Potter's
hat and the dented lantern to the jail and return Maude to the livery
stable.

As Gideon and Beecham eased the clothes off the corpse's rigid
limbs, the coroner kept up a muttered commentary: "Severe wounds
to the head. A fractured skull. Right arm broken. Those bruises on
the torso and legs could be from hooves. Deep contusions on both
thighs, looks like that rig ran right over him."

After leaving Beecham's house, Gideon headed for the state's
attorney's residence. He trudged along in the darkness, wishing he'd
brought a lantern like the one they'd found with Potter's corpse.

Alvin Fish's elegant limestone two-and-a-half-story house was
two blocks from the courthouse. The windows were draped; no lights

were visible. Gideon rapped on the door. A minute passed before he heard footsteps.

The door opened, and Fish peered out. The attorney, backlit by candlelight, kept his right hand behind the jamb.

Gideon saw emotions flit across the sallow face: fear, puzzlement, then anger as Fish recognized who it was standing on his doorstep.

"Sorry to bother you, Mr. Fish," Gideon said. "But there has been a suspicious death on the Halfmoon Valley road."

"Couldn't it have waited until morning?"

If I'd waited, thought Gideon, you would have criticized me for delaying telling you. "The dead man is Phineas Potter."

Fish staggered back.

"A wagon ran over him. He had many severe injuries, including a head wound that could have been caused by someone clubbing him with a rock. His body was concealed." For as long as Gideon had known Fish, it had been the attorney's avid ghoulish practice to assist the coroner in cutting up corpses. "Dr. Beecham will do the autopsy first thing tomorrow. He asked if you want to help."

Fish backed away farther and sat down heavily in a chair. As Gideon stepped over the threshold, he saw a cocked pistol in the attorney's right hand.

"Mr. Fish, I've heard that you were friends with Mr. Potter. Do you have any idea why—"

"Leave," Fish blurted. He poked the pistol toward the doorway.

"I need to start investigating his death right away. Find out whatever I can about—"

The muzzle of Fish's firearm swung toward Gideon and settled on his chest. "I said leave! Now!"

Gideon quick-stepped out the door.

★★★

Gideon and True ate a late supper and went to bed. He told her about finding Potter's body, and the man, John Horne, who had gone missing. Also the mixed-race couple rumored to have disappeared from Annie Picard's house. He described being accosted by the tinner, Melchior Dorfman, on the road, and Dorfman's belief that someone was kidnapping colored people to sell them into slavery.

"Poor Mr. Potter." True caressed her husband's chest. "Robbed and killed. And people gone missing, maybe kidnapped. I don't like this violence."

"I don't like it, either." Gideon's mind snapped back to when he had first come to Colerain County almost five years ago. Riding through the Seven Mountains south of Adamant, he'd been waylaid by three highwaymen. It had been a close thing. If he hadn't immediately galloped Maude out of the trap, he believed he would have been killed—and for next to nothing, since he had only a few cents left after his travels. The bandits had shot at him as he fled. They missed him, but a pistol ball had taken the tip off one of Maude's ears. Now every time he got on his mare, he noticed that cropped, disfigured ear.

He lay warm and comfortable in the bed. He wanted to change the subject and talk about things that weren't sad or frightening. "What did you do today?" he asked.

"I split some more of that ash wood."

A man of Gideon's acquaintance had delivered a wagonload of ash billets, which now lay in their back yard. True's grandmother had taught her how to pound the billets on their ends, separate the wood into splints, shave the slivers thin, and weave them into baskets.

"I've made a bunch of baskets," she continued. "Egg baskets, berry and garden baskets. Mr. Tuttle at the dry goods says he'll buy all that I can make."

"That's good. We can use the money." Gideon felt himself starting to drift off to sleep.

"I'll also sell them to neighbors and people in the church. I started making some big ones, too—clothes hampers and pack baskets. And I want you to teach me how to shoot."

"What?" He came fully awake.

"Shoot a gun."

"We don't have a gun. Other than my shotgun."

"A pistol, I mean."

"We don't have a pistol."

"I want one."

"Why?"

"When I ride out on Jack, I want to be able to defend myself."

"Why do you want to ride out on Jack?"

"To visit my gram in the Panther Valley," True said. "And my folks at the ironworks."

Jack was their not-very-ambitious or overly energetic gelding, used mostly to pull their wagon, and, as it had turned out, a solid riding mount.

"I don't know," Gideon said. "It's chust that women, well, they don't shoot." He heard his Dutch accent come to the fore, as it often did when he was flustered.

"My gram shoots. She's probably as good a shot as you are, maybe better."

"True, honey, it's not like we live in Texas or the Missouri Territory. Anymore there aren't wild Indians running around in Pennsylvania killing people."

"No, but there's plenty of bad men. Look what's happened in this county since you've been sheriff. And what happened to Mr. Potter."

"Don't you have enough to do? With your gardening, cooking, keeping house? And now basketmaking?"

"I intend to ride out on Jack. I want you to show me how to hitch him to the wagon and drive him. No reason I can't go and fetch my own ash wood."

"Well, maybe."

"I figure a pistol makes more sense than a heavy old rifle."

"A pistol costs money."

For a while, True stayed silent. Gideon wondered if she was considering her rights, or rather her lack of rights. By law and by custom, a husband controlled his wife's possessions. He could sell whatever she owned—even her clothes—and take any money she earned. He could decide what they would buy and what they would not buy.

True propped herself up on an elbow. "Do you want your wife to be safe?"

Gideon didn't like the way this conversation was going. True had changed since last summer. In a good way, mostly. She was no longer mired in depression, as she had been after David's death. Gideon had found it miserable when she kept to her bed for days on end. They had barely been husband and wife. Things were much better these days. But now she was almost . . . fierce. And persistent. Annoyingly so.

"The only reason women don't shoot," she said, "is because you men won't let us."

He sighed and turned away from her in the bed.

She pressed against him, reached around and made sure he couldn't sleep.

Ranaway, a negro named Arthur, has a considerable scar across his breast and each arm, made by a knife; loves to talk much of the goodness of God.

Chapter 5

———∞∞∞———

THE LIVERYMAN CAME JOGGING UP THE STREET LEADING TWO horses, both saddled. One was a dark bay gelding that looked to Gideon like his own mare Maude, nondescript but fit. The other seemed like a steed out of a dream: a white stallion whose coat glowed in the morning sun. A good fifteen hands tall, with a broad chest, sloping shoulders, and a short neat back carrying to a muscular hind end. An arching neck and a chiseled head. A soft eye. Gideon always looked at the eye. The stallion was a generous-appearing horse, he decided; a horse he would love to ride.

He had wanted to see some Southern horseflesh, always so highly touted. Curran, the manager at the American, had told him that the horses of the guests from Virginia would be delivered at half past seven.

The men came out of the hotel to get their mounts.

Gideon greeted them and introduced himself.

"Pleased to meet you, Sheriff," said the older of the two men. Stocky, solid, his eyes a startlingly pale blue. He offered his hand. "Tazewell Waller, sir, of Red Rose Farm, Harpers Ferry, Virginia. In the Shenandoah Valley."

Waller's voice was smooth and mellifluous: "Sir" was "suh" and "farm" became "fahm." It made Gideon think of how harsh and nasal his own Dutch accent must sound.

"May I introduce my assistant, Mr. Franklin Blaine," Waller said. Blaine was lean and muscular, a few inches taller than his employer.

His sandy moustache and spade-shaped beard were neatly trimmed. He wore his slouch hat at a rakish slant.

After shaking hands with Blaine, Gideon turned back to Waller. "I understand that you are looking for a runaway."

"My servant Leo. He eloped from my farm in September of 'thirty-five."

"That's a year and a half ago."

"Indeed. I looked for him at first near Red Rose, then nearby in Maryland." Waller cocked his head in a thoughtful way. "It gnawed on me, him getting away like that. Absconding, for no reason whatsoever. And stealing a prime hand to go along with him. Though I still have an affection for the lad."

"What brought you to Pennsylvania?" Gideon asked.

"I received a report, heard a rumor." Waller's voice trailed off. Then he resumed: "It matters not. I am here. And I expect your help in finding that boy. A slippery little fellow, Leo. Perhaps you've seen him. Thirteen years old. A fine-built lad, on the small side."

Gideon shook his head.

"Mr. Blaine has been in Pennsylvania for almost a month," Waller continued. "South of here, in a settlement called McDonough, he spoke with a man who said a colored boy answering to Leo's description lived there for quite a while before leaving recently. The man suspected he may have come to your town."

"I haven't seen him."

"But you did see him in McDonough, sir," Blaine said. "The man I talked to was a constable named Thaddeus Kirkwood. Poor fellow was all crippled up. He told me that last August, you broke his leg with a club."

Since Blaine had not asked a question, Gideon did not answer. He had disabled Kirkwood by breaking his leg, but only after the man attacked him and tried to kill him.

"This Kirkwood fellow told me that Leo watched the two of you fight," Blaine continued. "Is that so, Sheriff?"

"I noticed a boy there. I haven't encountered him since."

"Kirkwood said the lad was calling himself Otis Johnson," Blaine said.

"I see that you have a number of the sable race living here in Adamant," Waller added. "May I ask you to inquire among them? I am offering a substantial reward for Leo's recovery."

Blaine got a piece of paper out of his pocket and handed it to Gideon. A written description of the boy, it announced the two-hundred-dollar reward. "We will have this printed and put up around town," Blaine said.

"Someone may be hiding him," Waller said. "Of course, that would be in violation of the Fugitive Slave Act."

Gideon knew of the statute, a federal one, but had never found a reason to study it, let alone enforce it. He handed the paper back to Blaine. He glanced again at the livery worker holding the Virginians' horses: a black fellow named Collins, who worked at the stable where Gideon kept his own horses. Collins stood with his face averted and his eyes directed at the ground. Not at all the way he behaved when Gideon visited the livery.

Gideon had never spoken to Collins beyond instructing him in caring for Maude and Jack. The man's background, his whole life, were a mystery to him; Gideon realized he didn't even know Collins's first name.

Gideon nodded at the white stallion. "That's a fine-looking horse. Are you taking him out for some exercise?"

Waller smiled. "Leo loved that horse. I call him Boaz. A biblical name; it means 'swiftness.'" Waller looked up at the sky, a full soft blue. "We plan to ride out in the countryside and ask after Leo at farms and taverns. Perhaps he has found work with horses, or with other livestock."

"On Sunday evening I saw the two of you at the church where the abolitionist was speaking," Gideon said.

"Ah, yes. That shaggy-haired fellow seemed unable to persuade his audience that servitude should be abolished."

"After the speech, where did you and Mr. Blaine go?"

"We came back to the hotel."

"And you stayed there all night?"

"Yes. I understand that a gentleman was killed that evening. A newspaperman. Do murders happen often in your county, Sheriff?"

Gideon wondered how the Virginian knew about Potter's death. Probably Alonzo or Gaither Brown, or both, had gone to a tavern last evening and gabbed. The news would be all over town.

"Do you know anything about that murder?" he asked.

The friendly expression vacated Waller's face. "Other than that it happened, certainly not."

"Do you know anything about the recent disappearances of a black man named John Horne, and two other people of color?"

"Sir, why would we know of such things? We are here in search of my servant, and for no other reason."

Waller stepped forward and took the stallion's reins from the liveryman. He looked back at Gideon. "When we find Leo, we may require you to hold him in jail until we can arrange to take him home. Good day to you now, sir."

★★★

On Lawyers Row, Gideon knocked on the door of the state's attorney's office. No response, at first; then a weak voice said: "Enter."

The Cold Fish sat with his elbows on his desk, his head between his hands. No law book lay open, no brief spread out before him. Fish's eyes were rimmed with red. He had not shaved, and his heavy beard made his sunken cheeks look gray. Gideon smelled the sickly sweet scent of alcohol.

"Mr. Fish, I hope you can help me with something. What are my responsibilities under the federal fugitive slave law?"

Fish stared at Gideon for almost a minute, making Gideon wonder if the attorney had heard him or understood his question. Finally Fish heaved a liquor-tinged sigh and rose unsteadily. He balanced himself with a hand on his desk, then reached for a leather-bound volume on a bookshelf.

"The Fugitive Slave Act of 1793," he said listlessly. "It requires that a person held to servitude or labor, who flees to another state, be returned to his master in the state whence he fled." Fish slumped back down in the chair. He fixed a pair of oval-lensed eyeglasses on the bridge of his nose; they sat there askew. He flipped through pages, laid the opened book on his desk, and pushed it toward Gideon.

"I . . . might not understand it," Gideon said.

Fish stifled a belch. "No doubt." He cleared his throat. "In essence, the Act guarantees the right of a slave owner to recover his property. It directs the legal apparatus of the state—you, me, magistrates, judges—to assist that person or his agent in reclaiming a slave who has fled to any state where slavery has been abolished."

"Such as Pennsylvania."

"That is correct. The state legislature passed an act for the gradual abolition of slavery in 1780. It phases out slavery. In point of fact, there are still slaves living here in the Commonwealth. They were slaves before the act was passed, and they will remain enslaved until their death."

"I thought Pennsylvania was a 'free state.'"

"It is so considered."

No further explanation seemed forthcoming. "Mr. Fish, have any fugitive slaves ever been caught here in Colerain County?"

Fish took off his spectacles and slowly rubbed his nose. "Around ten years ago," he said, "two Southerners came here. They apprehended a pair of negroes, claiming they were runaways. The men had been working at the tannery. The slave hunters chained them together and paraded them through the streets. Entertainment for the masses. The two were lodged in the jail until a hearing took place before Judge Biddle. From the evidence adduced, the judge permitted the Southerners to take away those miserable blacks."

Gideon caught his breath. Judge Hiram Biddle had been his mentor and closest friend. They had hunted grouse and woodcock together in the brushlands around Adamant, sipped whiskey in the judge's study—the room where Biddle had later taken his own life. Upon his death, the judge willed to Gideon a beautiful English shotgun, his hunting dog Old Nick, the gelding Jack, and a wagon. In the two years they had known one another, the judge had never said anything to Gideon about having returned two fugitives into slavery.

"I was in private practice at the time," Fish said. "Some men in town, strong abolitionists, engaged me to argue the case on the negroes' behalf. I relied on Pennsylvania's new anti-kidnapping law. However, Judge Biddle ruled that the federal fugitive act took precedence over the state statute." Fish rooted around in a drawer, got out a pamphlet, and tossed it across his desk. "The Pennsylvania Fugitive Slave Act of 1826. Probably even you can understand it. It lays out the procedure that must be followed to repossess a slave who has fled to this state. However, I doubt very much that Judge Campbell would find that the Pennsylvania statute overrides the federal one. And, as the state's attorney for this county, I would not waste my time prosecuting anyone under such a weak and ineffectual law."

Gideon picked up the pamphlet. He would read it at the jail. He had another reason for visiting Fish: "Dr. Beecham should have finished the autopsy on Phineas Potter by now. I believe it will show that Potter was run down by a wagon and then struck one or more blows to the head with a rock. He was murdered, Mr. Fish. So far, I have not found out why Potter was on the Halfmoon Valley road on Sunday night. And I need to learn as much about him as I can."

When Fish did not respond, Gideon continued: "I understand that you and he were friends."

Fish fidgeted. "We were acquainted."

"What can you tell me about him?"

Fish opened another desk drawer. For a moment Gideon wondered if Fish would get out a pistol and, as he had done last night, use it to send the pesky sheriff fleeing. Instead, the attorney removed a sheaf of papers and set them on his desk, clumsily trying to square their edges. "I did not know Mr. Potter all that well," he muttered.

"My deputy says the two of you dined together at the hotel."

"I met Mr. Potter there now and then."

"Why was that, Mr. Fish?"

"He was interested in various laws."

"Which ones?"

"The fugitive slave laws, as it happens. Both federal and state. I told him essentially what I have just told you."

"Was Mr. Potter a close friend?"

Fish looked off to one side. "An acquaintance, a friend. What does it matter now?"

"As I said, I'm trying to find out more about the man. It may help me learn who killed him."

Fish riffled through the papers on his desk.

"Did Potter have many other friends?" Gideon asked.

"I cannot say."

"Any enemies? Anyone who hated him and might have wanted to harm him?"

"You ask me about matters of which I have no knowledge." Fish raised his face and glared. "You forget yourself. I am the state's attorney. As sheriff, you are my employee. I do not appreciate being interrogated by my subordinates."

"Potter's death is not the only suspicious thing that has happened lately. A black man named John Horne has gone missing."

"That name means nothing to me."

"He lived in Halfmoon Valley in a cabin not far from where Potter was killed. And there are two others, a man and a woman, both of mixed race. They disappeared from a house in Hammertown. It's possible that all those people were kidnapped to be sold into slavery."

"Then it appears you have several situations to investigate."

"I wonder whether Potter's death and these disappearances could be linked."

Fish waved his hand. "Do your job. Tell Dr. Beecham I will review his report. Now go."

Stop the Runaway!!!—$25 Reward. Ranaway from the Eagle Tavern, a negro fellow, named Nat. He is no doubt attempting to *follow his wife, who was lately sold to a speculator named Redmond.*

Chapter 6

—⚮—

THE CORONER, A CHEERFUL ROTUND MAN IN HIS MIDDLE YEARS, SAT across from Gideon at a table. His wife had made coffee, too watery for Gideon's taste, but out of politeness he took a few sips.

Enumerating Potter's injuries, Beecham used a pudgy index finger to fold down the outspread fingers of his other hand. "Fractured skull. Fractured left and right femurs. Right arm broken in two places." Gideon noticed that Beecham still had blood beneath his fingernails. "The right scapula shattered. Eight broken ribs, two of which punctured the lungs." The coroner had run out of fingers. He went on: "Lacerations of the liver and spleen, with massive internal bleeding." He sat back in his chair. "That rig must've been going like a coach and six on a turnpike. Why didn't he get out of the way?"

"Maybe he expected them to stop," Gideon said.

"The rock you found? The hairs on it match the hairs on Potter's head." Beecham glanced through an open door from the parlor into the surgery, where the body lay under a sheet freckled with maroon spots. "Want to take a look?"

"No, thank you."

"How about the liver and spleen? I have them in jars."

Gideon shook his head and rose. "When your report is ready, Mr. Fish wants to see it."

After leaving the doctor's house, Gideon strode down High Street. He crossed Spring Creek on a covered bridge with a sign that read WALK YOUR HORSE OR GET A 2 DOLLAR FINE—a rule he had never bothered to enforce. On the right, farther down the creek, were a gristmill, a sawmill, and a nail factory, all powered by the constant reliable flow from the Big Spring. In that same area were a tannery, a brickyard, and the livery stable where Gideon kept his horses. Scattered among those businesses and on a low hill above them were boardinghouses, smaller frame dwellings, and cabins, most of them occupied by laborers and their families.

To his left beyond the bridge lay Hammertown, where it was easy to get drunk on rye whiskey, gin, rum, beer, wine, cherry bounce, applejack, and various other beverages sold in saloons and out the back doors of houses. Fights broke out in Hammertown with some regularity. Gideon and Alonzo tended to ignore them unless someone got their fingers bitten off or an eye gouged out or an inch or two of knife stuck into some part of their anatomy.

Loose women plied their trade—there was no law against it—in rooms above saloons, in some of the houses, and in alleys. The going rate was seventy-five cents.

Strolling into Hammertown, he passed a fat man sitting on an overturned crate in front of a saloon. The man wore a stained collarless shirt and pants held up by suspenders. When he saw Gideon, the man leaned forward and pointedly squirted tobacco juice onto the ground between his legs.

A smudge-faced boy draped in grimy oversized clothes came struggling down the street carrying two wooden buckets dangling off the ends of a yoke. When Gideon stopped him, the boy crouched to let the water-filled buckets rest on the ground.

"Have you seen a colored boy about your age?" Gideon asked. "He would have shown up here in the last few weeks."

The boy narrowed his eyes. "Maybe," he said, drawing out the word. Gideon dug a nickel out of his vest. The lad grabbed it. "No, sir, I ain't seen no blackbird like that. But if I lay eyes on him, you'll be the first to know." He cackled, straightened, and went lurching off under his load.

On Hammertown's western edge Gideon climbed a set of stone steps to a weather-beaten two-story house. Alonzo claimed that a wealthy family from downstate had originally built it as a summer retreat, adding: "Why they reckoned Adamant was any kind of a resort, I couldn't say." The site offered a view of the town, nestled among and upon its hills: the courthouse partway up one hill, with the jail above it; the burying ground occupying another prominence; and the Academy perched on a third.

After Gideon had come to Adamant, and before he'd met True, he had been tempted to visit Annie Picard's establishment. But he had never gotten up the nerve. He was glad of it now; it would be awkward to barge in and start asking questions if he'd patronized the place in the past.

He knocked on the walnut door with its ornate floral carvings, the wood dry and crumbling.

A big man opened the door. Gideon, a shade over six feet, had to look up to see the man's eyes. One of those eyes veered off sideways. A pale scar ran down the man's face from the corner of that wayward eye to the edge of his mouth.

"Whatta you want?" The voice rumbled up from a broad chest.

Before Gideon could reply, a woman joined the man in the entry. Annie Picard was short and stocky, her black hair shot with gray and pulled back in a bun. She wore a loose-fitting calico dress. She said to Gideon in a low raspy voice: "We are not open. Come back tonight."

Gideon identified himself as the county sheriff, though the badge on his coat should have made that plain. "I need to ask you some questions about two of your employees."

She hesitated, then flicked her hand for him to enter. Another flick of her stubby fingers sent the brawny doorman away.

The parlor, much better kept than the house's exterior, had Turkish carpets, plush chairs, upholstered couches, and a fireplace surrounded by marble panels. A gleaming brass candelabra hung from the ceiling, its candles unlit at this hour. A piano sat at the room's far end.

"I heard that a man and a woman lived here until recently," Gideon said. "Colored people."

Picard sat down in a chair, her dark eyes narrowed.

"I understand the woman was . . . available," Gideon said.

"If you are interested in a liaison, then you are too late." Picard spoke with a whimsical tone. "Of course, we see your deputy now and then."

Gideon was unsurprised to hear that.

"Those two people who lived here formerly," he said. "What were their names?"

"She is called Amanda Jones. The man is Felix Wiley."

"What did they do?"

Annie Picard gave him a condescending smile. "Amanda entertained our guests. Felix helped with the cooking and cleaning."

"Where were they from?"

"Philadelphia."

"Did you bring them here?"

"No. They came on their own."

"Why did they come to this house?"

A dramatic shrug. "Perhaps because we have such an excellent reputation."

"When did they arrive?"

"Last autumn."

"And they left . . . ?"

"Two weeks ago. I believe they took the coach."

"Do you know why they left?"

"Perhaps they missed *l'excitation* of the city."

"Please show me where the woman lived."

"The room has another tenant now."

"I want to see it."

"That I cannot permit."

"Would you rather I come back with a couple of deputies and go through your house room by room? And find the whiskey that you sell but don't bother paying taxes on, and pour it in the street?"

Picard rolled her eyes, then rose and led him up the stairs and down a dim hallway. She rapped on a door. A girl opened it. She was blonde, tall and slender, and, like Picard, wore a loose calico dress. "Go down to the kitchen," Picard told the girl. "You are too thin. Get something to eat."

"No," Gideon said to the girl. "You can stay."

Again Annie Picard gave an exaggerated shrug. "Do what he says."

Gideon didn't recognize the girl. She was probably off a farm with too many mouths to feed, or a house servant gotten in trouble by her employer and cast out. She wouldn't look him in the eye.

"This was Amanda's room," Picard said. "Felix stayed in a room behind the kitchen. You will not find anything of theirs. They took with them all of their possessions."

"That's not what I heard." Looking around, Gideon saw a bed, a chest of drawers, a couch rather more frayed than the ones in the parlor, a table and lamp. A book with a red cover lay on the table. Gideon picked it up. It was titled *Pride and Prejudice*, and its author was identified as "The author of *Sense and Sensibility*." He was mildly surprised that the girl could read. The room also had a mirror on a wooden stand and a washbasin. A small window looked out behind the house at two outhouses and an ash heap.

Hanging in the closet were a pair of low-cut gowns, one red and the other green. Also some petticoats. In the drawers, various underthings.

"Do these belong to you?" he asked the girl.

"Yes, sir."

"What's your name?"

"Catherine." She plucked at the sides of her dress and made an awkward dipping motion that Gideon realized was intended to be a curtsy.

"Did you know Miss Jones?"

The girl shot a glance at Picard.

"Don't look at her," Gideon said. "Talk to me."

"Yes, I knew Amanda."

"Where did she and Felix Wiley go?"

"Downstate, I think."

"Did they go on their own? Or did someone come and get them?"

The girl's shoulders hitched. "I don't know. One day they were here, the next day they were gone. Mrs. Picard gave me Amanda's room. It's nicer than the one I had. I can't tell you any more than that."

Gideon reckoned he would learn as much from any resident in this house. He nodded goodbye to Catherine, then had Picard show him the room where Wiley had stayed. He found nothing there, either.

The madam followed him to the door.

Before leaving, he asked: "Did Phineas Potter ever come here?"

A half smile came to Picard's face. "The newspaperman? I believe he had no fondness for women."

Ranaway, the negro slave named Jupiter—has a *fresh mark* of a cowskin on one of his cheeks.

Chapter 7

———◦◦◦———

WHEN GIDEON WAS A DEPUTY, THE SHERIFF WHO HAD HIRED him, a slight, soft-spoken man named Israel Payton, told him that if a serious crime wasn't solved within a few days—if no one reported anything suspicious, if a crucial piece of evidence failed to turn up, if a ne'er-do-well didn't brag about their misdeed—then the thing might remain a mystery forever.

Gideon knew he must quickly learn as much as he could about Phineas Potter, dead now for almost thirty-six hours.

Sheriff Payton himself had been dead for three years, felled by a stroke of apoplexy, after which the Colerain County commissioners had appointed his young deputy as the new sheriff. Who now went scuffing down the street in Hammertown past quiet empty saloons, leaning fences slapped together from mismatched boards, and drab cramped houses.

He tried to banish from his mind the image of Phineas Potter's broken corpse and call up instead a vigorous man with a firm jaw, a full head of wavy brown hair, and a friendly smile.

Gideon had felt the warmth of that smile a week ago. He and Potter had been approaching one another on Franklin Street. Potter looked preoccupied, maybe worried. Before they met, he glanced up and saw Gideon. A smile overspread his face. Gideon thought Potter might stop and strike up a conversation, but the fellow had made some remark—Gideon recalled an offhand "Good to see you, Sheriff"—and continued past.

Annie Picard said Potter had "no fondness for women." Was he instead attracted to other men? Could that predilection have put Potter in danger? Gotten him killed?

Potter was educated and apparently well off. Like any newspaper publisher, he had used his paper to promote his own views. Potter railed against the backwoods populism and imperiousness of former president Andrew Jackson, scornfully calling him "King Andrew." Last autumn the *Argus* had promoted the Whig nominee for president, the Ohioan William Henry Harrison, while lambasting Jackson's handpicked Democratic successor, Martin Van Buren of New York, who ended up winning the popular vote by a slim margin.

A Democrat had also won the vice presidency: Richard Mentor Johnson of Kentucky, renowned for his past affections toward one of his female slaves, whom he had openly treated as his common-law wife and who had borne him two children before dying in a cholera epidemic. Gideon recalled an article in the *Argus*, a reprint from some other newspaper, that deprecated Johnson's current lover—also a black woman—as "a thick-lipped, odoriferous negro wench."

Did printing that article, with its cruel description, mean that Potter was repelled by negroes? Or by women? Or was he just trying to sell papers? Or drum up Whig votes?

Most Democrats tended to support slavery, whereas Whigs opposed it. True to Whig values, the *Argus* strongly advocated abolishing slavery. But abolitionists didn't always agree with each other. Potter's stance on colonization—returning emancipated people to Africa—had infuriated Melchior Dorfman and no doubt other residents in Adamant.

Why did Potter favor colonization? Was he simply against slavery, or did he fear the political power of free men of color? Or did he hate the idea of amalgamation, the mingling of the white and black races?

Potter seemed to Gideon to be a bundle of contradictions. As so many people were.

A man belonging to the Colerain County Anti-Slavery Society worked on this side of Spring Creek: Hack Latimer, the tall, lanky fellow who had come rushing to the front of the church on Sunday evening to help protect the abolitionist speaker when the crowd got ugly. Maybe Latimer could shed some light on Potter, his friends and activities.

As he neared Latimer's sawmill, Gideon heard the creaking of the water wheel as it transferred power to the mill. He entered the open-sided shed to a din of gears clacking, belts groaning, wheels screeching, and the rhythmic rasping of the up-and-down saw as it bit through a log.

Seeing Gideon, Latimer gestured for them to go out into the relative quiet of the yard.

Once there, Latimer brushed sawdust off his shirtsleeves and shook hands with Gideon. He had deep-set eyes above prominent cheekbones. He was as tall as Gideon but packed less meat on his bones. Latimer set his boot on a stack of fresh oak boards whose smell reminded Gideon of cat piss.

"Have you heard about Phineas Potter?" Gideon asked.

"Poor devil," Latimer said. "I heard he was robbed and killed. Then they hid him under some brush."

"Mr. Latimer, I am trying to learn more about Mr. Potter. You belong to the anti-slavery society. He often wrote about your group in his paper."

"Phineas printed some good anti-slavery stories," Latimer said. "I can't say I agreed with him on colonization, though. Sending those poor folks back to Africa, after they helped build this country with their sweat and blood? That would be just plain wrong."

"I imagine others feel the same way."

"You bet they do. Get pretty riled up about it."

"Who?"

Latimer named several men, including Melchior Dorfman.

"Do you think any of them were mad enough to harm Potter?"

Latimer shook his head. "No. It just sounds to me like Phineas was in the wrong place at the wrong time and some highwaymen got him."

"Any idea why he might have been on the Halfmoon Valley road that night?"

"No idea."

"How long have you known Potter?"

"I met him when I was a little shaver—eleven years old. Right after the roof fell on my head. My folks sent me to the Academy." Latimer looked toward the pale limestone building on its hill. "Phineas was a student there. A couple years older than me. Quite the scholar, which I never was."

"You say a roof fell on your head?"

Latimer grinned. "I took an ax to the posts for a porch on a house my pa was building. The workmen were off having lunch. I was pretty rambunctious back then."

"Why did you chop down the posts?"

"To see what would happen. The last post I was hacking away at snapped, and before I could get out of the way that roof came down on me like a thousand of bricks. Knocked me out for three days. I been called Hack ever since."

Gideon winced inwardly. He, too, had suffered a bad concussion last year after falling off Maude. He'd lost a chunk of his memory for a while, although it had come back. Even now, headaches and dizzy spells plagued him at times, especially when he was tired. "After you recovered," he said to Latimer, "why did your parents send you to the school?"

"They wanted to reform me. Though I am dubious it succeeded." Latimer winked and clapped Gideon on the shoulder. "I purely hated it. Having to walk up that hill every day, sit in a stuffy classroom and listen to old Foote try to drum Greek and Latin into my head, along with lit'ature and history and physics—I reckon I already knew plenty about the law of gravity, didn't I?" He laughed.

"How long did you attend?"

"Four very long years."

"And you got to know Potter then. What was he like?"

"Always had his nose in a book. Kept to himself, didn't join in the fun and games. After a while, I told my parents I was done—I quit school. And Phineas went off to college."

"Then later he came back and started his newspaper. Did you get to know him then?"

"When he wanted to print something on the anti-slavery society, he'd meet with a few of us." Latimer named several individuals— a preacher, a merchant, an employee at one of the banks.

"Did you get to know Potter socially?"

"Phineas and me, we didn't run in the same circles."

"Was Mr. Potter"—Gideon struggled to find the right words— "was he physically attracted to men?"

The smile vanished from Latimer's face. "I won't speak ill of the dead. Phineas never tried nothing funny with me. And I never saw him in the places I frequented."

"Such as?"

"Hammertown, Sheriff. I admit it, I used to wet my whistle there. It's right on my doorstep." Latimer indicated a small house near the sawmill. "That's where I live, to keep an eye on things. Else the lumber tends to sprout legs and wander off."

"Are you married, Mr. Latimer?"

"You sure are full of questions," Latimer chuckled. "I was all set to get hitched a few years ago, but the woman said I had to quit drinking and smoking. I told her to find someone else to boss around. But nowadays, I'm a reformed man. I don't waste my money on booze or tobacco."

"Do you know if Potter had any close friends?"

"I couldn't say."

"Did he have a horse?"

"I think I've seen him on a horse a time or two."

"Any idea where he kept it?"

Latimer shook his head.

"Have you heard that several colored people have gone missing in the county recently?" Gideon named them.

"I heard a rumor about that," Latimer said. "But I can't tell you anything. I just saw wood and sell lumber. Plenty of building going on in town these days. I'm taking the mill over from my pa. Sheriff, if we are done here, I need to help my sawyer set up the next log."

Gideon thanked Latimer for his time. He headed for the covered bridge, crossed the creek, and trudged back up High Street to the center of town. His stomach reminded him that it was noon, and he set off for home.

Between mouthfuls of fried pork and steamed poke shoots, he told True about meeting the Virginians Waller and Blaine and then talking to Annie Picard and Hack Latimer.

"It disgusts me," True said, "those two slave hunters here in Adamant. I bet Waller fathered that boy on one of his slave girls."

"That could explain why he's so anxious to find him." Gideon told True about the big reward.

She frowned. "He catches him, he'll drag that boy back to his plantation and whip or brand him to set an example for the ones who haven't run."

"Honey, do you recall me telling you about the lad I met in Greer County last year when I got into that scrap?"

"When you fought with that constable, the one who cracked your ribs."

"Yes. After the fight, the boy warned me that the man's brothers were coming. He said he'd send them in the other direction. If he hadn't done that . . . Anyway, I'm pretty sure he's the one Waller is hunting." It hit him, then: the bind he'd be in if Waller caught the lad and asked Gideon to hold him in the jail before returning to Virginia.

"Must you help that wicked man?" True asked.

"If I don't, I could lose my job."

"Then maybe you have the wrong job."

Gideon was astonished to hear True say that. His wife had been saying and doing many surprising things lately. True had grown up in this county; she knew it and its residents in ways he never would. "What can you tell me about Annie Picard?" he asked. "Is she really French?"

"She is. Years ago, a gang of French people came through here. On foot, pushing handcarts with their belongings. I heard they stopped in Adamant and bought supplies. Then they kept walking, up onto the mountaintop, where they started that Frenchtown."

Once when riding on Maude, familiarizing himself with the county, Gideon had passed through that settlement. It was on the Allegheny Plateau, a high rolling upland north and west of Adamant, a place with thin soil, where winter came early and stayed late.

"A man from downstate owns a big tract of land up there," True said. "He settled a debt with some other silk stocking over in France by giving him thousands of acres. Then the Frenchman sold the land to a bunch of families, probably telling them how good it was for farming. Imagine how those folks must have felt when they crossed the ocean, pushed their carts all the way up there, and found out what a poor bargain they'd made.

"Annie Picard didn't come till later," True continued. "Maybe she heard about Adamant from the ones in Frenchtown. Those folks are poor, but Annie's rich—leastwise she had the money to buy that fancy house. Gid, I knew a woman who ended up there. Bess Calhoun; her husband got killed in an accident at the ironworks. Afterward, the ironmaster kicked Bess out of their cabin. She went to Hammertown and whored for Annie Picard. Later she threw herself in the creek and drowned."

"I remember you telling me that sad tale."

"So you went and talked to Hack Latimer," True said. "I wouldn't trust that man."

"Why not?"

"I dislike the way he looks at me on the street. Same with your deputy Gaither Brown, not to mention a bunch of other men." She set her jaw. "Hack is a gambler. Dice, cards, cockfights, he'll bet on anything. He likes his wenches. He's a hard drinker. That's what Jesse says." Jesse Burns was the youngest of True's four brothers, all older than she, all employed by the ironworks in one capacity or another. "Jesse told me he made a bet with Hack last fall. Hack wagered you'd lose the election, since nobody in Colerain County would vote for a Dutchman as sheriff. Jesse bet that you'd win."

Gideon was amazed to learn that his irascible brother-in-law had believed he could be elected and then bet on him like a horse in a race.

"Everyone thinks Hack is a changed man," True said, "ever since he stood up at camp meeting last summer and hollered about giving his soul to Jesus while the old women bawled and trickled snot and yelled 'Praise be to the Lord, our Judah is saved!' That's his real name, Judah Latimer. Hack joined the abolition society and the temperance one, too. But Jesse says he didn't stop drinking or smoking or any of his other vices."

Gideon mopped up grease on his plate with some bread and put it in his mouth. "Can you tell me anything about Phineas Potter?"

"Well. He was a real handsome man."

Gideon grinned. "So you look at the men even though you don't like it when they look at you?"

She punched him in the arm. "Have you thought any more about what kind of gun I should get?"

"I thought we decided that you didn't need a gun."

"Maybe you decided that. But my mind is made up. I am getting a pistol to protect myself when I ride out on Jack. You can help me or not."

Ran away, negress Caroline—had on a *collar with one prong* *turned down*.

Chapter 8

———— ∞∞∞ ————

A	T THE JAIL, GIDEON TOLD ALONZO ABOUT HIS VISIT TO ANNIE Picard's house. "The rumors may be true. Two mixed-race people, a man and a woman, disappeared from there recently. Picard said they went back to Philadelphia of their own free will. But I don't think she was telling the truth."

Alonzo kept mum. Gideon considered that unusual. Alonzo was a talkative soul, sometimes too talkative. Soon after Gideon had become sheriff, he'd been urged to hire Alonzo as his deputy by one of the county commissioners. Alonzo looked rather dull but was in fact quite intelligent. The man had helped Gideon in countless ways: introduced him to dozens of people, taught him to be a better marksman, showed him different parts of the county on maps and on the ground. Told jokes and made quips that entertained Gideon and helped keep his spirits up.

"What can you tell me about Madame Picard's establishment?" Gideon asked.

Alonzo formed his rough features into an expression of innocence. "Why should I know about her house of ill repute?"

"She says you're a patron."

Alonzo's eyebrows lifted and he fingered his ear.

"For starters, who is that big wall-eyed thug that answers the door?"

"A manservant she brung over from the land of the frog-eaters."

"Does he have a name?"

"I have heard him called Pierre. He got in some trouble over there, one of their riots or revolutions or some such. He dodged the machine they have, the one that cuts off your head."

"He looks like a rough customer."

"I should go sweep the cells," Alonzo said.

"They can wait. During your visits to Annie Picard's, did you, um, get to know Amanda Jones?"

Alonzo shook his head. His face was weathered, but Gideon thought he detected a flush.

"Have you heard anything about her?"

"Only that she's a screamer."

"Meaning?"

"When she does the deed, she's noisy. Inspiration for the customer, gets things over and done with quick." Alonzo looked toward the cells. "I really do need to sweep. I try to redd 'em up once a week, and it's been a while. They are filthy."

"Oh, all right. When you're done, go ask around at the livery stables and try to find out where Potter kept his horse. Get a description of the horse if you can. And maybe someone knows why he went to the Halfmoon Valley that night."

Gideon sat down at the desk with the Pennsylvania fugitive slave statute that Fish had given him—the recent law that the state's attorney said was inferior to the federal one. He reckoned that it was this law that the tinsmith Melchior Dorfman had said the black people in Adamant expected Gideon to enforce.

Before opening the pamphlet, he thought about how disturbed Fish had been last evening on learning of Potter's death—and how stunned and despairing he had seemed this morning, with his breath reeking of liquor. Gideon had never known Fish to drink. Rumor had it that he was a teetotaler, that strange new word that temperance advocates were using to describe total abstainers who never let a drop of alcohol touch their lips.

Of course Fish would be shocked by the news that a friend had been murdered. But had relations between Fish and Potter gone deeper than mere friendship? The thought of those two together made Gideon's flesh crawl. Then again, the thought of Fish with a woman was no less repugnant, Fish being so ill-made and hateful.

Gideon disliked the state's attorney deeply. The Cold Fish ridiculed his Dutch accent and slighted his intelligence. He was always pointing out Gideon's youth and inexperience, railing at him for any mistake, and generally making it hard for him to do his job.

Gideon opened the pamphlet. *"The Pennsylvania Fugitive Slave Act of 1826. An Act to Give Effect to the Provisions of the Constitution of the United States, Relative to Fugitives from Labor, for the Protection of Free People of Color, and to Prevent Kidnapping."*

Three pages of legal verbiage that seemed largely aimed at preventing people from abducting free negroes and carrying them into slavery. But the law also made it harder for someone from outside the state to come to Pennsylvania and reclaim anyone who had run to freedom.

The law required a slave owner or his representative to obtain a warrant from a Pennsylvania judge or justice of the peace. To do that, they first had to present an affidavit with the name, age, and description of the runaway, issued and legally authorized by an official in their home state. Someone from Maryland or Virginia couldn't just show up, nab a fugitive as you might round up a horse that had strayed, go before a Pennsylvania judge or magistrate, and declare: "This is my property, and I'm taking him home." And yet, thought Gideon, according to the Cold Fish that was exactly what had happened ten years ago in Judge Biddle's courtroom.

The Pennsylvania law specified that anyone who tried to carry a negro or a mulatto out of Pennsylvania without following the correct procedure could be charged with felony kidnapping and imprisoned for up to twenty-one years.

Gideon doubted that Tazewell Waller had an affidavit or a warrant to recover his runaway; if he did, he would have come straight to Gideon and presented it. Instead, Waller referred to the federal act of 1793, which made it much easier to reclaim a fugitive.

But what if Waller followed the Pennsylvania law to the letter? What if he or any Southerner marched a person to the jail, handed Gideon a properly obtained warrant, and said "Please lock my servant in one of your cells." According to the state statute that Gideon had just read, it would be his legal duty to jail the runaway and let the unfortunate soul be hauled back into slavery. If he didn't do that, he could be prosecuted himself.

And the federal law was even more stringent. The Cold Fish had said it directed state officials, including sheriffs, to actively *help* a slave owner or his agent reclaim a fugitive.

How would he feel if he were forced to help Waller capture that boy—even if he wasn't the same lad who had helped Gideon out of that jam last summer? And how would True react? She seemed to have thought more about slavery than he had. She was dead set against it. Maybe because she'd been one step above such servitude when she worked as a chore girl in the ironmaster's house in Panther. Gideon knew that something bad had taken place there; he believed the ironmaster had molested True and perhaps done worse. But True had never told him exactly what happened back then.

Just as he had never told her what had befallen his mother thirteen years earlier in Lancaster County in the kitchen of their family's home.

He got up from his desk. Alonzo was still busily sweeping the cells. Gideon called to him: "That's enough cleaning. Go see if you can find where Potter kept his horse. Also, I need you to go with me to Hammertown tonight. Let's meet at the covered bridge at nine."

"Armed?" Alonzo replied.

"That won't be necessary."

Gideon left the jail and went to Melchior Dorfman's shop. When he stepped inside, the tinner looked up from his work.

"Have you heard anything about John Horne?" Gideon asked.

"No. But I'm sure he's been kidnapped and is being held against his will somewhere." Dorfman held a mallet in his right hand, a sharp iron punch in his left. "I think John has been so badly used in the past that he may not even be in his right mind at this point. I've told everyone I know to ask their friends and neighbors if they've seen or heard anything."

"I spoke with Madame Picard about the two other people you mentioned," Gideon said. "She told me they left two weeks ago of their own free will. The next time the coach comes, I'll talk to the driver and see if he remembers them. And the two Virginia men are still looking for the boy they call Leo Waller."

"If that child is in Adamant," Dorfman said, "and if those men try to take him, they will find they kicked a hornets' nest."

"Mr. Dorfman, I uphold the law in Colerain County. I won't tolerate mayhem or violence, not from those men and not from you or anyone else. In the meantime, I will continue to investigate Phineas Potter's death." Gideon knew he needed to bring up the subject, and he was ready for Dorfman's anger: "I was surprised to meet you on the road so soon after we recovered his body. And not far from where he was killed."

Dorfman glared. "What's your point?"

"Sometimes a person who commits a crime will go back to the same place afterward."

The tinner slammed his tools down on his bench. He rose and stood squared on to Gideon. He took a step forward. "You're just like the rest of them."

Gideon did not back up. "Mr. Dorfman, I am not blaming you or accusing you of anything. I am just trying to conduct a thorough investigation."

"I told you I had been to John's cabin. That's all I did. And that's the God's truth."

"Did you or anyone you know hate Potter for his views?"

"Hate him enough to kill him? Don't be a fool."

Gideon shrugged. "Maybe someone decided he had kicked a hornets' nest."

RAN AWAY, a Negro Boy, named PETER, about 18 or 20 years of age, five feet seven or eight inches high, well proportioned in make, has a pleasing countenance, smiles when spoken to, and is very intelligent. He is easily frightened by the whip, and may be made to tell the truth readily.

Chapter 9

⬩⬩⬩

PHINEAS POTTER'S PRINTING BUSINESS WAS ON THE SECOND FLOOR above a furniture-maker's shop. Gideon was surprised to hear someone moving around inside. He called out "Hello?" and then tried the door and found it unlocked.

A young man looked up from the printing press.

In the office were newspapers and pamphlets on shelves, wooden racks of type, ink scuffs on the walls along with sample handbills ornamented with livestock, houses, boots, wagons, plows—one showed a black man in profile, down on one knee and raising clasped and shackled hands above the message AM I NOT A MAN AND A BROTHER? Bills with that image had been put up around town advertising the abolitionist's speech.

Gideon said he was the sheriff and asked the young man's name.

"Lemuel Robinson, sir."

Robinson looked about sixteen years old. The young man wore ink-stained gloves. He had a chunky build, dark hair, a wide mouth. It looked like tears had tracked down through the grime on his cheeks.

"You are an apprentice?"

"Yes, sir."

"Why are you still at work?"

"I . . . I didn't know what else to do. I know I'll have to leave here soon."

"I'm sorry your master was killed."

Robinson looked at Gideon through shining eyes. "Mr. Potter was teaching me to be a printer. He took care of my food and lodging."

"Did he tell you why he was going to Halfmoon Valley that night?"

"No, sir."

"Did he have a horse?"

"Yes."

"Where did he keep it?"

Robinson shook his head. "I don't know."

"Did Mr. Potter talk with you about stories he was working on for the paper?"

"Sometimes."

"Was he working on anything in particular?"

"He was planning to write about the speech by the abolitionist from Connecticut."

"Anything else?"

"Not that I know of."

"Were you at the speech?"

"No, I stayed home. At Shaw's."

It was a boardinghouse.

"Did Mr. Potter ever talk to you about slavery or abolitionism?"

"He talked about those things all the time. He even sent money away so that black people, the ones who'd been freed, could go live in Africa."

"Where are his notebooks?"

Robinson showed Gideon a cluttered desk with three bound books sitting in one corner. Gideon leafed through the top one: at a glance, Potter's writing looked almost indecipherable. He put the books under his arm. "Have you ever been to his house?"

"A few times." Robinson stammered: "He'd invite me to supper now and then. He would talk about all kinds of things, politics, history, world events, how to find out the news." The apprentice gestured toward one of the many stacks of newspapers. "We get over a hundred papers each month, from all over the country. We get them for free—that's one of my chores, to go pick them up at the post office and to take copies of the *Argus* there to be mailed out. Then I read through the papers looking for stories, interesting things like wars and plagues and shipwrecks and elections—anything and everything."

"You then set the stories in type?"

Robinson nodded. He pointed at the heavy cast-iron press that dominated the room. "Mr. Potter bought it in Philadelphia. Isn't it beautiful?"

A pair of ornate brass finials decorated the top corners of the press's head-high iron frame, which also bore inlaid brass ovals depicting the profiles of two men, George Washington and some other bewigged gent that Gideon couldn't immediately identify.

"Does Mr. Potter have family in the area?" Gideon asked.

"His sister, Mrs. Philomena Hutchinson, she lives in Walkersville."

Walkersville was the county seat of Greer County, adjoining Colerain County to the south.

"Her husband's name?"

"Glenn Hutchinson. They have the inn on the town square."

"Lemuel, do you know if Mr. Potter ever helped runaway slaves? Did he hide them, here or at his house? It's all right. You can tell me."

Robinson's shoulders twitched upward. "I don't know. Maybe. He was a kind man." Robinson looked at Gideon with his sad eyes. "Are you going to make me leave, Sheriff?"

"That's not for me to do."

"My parents sent me here because I have too many brothers and sisters. There was never enough food. And I wanted to learn a trade." His eyes filled with tears. "I have two years left on my contract."

"Do you know if Mr. Potter had any enemies?"

"None that I know of."

"Did anyone owe him money? Or did he owe anyone money?"

"I don't know."

"Any odd incidents lately? Someone angry about a story that ran in the paper, or anything else?"

"Not really. Well, there was one thing. Two men came in the other day. They were from Virginia. They asked Mr. Potter to print some bills for a runaway they were hunting."

"And . . . ?"

"Mr. Potter wouldn't take the job. One of the men, the older one, got real mad."

"Did the man threaten him?"

"I don't know if it was a threat or not, but he said, 'You'll regret this.' Then they left."

"Thanks for talking with me," Gideon said. "If you think of anything else, you can find me at the jail." Then he added: "I hope things work out for you, Lemuel. I really do."

This statement of concern was too much for the young man. Tears ran down his cheeks as he wordlessly turned back to the printing press.

$5 REWARD for the apprehension and delivery of negro boy **ALFRED**, who escaped my farm. He is about 5 feet high, tolerably black—had on a low-crown white hat, white kersey over jacket, pants blue & red.

Chapter 10

⊶⊷

A ROSY EVENING LIGHT BATHED ADAMANT'S DWELLINGS BOTH humble and refined. Gideon climbed a dirt street to the Academy, a four-story building with windows arranged symmetrically in its gray limestone facade.

A boy who looked to be twelve or thirteen answered Gideon's knock and said he'd go find the headmaster.

Waiting in the entry, Gideon thought of another boy of about the same age who had been born into slavery, fled from his master, evaded capture in Virginia and Maryland, crossed into Pennsylvania, traveled north to a desolate, violence-ridden hamlet in Greer County—and who might now be hiding somewhere in Adamant. A boy who probably had never been taught to read or write, or attended school, or learned things that would set him on the path to becoming a doctor, a lawyer, a teacher, a newspaperman, a sheriff.

A boy who might be just as intelligent as the youngster now fetching the headmaster—and surely a lot more determined, to have survived thus far.

Back came the student. "Mr. Foote says to go on up."

Gideon often visited Foote in his rooms on the top floor of the Academy, which the headmaster called his "aerie." Horatio Foote had good whiskey on offer and a trove of knowledge about the natural world and Adamant and Colerain County.

As Gideon reached the landing, he heard a strange chuckling sound.

He stepped through the doorway into a suite of connected rooms that collectively resembled a library, a menagerie, a museum. Books filled floor-to-ceiling shelves. A box turtle trundled across the carpet. Glass-fronted cases displayed polished stones, fossil annelids, iridescent beetles. Mounted furred and feathered animals stared glassy-eyed from the walls.

Gideon smelled something musky and disagreeable.

The headmaster stood with his back to Gideon, facing an iron cage about five feet square. On the floor of the cage, a dark animal paced back and forth. Three feet long, with a bushy tail, a sinuous body, and a broad triangular head. It leaped onto a section of tree branch fixed to the back of the enclosure and stared at Gideon with small baleful eyes.

"My new creature," the headmaster said in a wondering tone.

Foote had a long narrow nose and a head of wispy white hair. White sideburns extended most of the way to his pointed chin. In one hand he held a small gray bird, dead. Tentatively he extended the bird through one of the rectangular cage openings.

The creature sprang from the branch, hit the grating with a bang, and seized the bird in its jaws, causing Foote to jerk his hand back.

On the floor of the cage, the animal held the bird down with its front paws, tore it apart with its teeth, and gulped the pieces down.

"What in heaven's name is it?" Gideon asked.

"I am not completely sure. I purchased him—and the creature is definitely a 'him,' for he has a baculum—for fifteen dollars."

"A baculum?"

"*Os priapi.* A penis bone. Possessed by ursids and mustelids; absent, of course, in *Homo sapiens.* Or the males of our species would wander about embarrassed much of the time. There! You can see it when his ventral parts are visible."

The creature jumped back to the tree branch and sounded the querulous chuckling that Gideon had heard earlier. "That's quite an interesting feature of anatomy," Gideon said.

Foote explained that a local trapper named Meshach Browning had caught the creature. Gideon knew Browning all too well: a grime-encrusted, strong-smelling individual who lived in the mountains south of Adamant and who frequently brought the skins of wolves and panthers to the jail for bounty payments.

"When Meshach captured this fellow," Foote said, "knowing of my interest in natural marvels, he brought him here in a stout wooden box—which this devil had just about chewed through by the time he arrived."

"He looks like a big weasel."

"Indeed. The musky smell indicates that he belongs to Family Mustelidae. Meshach calls him a wejack. He may be a fisher marten, *Mustela canadensis*, so named by von Schreber. Meshach says the wejack is one of the few beasts that can kill a porcupine. It darts in and bites the porcupine's face again and again, avoiding its quills. When it has subdued its prey, the wejack flips the porcupine over and devours it from the belly up. Or down, as the case may be. I would dearly love to see that. If you happen onto a porcupine, could you bring it here? Now let us share a drink in celebration of my new acquisition."

From a thick columnar vessel Foote poured an amber liquid into two glasses. The large vessel resembled the numerous containers sitting on shelves in the room, each housing some embalmed biologic specimen, which Gideon generally avoided looking at too closely.

The headmaster handed Gideon one of the glasses and motioned to a pair of chairs facing the wejack's cage.

"What will you do with him?" Gideon asked as he and Foote settled into the chairs.

"Observe him. If he dies, dissect him and then stuff him."

"And if he doesn't die?"

"Perhaps he will become indolent. Trusting."

The creature slammed into the front of the cage and sounded its agitated chuckling again. Gideon doubted very much that the wejack would oblige Foote in any way.

"Have you heard about Phineas Potter?" he asked.

Foote gave him an inquisitive look.

"He's dead," Gideon said.

"No!"

"His body was found along the Halfmoon Valley road. Killed late Sunday night or early Monday morning."

"Dear God, what happened?"

"He was run over by a wagon."

"An accident?"

"Maybe. I suppose he could have been on the road and got hit accidentally. But someone also bashed him over the head with a rock."

A sharp intake of breath from the headmaster.

Gideon sipped his whiskey. "They hid his body under a pile of limbs. I found a lantern, badly damaged, that had been thrown off into the brush. I wonder if Potter was signaling to someone when he got hit."

Foote took a gulp of whiskey. "I can't believe Phineas is dead."

"He was at the speech Sunday evening. I saw you there, too. Did you talk to him?"

"Briefly. He told me he's been trying to drum up subscriptions. The *Argus* hasn't been as profitable as he'd hoped. And he wanted to make people think about the problems the country is facing—banks failing, the flood of counterfeit money, alcohol abuse. Violence in the cities. And the wickedest sin of all, slavery."

"Were you and Potter friends?"

"He was my pupil, and that can create a certain barrier. But later we became friends. I admired his principles. He editorialized often about abolishing slavery. He was keen to set up a country for freed slaves in Africa and return them there. Phineas felt that blacks and whites could never coexist on equal terms in this country. That the cruel and barbarous things the white man has done to the negro has made it impossible for the two races to dwell in harmony."

"Maybe he was right," Gideon said.

"Think of that uprising in Virginia a few years ago, Nat Turner's rebellion," Foote said. "Dozens of whites murdered. And the riots in the cities, when whites turn on blacks and beat them, burn their homes and churches. Cincinnati last year. Washington, Philadelphia, New York. Even my home state of Connecticut, the Canterbury Female Boarding School: the people in that otherwise peaceable town tried to burn the school down because the headmistress had the temerity to admit colored students. When the fire didn't catch, they broke in with iron bars and terrorized those poor girls."

"Do any black students attend your academy?"

Foote shook his head.

"Would you accept them?"

"Of course. But I wonder if the people of Adamant would countenance it. I hear that Sarah Dorfman, the tinner's wife, is schooling colored children in her home. And doing a fine job of it."

"What was Potter like as a student?"

"One of the most intelligent young men who ever attended the Academy. A good-hearted boy who became a fine man."

"Can you think of any reason why he might have been on the Halfmoon Valley road in the middle of the night?"

Foote raised his glass and drained it. "The Halfmoon Valley. The place got its name from the half-moon markings hacked into the bark of trees. They were found by the first settlers. It is supposed that the lunar images denoted an Indian trail." Foote picked up the columnar vessel and poured himself another drink, then raised his eyebrows at Gideon, who shook his head and covered the top of his glass with his hand.

Gideon asked again: "Can you think of why Potter might have been on that road at night?"

"No," the headmaster said.

"Are you certain?"

Foote closed his mouth tightly and looked aside.

Gideon tried not to let himself feel hurt—Foote had always been forthcoming with him. He would try a different tack.

"In looking into Potter's associates," Gideon said, "I learned that he was connected with Mr. Fish, the state's attorney. Do you know if he had any other friends?"

"Many people were acquainted with Phineas. I do not know of any particularly close friends."

"Potter was unmarried." Gideon decided to ask Foote the question he had posed to Hack Latimer earlier, and that he had thought of, and left unasked, when talking to Lemuel Robinson, the newspaperman's apprentice: "Was he attracted to other men?"

Foote said curtly: "I do not choose to answer such a question."

Gideon couldn't recall the headmaster ever replying to him in such a snappish way.

"As a teacher, I have learned not to be censorious," Foote said. "I am unmarried myself, as you know. Sometimes life turns out a certain way. One fails to find a compatible partner. And all of us are calibrated differently. Who is to say what is 'natural' and what is not?"

Gideon paused to ponder that statement, thought for a moment of True, who might have said the same thing. "Earlier today I spoke with Hack Latimer. He said he knew Potter when they were in school here. Latimer told me he attended the Academy for several years, and that he was an indifferent scholar."

"Yes. His attention span was virtually nonexistent."

"A result of his concussion? He told me that when he was a boy, a roof fell on his head."

"Perhaps his behavior stemmed from that injury. He was disruptive. Always playing pranks. Big for his age, and a bully."

"Yet he seems to have turned out all right," Gideon said. "He runs the sawmill. And he belongs to the anti-slavery society. You are also a member, correct?"

Foote nodded.

"Do the people in the anti-slavery society hide runaway slaves? Do they help fugitives get away to the north?"

"I have never considered question and answer to be a civilized form of conversation," Foote said.

"I am sorry. I'm just doing my job. And I am not sure I really want to know the answer to that question." He explained to Foote about the three colored people who had gone missing. "There's a rumor that they were kidnapped to be sold into slavery in the South."

"Abominable."

Gideon followed the headmaster's gaze. The wejack in its cage looked like a coiled brown muscle that might lash out at any moment. Perhaps reacting to the two men's stares, the creature began pacing back and forth again. Suddenly it vaulted onto the side of the cage, clung to the iron mesh, and sounded its anxious chuckling.

Gideon downed the rest of his whiskey and rose from his chair. "Thank you for the drink, Mr. Foote. If you think of anything else, you know where to find me."

Ran away, my man Peter. He has a *sister* and *mother* in New Kent, and a *wife* about fifteen or eighteen miles above Richmond, at or about Taylorsville.

Chapter 11

F OR THE SECOND TIME THAT EVENING, GIDEON SMELLED A DISA-greeable rank odor. He emerged from the darkness of the covered bridge into the day's fading light.

Alonzo stood waiting.

Gideon wrinkled his nose. "What's that smell?"

"What smell?"

"Like rotten eggs."

"Oh. It might be me. I had a mess of ramps for supper."

Gideon blew out his breath. "You reek."

"I tell you, ramps are just the thing for cleaning the blood in springtime," Alonzo replied. "Keep your fiddleheads and dandy lines and pokeweed, and give me a good gorge of ramps any day."

"Don't get too close to me," Gideon said.

They made their way into Hammertown, Alonzo whistling fragrantly. They had not brought lanterns, but the light from the brightening stars and lamplight leaking out through house and saloon windows let them see well enough.

Alonzo said he'd been unable to learn anything about Potter's horse. Perhaps he kept it in a private barn rather than in one of the livery stables.

Gideon told Alonzo that this evening he hoped to find out more about Potter and the missing people. He didn't mention that he also would be looking for a spare-built, small-for-his-age colored lad. Again Gideon wondered what he would do if he encountered the boy. Warn him of the reward on his head? Urge him to leave town?

Or, at some point, would he be obliged to secure and detain him?

They detoured around garbage and pig manure in the street. A woman's high-pitched laughter rang out. A dog's sharp barking set others yapping.

They entered the tavern called the Guinea Hen. Tallow lamps threw a wavery light. Customers were few on this weekday evening. Four workmen in dirty clothes sat around a table using redware mugs to dip drinks out of a porcelain bowl. A three-handed card game occupied another table. A broadside tacked to the wall caught Gideon's eye: labeled LIFE IN PHILADELPHIA, it showed a cartoon of an extravagantly dressed black couple, the man in a swallowtail coat and the woman wearing a large, flower-bedecked hat. The caption said: "How you find youself dis hot wedder, Miss Chloe?" "Pretty well, I tank you, Mr. Cesar, only I aspire too much."

Gideon joined Alonzo at the bar. The tavern was redolent of harsh tobacco smoke and stale beer. "This place smells almost as bad as you," Gideon said.

"I'll get you some ramps," Alonzo replied. "Your wife can cook them up and then you won't smell me."

The saloonkeeper had a stoop to his back and a patch of white in his dark hair.

"What can I do you for?" The man pulled back. "Christ! You smell bad enough to make a baby cry."

Gideon glanced at Alonzo before addressing the man. "You probably heard that the newspaperman Phineas Potter was killed two nights ago."

"I have been brokenhearted ever since," the saloonkeeper said. "Damned do-gooder complained in his rag about liquor and gaming and cockfights and pretty much everything else pleasurable in this world."

"Did he ever come in here?"

The man scoffed and shook his head.

"How about a black man named John Horne? He wears an old blue uniform coat. Might have a dog with him. Also a mixed-race man and woman named Felix Wiley and Amanda Jones."

"The coloreds don't come in here. Try the Horse."

"Do you know Hack Latimer?"

"He's a rig and a half, that one. I wish he'd step in the door this very minute and settle his debts."

"He owes you money?"

"He sure does. No ifs, ands, ors, buts, shits, or pisses about it." The man grimaced and stared at Alonzo. "It's you. You smell like a rat that got caught in the wall and died there."

They went on to the House of Lords and then the Buckhorn. At each, the proprietor had heard about Potter's death but said the news-paperman wasn't a patron. They did not know of John Horne or the mixed-race couple and seemed indifferent to the fact that they had gone missing. Both said that Hack Latimer had run up a tab, and expressed a desire that the sawmill man make good on his debts. Back outside, Alonzo huffed. "That barkeep, saying I smell like a snapping turtle that's been dead on the crick bank for two weeks. I tell you, nobody credits how good ramps will set you up after a winter of beans and salt pork."

The Broad Ax had more drinkers and card players. Again Gideon heard that Phineas Potter never patronized the tavern, Hack Latimer owed money, and John Horne and the two other colored people were nonentities.

They went back out in the street. Suddenly Gideon stopped and retraced his steps into the tavern.

On a vacant corner table sat an empty shot glass and a half-full tankard of beer. A man had been drinking by himself at that table two minutes ago. Gideon tried to recall the man's face. Dark-complected, he thought, with a hooked nose. No beard, but the man needed a shave. There was something vaguely familiar about that rough visage shadowed beneath a hat brim. And why had the man left so suddenly, without finishing his beer? Gideon looked around and saw a back door.

He asked the waitress about the fellow.

She shook her head. "I don't know his name."

"Is he always by himself, or does he come in here with friends?"

She thought for a while. "By himself. Always sets right there if that table is empty."

"Does he do or say anything?"

"Not that I recall. He just drinks and watches who goes in and out."

Alonzo tapped Gideon's arm. "Let's get going."

"All right. We need to check the Horse."

Gideon had always thought it a feeble name for a saloon. Why not the Red Horse, the White Horse, or the Horse and Rider? Or maybe it should be the Black Horse, since it was the only establishment in Hammertown that seemed to welcome colored patrons.

Upon entering, Gideon immediately spotted Melchior Dorfman at a table with three other men. They all had glasses of whiskey in front of them. The tinsmith was holding forth while the others leaned forward, listening. Gideon recognized one of Dorfman's companions as a freighter—the same stocky, strong-looking fellow who had joined Dorfman in the front of the church on Sunday evening when they'd formed a knot around the abolitionist speaker to protect him from the crowd. He'd seen the two other men working on a house-building crew in town.

Smoke clouded the air above the men. Dorfman held a small cigar between his fingers, waved it while making a point.

Gideon approached the table. "Gentlemen," he said. The men looked up warily. "I'm sure you know Phineas Potter was killed on the Halfmoon Valley road late Sunday night or early Monday morning. I'm looking for information about his death. Have any of you heard anything?"

The freighter and the two carpenters shook their heads and shrugged.

Gideon turned to Dorfman.

"I already told you I was home in bed," the tinner said testily.

"You also told me you never come here to Hammertown."

"What's that stench?" Dorfman looked around, then aimed his cigar at Alonzo. "Someone drag a dead cat in here?"

Nervous laughter from the freighter and the carpenters.

"May I ask what you men have been discussing?" Gideon said.

"Not really any of your business," Dorfman said. "But we're figuring out how to do your job for you. How to find John Horne. Because we don't think you are trying very hard to locate him."

"Since you told me he was missing, I've been asking around town."

"With no results," Dorfman said.

"None so far."

"Have you questioned anyone in Halfmoon Valley?"

"Not yet. But I will go there. I'm also looking for the two other people who went missing from Annie Picard's house. Do any of you know anything more about them?"

Again Dorfman's friends shook their heads.

Gideon turned to Alonzo. "Let's go."

Outside again, the buildings dark and hulking, alleys entering the street from north and south.

"A dead cat," Alonzo said disgustedly. "I don't smell no worse than the cheroot the tin man was sucking on."

Somewhere a voice rose in song:

> *The time is swiftly rolling on*
> *When I must faint and die.*
> *My body to the dust return,*
> *And there forgotten lie.*

The ballad, slow and in the minor mode, was accompanied by a fiddle, the instrument wavering, seeking, finding an approximate unison with the words. Gideon knew the song: "The Dying Preacher." He thought it was Southern.

> *Through heat and cold I've toiled and went,*
> *And wandered in despair;*
> *To call poor sinners to repent*
> *And seek the Savior dear.*

"Let's get out of here," Alonzo said. Gideon hissed him quiet. He wondered where the music came from. An upstairs window?

The baritone voice, pure, unhurried, slid up into the notes:

> *My little children, near my heart,*
> *And nature seems to bind;*
> *It grieves me sorely to depart*
> *And leave you here behind.*

Gideon felt a sudden stab of grief at the thought of his own son, David, gone now for almost a year and a half.

A shout from somewhere: "Sheriff!" Then quick footfalls.

From another direction came the thudding of hooves. At the edge of his vision Gideon saw a gray horse enter the street from an alley, its rider in shadow. The horse picked up a fast trot and headed west into the night.

"Sheriff Stoltz!"

Gideon swiveled his head, saw Tazewell Waller and Franklin Blaine emerge from the darkness.

Waller lurched up to Gideon.

"Have you found him yet?" Waller demanded.

Gideon smelled whiskey on Waller's breath.

Blaine stood a few feet behind. He placed his hand on his employer's arm. Waller shook it off.

"Two days," Waller said loudly. "We have been all over your damn county, and we haven't found hide nor hair of Leo."

"This is a pretty big county," Alonzo said. "Which it would take you way more than two days to ride all over it."

"Let's get back to the hotel, Mr. Waller," Blaine said.

"Not until this yokel tells me when he's going to deliver my boy."

Gideon recalled the Cold Fish saying that he would not prosecute anyone for violating Pennsylvania's fugitive slave law. But Waller and Blaine would not know that.

"If you want to reclaim a fugitive in this state," Gideon said, "you must locate him first. It's not my job to do that. But if you do manage to find this boy, be aware that you are not allowed to capture him. You must first present a warrant . . ."

"What do you mean, 'a warrant'?" Waller bellowed.

"Under Pennsylvania law, you must obtain a warrant from a judge or a justice of the peace before taking a fugitive into custody. To do that, you need an affidavit . . ."

"I don't need any damned papers."

"Mr. Waller, I tell you in all honesty that you do need both a warrant and an affidavit. Why don't you come to the jail tomorrow, and I will explain how the law works."

"I don't answer to any law passed in this blasted abolitionist state. The Constitution of the United States gives me the right to recover what is mine. And by God, that boy belongs to me."

"There's no need for us to stand here arguing," Gideon said. "But I must warn you, there are harsh penalties for breaking the law. The law as it stands in Pennsylvania."

He turned and began walking away. Then stopped when he saw Dorfman and his friends come out of the Horse.

The baritone voice and its partnering fiddle rose up again in the darkness, the sound floating through the air:

> *Though I must now depart from thee,*
> *Let this not grieve your heart;*
> *For you will shortly come to me,*
> *Where we shall never part.*

Dorfman and his three companions halted for a moment and stared at Waller and Blaine. Then they began walking again.

Gideon and Alonzo placed themselves between the Southerners and the four men.

The cigar in the tinner's mouth glowed orange.

Gideon saw Dorfman's freighter friend draw something out of the back of his trousers, keeping it hidden in his hand.

"Stop!" Gideon shouted.

The two carpenters hesitated. Dorfman and the freighter kept coming.

"Twenty-one years at hard labor!" Dorfman yelled. "That's what you get for kidnapping a colored person in Pennsylvania!"

Gideon held up his hand. "Mr. Dorfman, stop now!"

Out of the corner of his eye he saw Waller reach inside his coat and pull out a pistol. Before Waller could aim the gun, Gideon seized the man's hand in both of his and raised it, pointing the weapon in the air.

Waller struggled to level the pistol. He was breathing heavily, and his eyes started from his face.

Gideon held up Waller's hand with all his strength. "Stop right now, Mr. Waller. You've done nothing unlawful so far."

He was taller than the man. Stronger, too. If he wrenched Waller's arm backward, he could break it. He hoped he wouldn't need to do that. And he hoped Dorfman and his friends would keep their distance.

He felt Waller quit trying to bring the gun to bear.

Gideon moved Waller's arm down and to the side. Alonzo took the pistol from the Virginian's hand.

Dorfman and the freighter had stopped five paces away.

"You men go home," Gideon said.

The freighter slipped whatever he'd drawn—a razor? a knife?—back into his belt.

"God damn you, slave man!" Dorfman said. "When you die, the devil will make hash out of you in hell!"

A shower of sparks as the tinner threw his cigar on the ground. He spun on his heel and stalked off, his friends following him.

Waller stood next to Gideon, panting.

Gideon said to Waller: "My deputy and I will escort you and Mr. Blaine back to the hotel. I will hold on to your pistol. When you are ready to leave town, I'll give it back."

Gideon went to where Dorfman had been standing. He picked up the tinner's cast-off cigar, stubbed it out on his boot sole, and pocketed it.

$100 REWARD, ran away from the subscriber, residing in Pleasant Valley, Md., a MULATTO BOY named MEHLON HOPEWELL, about 22 years old, 5 feet 7 or 8 inches high, had on when he left, a homemade lincy frock Coat, Cloth cap, dark pantaloons and a new pair of boots. He is a boy of good countenance and wore his beard on his chin unshaven. He took a horse belonging to Dr. Rush Claget, which he turned loose in the mountain near Smiths town.

Chapter 12

———⟨∞⟩———

OTIS LAY IN BED IN THE ROOM HIGH UP IN THE FANCY HOUSE. HE was bored. It was nighttime, and he knew he should be sleeping, but he wasn't tired after napping off and on all day.

He reckoned he shouldn't complain. The meals came regular, brought by a sour-faced old white lady who clapped the plate down on the table, took out the pot he did his business in, and locked the door behind her.

He always tried the door afterward, just to check.

The room where they'd squirreled him away had a bed with sheets and a quilt, a small table, a chair, and a dormer window. He could look out the window at a tree. The tree's leaves had started out tiny and pink and gotten bigger and greener in the days he'd been here. Three days so far: each day he scratched a mark on one of the chair's legs with the knife that came with his food.

Through the window he could also see an alley, a small open-fronted building that appeared to be a carriage house, and the back of another house like the one he was in, a rich man's house, big and built of gray stone.

He had spent hours standing at the window watching the tree's leaves lifting in the breeze. Little black bugs flitted among the leaves, chased by small birds. Some of the birds had blue heads and yellow bodies, while others had black-and-orange backs and white bellies. Another kind, bigger, had a black head and a black back and a white breast with a big red patch in its center, like someone who had been stabbed in the heart with a knife.

The birds' singing woke him every morning before dawn.

The woman who brought his food told him to keep quiet and wait.

He had never been good at waiting. Especially when he didn't know what he was waiting for.

He lay in bed staring at the ceiling in the darkness and told himself this place was a whole lot better than the barn he had lived in in McDonough, and the food was way better and a lot more of it than what they'd given him there.

His mind turned to his mama. She had always known that he would run; he must have told her a hundred times that someday he would run north from Red Rose and get free. His mama let him study a big map on the wall in the office of the big house. She told him that north was at the top of the map. She pointed out the coiling blue river, the Potomac, which he would have to get across before making his way north.

His mama, Flora, worked in the big house as a maid. He had heard Waller call her "one of the comely colored flowers of Red Rose."

Mr. Tazewell Waller. Who always had to be called "Sir" or "Master," otherwise you'd get cuffed on the head, or worse. Well, he didn't have to call him that anymore. Just "Waller." Plain old "Waller" and nothing better than that.

His mama had run once. She took him with her, her baby boy called Leo. They caught her before she even made it across the river. Waller did not have them whip her or brand her or take a slice out of her ear, because he prized how she looked. He didn't sell her, either.

Otis did not recollect those events.

He thought his mama must be crazy, the things she sometimes said. Mean, spiteful things about the other servants, and sometimes about him, too. She told him that someday she meant to have her own big fine house, and she would be the mistress in it. Then in the next moment she would take a knife and cut herself, slice the back of her hand or her arm or leg and draw blood. Mumbling out of the corner of her mouth and rolling her eyes like a calf with the strangles. Once she'd held a razor to her neck, but he blubbered and she put it down. She told him that Waller had put her name in every newspaper in the land, telling about her in all her particulars—small and pretty, eyes set wide in her face, a voice good for singing, a light and lively way of moving—so that she could never get away from him again.

He knew his mama hated Waller even more than he did.

When he and Dan ran, they went at night. They snuck across the river on the new railroad bridge. He went with Dan because Dan was older and stronger. Otis had been twelve then, not very tall, with arms like sticks. Dan was at least four years older, with muscles from working in the fields. The patrols would have a hard time seeing Dan at night, dark as he was. Whereas he, Otis, was a pale shade of brown, like fancy light molasses.

He and Dan ran off just before fall. They filled a sack with food and put on all the clothes they could wear. He had a little brass compass that his mama smouched out of the office desk. He knotted the compass inside a kerchief along with two silver half dollars his mama gave him, then tied the kerchief to the rope that held up his pants. She said she'd make sure the overseer would not report him and Dan missing.

The bridge was a fearful thing: he tried not to look down between the ties at the water flowing swift and black below. After they pussyfooted across, they ran hard. Resting in thickets by day, walking and trotting at night. They heard no hounds, saw no determined watchful men on horseback. The river was off to their left but they didn't see it: they went across country, since he knew from the map that the river twisted back and forth like a snake, and following it too close would slow them down. They used the compass, going in the direction the little arrow pointed. At night they found their way by heading for the bright star that the two stars in the drinking gourd pointed at.

Knowing as they ran that Waller would come after them. He was like the winter: there was nothing you could do to keep it from coming.

The third night, fearing they were going too slow, he had an idea. If they could get themselves a horse, he told Dan, they could make it to Pennsylvania quicker, and then they'd be free.

That very night they came to a farm with a dark horse in a field like he'd been put there for the taking. The horse snorted and dashed around until Otis was able to talk him into standing still. Dan took down the rails while he stroked the horse's neck and spoke softly to him—he'd always had a way with horses, also cows and bulls and oxen, even scatterbrained chickens. He could whisper peace into their heads.

He took a hank of mane in both hands, and the horse didn't shy or flinch, just set its legs for balance. A step back, and he swung his leg up and over as he vaulted onto the horse's back. A big broad-backed horse that could carry them both. He reached one hand down to help Dan. They heard a commotion, dogs barking and a man hollering. The horse started fidgeting. He tried to keep it still by talking softly to it, a light pressure with his legs, one hand woven into the mane and the other hand gripping Dan's hand. His hands sweaty on account of he was scared, having realized that stealing a horse was a bad idea—if they got caught, they might get hung as horse thieves.

He lost his grip on Dan's hand. Dan fell and cried out. The horse leaped through the gap in the fence.

A while later, he heard a shot.

The horse galloped through the darkness while he kept his balance as best he could, one hand in front of the other, fingers twined in the mane. He slid partway down the horse's side before he could scramble back up again. After that he concentrated on riding. Sitting quiet, breathing deep. Addressing the horse until it heard him in its mind and calmed down. Not until they were going along at a walk did he let himself consider the fix he was in: He had no food, Dan being the one who carried the sack. No string for making snares, nor the barlow knife they'd made off with, nor the flint and steel and tinderbox and frying pan. He had the compass, the two silver half dollars, the clothes he was wearing, and his own wits.

He rode the horse on an empty road through forest where the ground was free of brush under the thick straight trunks of tall trees; then past a plowman's oak, stark as a shout in the middle of a starlit field. Where the footing allowed it, he pushed the horse to trot and canter, putting miles between them and the farm where he had lost Dan. At first light, with quail calling all around, he found a briar patch. He got down off the horse, and, since the horse wouldn't fit in the brambles with him, and he had no way of hiding or securing him, he whacked the horse on the rump and sent him home.

All day he lay in the patch and tried not to think about what might have happened to Dan. High above, vees of geese arrowed south through the smoky air, opposite his own orientation.

That night, and the nights following, he aimed himself at the bright star and went on with pat and charlie. Tired, cold at times, rained on so that he shivered, and hungry always. He ate apples and pears out of orchards. Broke up a pumpkin and ate the flesh. Late huckleberries and ripe simmons in the scrublands. Grapes that puckered his mouth. He smashed walnuts and hickory nuts between rocks and teased the meats out of the shells. He chucked a stone at a rabbit and stunned it, then twisted its neck and tore off the skin and plucked the meat off the bones with his fingers and ate it raw though it came near to sickening him, hot and blood-tanged and gummy as it was.

Toward dawn one morning he saw a black man come out of a cabin to use the jakes and chanced calling out. The man and his woman took one of his half dollars in exchange for a meal of bacon and eggs and yams and pone, a day of resting on a shuck tick, a goodly amount of smoked meat and hard-cooked eggs and cheese and dried apples and a pot of grape jelly, plus a sack to carry the food in.

Lying up another day, sprawled on his back in a thicket, watching clouds stream across the sky, he wondered if Waller had put a notice about him in the newspapers and how much of a reward he was offering.

He reckoned it was a big one.

He decided he needed a new name: Otis. Otis Johnson. His mama had called him Leo, after her own pa, a grandpa he had never met, but from now on he would be Otis. He liked how the name slipped off his tongue. The hiss at the end of it, like water running away over stones.

Ranaway my negro man Dennis, said negro has been *shot* in the left arm between the shoulder and elbow, which has paralyzed the left hand.

Chapter 13

————∞∞∞————

GIDEON, TENSE UNDER THE QUILT, TWITCHED AS HE DREAMED: *He's standing in the bright sun with his brother and sisters in the field of sweet-smelling new-cut hay. Their* dawdy, *scythe over his shoulder, vanishes over the hill to begin cutting on the far slope. Gideon grins at Friedrich and the girls, puts down his rake, and heads for the house.*

There's a jump in time, and he's going in the door, his mouth watering at the thought of the pie his memmi *is baking. She'll scold him half-heartedly for shirking his work, then cut a piece out of the still-warm pie: peach, that's what it is, and she ruffles his hair and smiles at him as he takes a big bite and the delicious sharp-sweet flavor floods his mouth. He's her* erschtgeboren, *her firstborn, and her favorite. She calls him her little* wutz *because sometimes he eats like a pig, but he just laughs, he knows she's teasing him because she loves him.*

He enters the kich, *which is strangely different. The floor is not wooden boards but dirt. Suddenly he realizes that his* memmi *is buried under the dirt—she's trapped there, and it's up to him to save her. His heart hammering and his sight blurring, he falls to his knees. His fingers claw at the dirt. He scoops it up in his hands, slings it aside, plunges his hands in again and again. But the dirt keeps falling back into the hole he's making. He digs harder, faster, his hands are bleeding and he's running out of breath. His arms fall limp at his sides, and he can't dig anymore.*

He looks around frantically and sees a hand sticking up out of the dirt. He's been digging in the wrong place! The hand pale, withered, and unmoving. Dead. Then he sees it, a dark stain beneath the hand, spreading through the dirt, getting closer and closer, coming toward him—

"Gideon!" True shook his shoulder.

He woke with a gasp.

"It's all right," True said. "I'm here with you."

Getting up on his elbows, he felt sweat pouring down his sides.

True stroked his cheek with her hand. "You had a nightmare." She kissed him on the lips. "You're awake now. At home. In our bed."

A shudder ran through him.

True asked: "What was it? What was your dream?"

"I don't remember," he lied.

"You can tell me."

He shook his head.

"What's troubling you, Gid? Maybe I can help."

He put his hand on her shoulder and gently pressed her back down on the bed. "You are helping me. Just by being here. I'm sorry I woke you. Now go back to sleep."

"You should tell me," she said.

He didn't answer.

She sighed, then turned away. He lay back down and drew the quilt up to his neck. After a while he heard True's breathing go slow and regular.

A dream, he told himself. Just a dream.

Not what he had really seen that day when his ten-year-old self snuck away from the haying and went into the kitchen and found his *memmi* lying on the floor, the front of her dress torn open, her skirt and *unnerrock* up around her waist. Stab wounds on her breasts, her throat slit. Blood pooled beneath her.

He tried to push the image out of his mind, as he always did.

For a moment he considered waking True again and telling her what he'd dreamed.

And then telling her everything that had happened back then.

How no one was ever arrested for killing his *memmi*.

How for months the sight of her dead body would flash before his eyes and overwhelm his mind. Reduce him to a cowering, whimpering child. Even thinking about it now made his neck tense up and his breathing go shallow.

He would tell True how the murder finally drove him to leave the farm, sparking his father's great anger. He rode north and west on his young mare, Maude. Finally stopping here in Adamant, where he'd found this beautiful woman, fallen deeply in love with her, and joined himself to her in marriage.

If his *memmi* hadn't been killed, he never would have met and married True. He frowned and shook his head. He didn't know how to make sense of it all.

He wished he could leave those troubling memories behind. It sometimes seemed that the murder had become the lens through which he saw the world and his place in it. It was why he worked so hard to solve crimes—especially when a person's life had been stolen from them and from those who had loved them.

Why hadn't he told any of this to True?

Was it because he felt ashamed to have lost his mother like that? Ashamed that such a thing could have happened to his *memmi* and to him and their family? As if they'd deserved the evil that had come crashing down on them?

Dawn was near; a dim light shone in through the small window. He looked at True lying next to him, her hair fanned out black against the pillow.

No. He wouldn't trouble her with this. He wasn't brave enough to do that yet.

He went over yesterday's many events in his mind. Talking to the barber George Watkins and meeting the Virginians Waller and Blaine, Annie Picard, Hack Latimer, visiting Headmaster Foote, going back to Hammertown with Alonzo to check the saloons, looking fruitlessly for information regarding Potter's death and the missing persons.

His mind suddenly pictured the man who had been sitting at the table in the Broad Ax. The man with the dark complexion and hooked nose. Wiry, spare, furtive in the way he'd looked off to the side when Gideon glanced in his direction. He should have gone straight to the table and questioned the man then and there. He knew he had seen him before, but try as he might, he could not remember where or when.

And then he and Alonzo had gone on to the Horse, where Dorfman and his three friends sat talking and drinking.

He thought of the haunting music they'd heard floating through the darkness. And Tazewell Waller, with his blotched face and whiskey breath, pulling a pistol. They'd been lucky to avoid bloodshed. He wondered if he should have arrested Waller, charged him with disturbing the peace. But the Virginian would have insisted that he'd drawn his weapon in self-defense. No, better to let the tension ease and hope it didn't flare up again.

What was happening in Colerain County?

Was someone really kidnapping people and selling them into slavery?

Why had Phineas Potter been on the Halfmoon Valley road that night? Investigating something, trying to get information to print in his newspaper? Or to meet another man for a tryst? Or to help a person fleeing from slavery?

And Leo Waller, or Otis Johnson, the boy Waller and Blaine were so doggedly pursuing: Was he in Adamant? Or somewhere far away?

A rooster crowed. Gideon lay there and listened. The wild birds started calling, each kind adding its own special song to the dawn chorus: the plaints of mourning doves, the bubbling of wrens, the trills and whistles of sparrows and warblers, the flutelike calling of thrushes.

He got up. Built a fire on the hearth and made coffee. Waited for True to join him in the new day.

$100 REWARD! My Black Woman, named EMILY, Seventeen years of age, well grown, black color, has a whining voice. She took with her one calico and one blue and white dress, a red corded gingham bonnet; a white striped shawl and slippers.

Chapter 14

"I DIDN'T LIKE IT, THAT SHERIFF COMING IN THE BROAD AX," THE HOOK-nosed man said. "When him and his deputy were looking the other way, I *absquatulated*."

From the upper story of the cramped dwelling came a *thud, thud, thud*. The sound went on for a while before stopping.

The hook-nosed man was William Jewell Jarrett. On the other side of the scarred table sat his friend and longtime associate Gulliver Luck.

"Absquatulated," a grinning Luck repeated. "Where'd you get that two-dollar word?" Luck wore a black coat, its lapels grease-stained and shiny with wear; on one side, a jagged tear had been mended with coarse pale thread like a lightning bolt across a night sky. Luck scratched his unshaven neck above the slack collar of a tattered shirt. He lifted a jug and drank.

"Never you mind where I got that word at, Gullie," Jarrett said. "And go easy on that applejack." Jarrett got up from his chair and crossed the room to a small window. He rubbed the dusty pane with a linsey-woolsey sleeve and peered out.

"I seen him before," Jarrett said. "That sheriff. But blamed if I can remember when."

"Well, you done the right thing, absquatulating."

"Had to leave half a glass of beer behind." Jarrett came back and dropped into the chair. "He was young for a sheriff. Yeller hair. Tall, with big shoulders on him. I heard the barkeep call him Stoltz. That name mean anything to you?"

Luck shook his head.

"He talked like a Dutchman," Jarrett continued. "Honked like a god-damned goose."

"Maybe someone will cook his goose for him," Luck said.

The door opened, and a big, sturdily built woman shuffled in carrying an armload of firewood. She dumped the wood in a box near the fireplace. She picked up a poker, broke up the coals on the hearth, and added several chunks of wood to the flames.

From the floor above: *Thud, thud, thud.*

"Must be they're hungry," the woman said. She had a square jaw. The corners of her mouth drooped down and the outer points of her eyes angled up, giving her a perpetual expression of angry astonishment. "The wench was harpin' at me this morning, saying she expects a better quality of food and lodging." The woman guffawed. She had crinkly mouse-brown hair with some gray in it. She wore a cotton dress with red and green vertical stripes. The dress's grimy hem brushed the tops of heavy half-boots.

Thud, thud, thud.

"How much longer we gotta listen to that?" Jarrett muttered.

Luck pushed the jug across the table. "Wet your whistle, Billy."

"We get us a couple more, we can head south," replied Jarrett. "Be about time. I hate this waiting."

Thud. Thud-thud. Thud.

"Must be the crazy one," the woman said. Her name was Liza Brodie. She cut up some bacon and dumped it in a skillet on a spider above the flames. The fat meat popped and hissed. When it had cooked, she used a wooden spoon to scrape the bacon and grease into a pot of beans bubbling under a crane.

She stirred the food, nudged the crane away from the flames. She ladled food onto three plates, then set the plates on the table along with a dish of cornbread. She sat down with the two men.

When he had finished eating, Jarrett pushed his empty plate aside, picked up the jug, and drank. "We are low on funds," he said.

It had been months since they'd cozied up to a traveler in a tavern who made the mistake of asking his new friends if they knew where he could buy any "good ground" and telling them he had the gold to pay for it.

Luck chortled at the memory. "That ignorant clodhopper from downstate? I reckon he has plenty of good ground now, don't he?"

"And no use for them eagles in his poke," Jarrett added. "Which they're almost gone, more's the pity."

Brodie stood. She pointed at the bean pot. "Gullie, you carry the grub and plates. Bill, get the water jar and the club."

Jarrett and Luck drained their glasses and rose.

The big woman picked up a double-barreled shotgun leaning against the wall. "Come on, you lazy whoresons," she said as she started up the stairs.

In the room above were three people. A young woman and a young man, both with light brown skin, sat side by side on the floor, their backs against a wall and their legs out in front. An older man with darker skin lay on his side. All three had iron collars around their necks, and fetters on their ankles from which chains led to a heavy eyebolt anchored in the floor.

Brodie motioned for Luck to serve the food.

Then Brodie, Luck, and Jarrett sat in chairs on the other side of the room and watched as the young man and the woman began to eat. The dark-skinned man remained lying on his side, the plate of food untouched next to him on the floor.

"Hey, you," Jarrett called to the man. "Eat."

The man wore a blue uniform coat with a row of tarnished brass buttons. Small twigs and pieces of leaves clung to his hair. His eyes appeared unfocused, and his mouth was slack. He lifted his head and brought it down on the floor.

Thud. Thud. Thud.

Jarrett got up and walked over to the man. "I told you, eat." He put his boot on the man's hip and waggled it back and forth. "What's the matter, vittles ain't good enough for you?"

The man in the uniform coat closed his eyes.

Jarrett raised his club, an old spoke from a wagon wheel, and brought it down, striking the man on the shoulder. "Eat, damn you," he said.

The man turned and lay on his stomach with his face against the floor.

Jarrett set his boot on the back of the man's head and put weight on it.

A muffled groan came from the man's mouth.

"Your nose is already flat," Jarrett said. "But I can make it flatter."

"Leave him be." Brodie handed the shotgun to Luck and went to where Jarrett stood. She was six inches taller than Jarrett. "Don't damage the merchandise, Bill. Now get out of my road."

She sat down beside the prone man, gripped his arm, and hauled him up to a sitting position. She patted him ungently on one cheek, then the other. With a spoon the big woman put some beans in the man's mouth. For a moment he just sat there. Then, dully, he began to chew.

Jarrett went back to his chair. He watched Brodie feeding the man in the blue coat. Then he shifted his gaze to the girl. She noticed him looking and lowered her eyes.

Jarrett smiled. "You got a name?"

She kept her head down.

"You been here a while, missy, and I ain't learned your name," Jarrett said. "That's my own fault, I reckon. But I can be mannerly if I set my mind to it. Can't I, Gullie?"

"Oh, yes," Luck said. "Bill can be mannerly. A fine fellow. A prince among men."

"Don't lay it on too thick," Jarrett said.

The girl had a pretty face and a slim figure. She wore a red dress, somewhat soiled, with a blue crocheted shawl over it. The shawl had holes and tears in it. The girl glanced at the young man seated next to her and moved her shoulder a little so that it touched his.

The young man kept eating. He did not raise his eyes from his plate.

"Girl, what's your name?" Jarrett said.

She spoke in a soft voice, the words failing to carry across the room.

"Say again?"

"Amanda," she said more distinctly.

"That's a purty name," Jarrett said. "Ain't it, Gullie?"

Luck grinned, showing broken brown teeth with the remnants of beans caught in them. "Amanda. That's Latin, so it is. It means 'much loved by everyone.'"

"Well, ain't that fitting." Jarrett laughed. "How do you know that, Gullie?" Without waiting for Luck to answer, Jarrett said, "You never seek to amaze me."

"I got some learning," Luck said in a complacent tone. He ran his thumb over the shotgun's hammers. "Been a preacher, too. Methody religion."

Jarrett resumed staring at the girl. "Amanda," he said. "Your friend there, he got a name?"

The young man's voice broke slightly as he answered: "Felix, sir."

Jarrett's smile took on a narrow-eyed aspect. "I asked her, boy, not you." He tapped his club against the side of his calf.

"Settle yourself, Bill." Brodie stood up from feeding the blue-coated man. She passed around the water jar. All three of the captives drank. Brodie took a ring of keys out of her apron and handed them to Luck, who gave her back the shotgun. She stood to one side and raised the gun's barrels.

Luck unfastened the padlock securing the chains to the bolt in the floor, then freed each chain by drawing it rattling through the ring on the shackles around the captives' ankles.

"Get up," Brodie said. "Get in line." After they complied, she nodded to Luck.

He ran a long chain through rings on the collars around each captive's neck, then locked the ends of the chain together.

The captives were taken downstairs and outside. They blinked in the light from the milky sky as they stood in the yard amid assorted junk and tufts of dry reddish grass.

The house they had exited was made of squared weather-blackened logs notched at the corners and with lime-and-horsehair chinking falling out from between them. It stood near a sway-backed barn and a corncrib built of logs left in the round. In the long-neglected fields around the house grew more of the reddish grass mixed with sweetfern and clumps of bear-oak and shin-high pines.

Brodie pointed with the shotgun. "Over by the corncrib."

The three captives shuffled to the spot, where the grass and weeds had been trampled down.

"Now do your bidness," Brodie said.

Hesitation, averted faces, sidelong glances.

"You, with the blue coat," Brodie said. "Drop your drawers and squat. Or get your pecker out or whatever. You don't go now, you will have a long wait. You don't want to be soilin' yourself."

She glanced at the sky. "Getting cold," she said. "Always was cold in this damned place. I believe it could snow." She looked back at the captives. They finished what they were doing.

"All right. In the crib."

Jarrett prodded the captives with the wagon spoke. He waited until the light-skinned man and the young woman had stepped over the sill. The man in the blue coat was last in line. When the man hesitated, Jarrett raised his boot, set it on the man's backside, and shoved him forward, sending him sprawling inside the crib and taking the two others down with him.

50 Dollars Reward. A negro slave who calls himself BILL GUY, about 5 feet six or 7 inches high, rather of a lighter complexion than the generality of blacks, extremely awkward and ungraceful in his address and particularly his walk, and has a wild and suspicious stare when accosted.

Chapter 15

PRING WENT OFF AND SULKED.

Clouds, cold rain, gusty winds, and one night a couple inches of snow. In the morning when Gideon walked to the jail, fallen maple flowers lay on the snow like scarlet blood drops on a white blanket.

Bills describing the fugitive Leo Waller began appearing on walls all over town, the two-hundred-dollar reward in large numerals with hands pointing to the extravagant sum. Gideon surmised that the Virginians, earlier refused service by Phineas Potter, had gotten the *Colerain Democrat* to print the advertisements.

True brought her work indoors and wove baskets out of the ash splints that she had prepared. The red setter Old Dick lay on the floor near the hearth, where a fire burned low.

It was the kind of weather when a body need not be hurried into the ground. Phineas Potter's funeral was scheduled for Saturday morning.

Gideon kept expecting the state's attorney to summon him and grill him on what, if any, progress he had made in investigating Potter's murder. But the Cold Fish remained uncharacteristically silent.

Gideon compared the cigar that Melchior Dorfman had thrown down in the street in Hammertown to the cigar butt he had picked up in the horse-trampled area near where the newspaperman's body had been found. They looked the same. At the tobacconist's shop, he learned that such cigars, made from cheap Pennsylvania tobacco, were big sellers, and scores of men in the town and county smoked them.

He went through Potter's notebooks. They were written in a personal shorthand that he could barely decipher. The last entries in one of the books concerned the abolitionist speaker and could have formed the basis for a news article. But Gideon found nothing indicating why Potter had been on the Halfmoon Valley road on Sunday night, nor anything that pointed to a possible suspect or suspects in his death.

Tazewell Waller and Franklin Blaine had not come to the jail to acquaint themselves with the requirements of the Pennsylvania Fugitive Slave Act. Waller's pistol remained locked in the armory. Gideon assumed the Virginians were still riding out in the countryside searching for their runaway.

He learned nothing indicating that the boy was in Adamant.

Nor did he hear anything more about the missing and presumably kidnapped people. He talked with the driver of the coach when it stopped at the hotel. The driver said that no colored people had used the conveyance. Then he growled: "They ain't wanted."

★★★

In a cold drizzle Gideon rode to the Halfmoon Valley. Following directions from Melchior Dorfman, he turned Maude onto a narrow road angling up the side of Muncie Mountain. Dorfman had said to look for a stone wall. Even in the fog, the wall was impossible to miss: four feet high and nearly as broad, dry laid, battered carefully, and capped with large flat stones. It snaked along following the contour of the land, enclosing perhaps two acres. No livestock grazed within it. No crop had been cultivated there. Weeds and brambles and saplings grew thick. The wall lacked a gate or a stile to provide access within.

How many thousands of hours had John Horne spent building his beautiful, useless wall? Why had he done it?

Gideon rode on to the cabin.

The door was shut but not locked. Inside, the air was as cold as the outdoors. A single room downstairs, a box staircase leading up to a loft.

Gideon righted the chair that Dorfman had told him about. The damaged table canted down on the side where its legs had been broken. A newspaper lay on the floor, an *Adamant Argus* from 1833: the same year Gideon had come to town, was hired as a deputy sheriff, and met and married True. He turned through the paper, its pages pliant, as if they had been turned many times. Nothing caught his eye, just the usual fare of wars, famines, shipwrecks, skirmishes with the Indians, scientific discoveries, political chicanery, new canals and sanitariums and prisons being built. Several stacks of newspapers sat against the wall. Apparently they were Horne's customary reading material.

Other than the overturned chair and broken table, nothing seemed out of place: cooking utensils in drawers, towels and napkins carefully folded, food in cupboards or stored in sacks dangling from the rafters. Plenty of mouse droppings on the floor, and some dry leaves that must have blown in while the door remained open between when Horne left or was kidnapped and when Dorfman came to check on him and then shut the door behind him.

In the loft were clothes hanging on pegs, a neatly made bed, a side table with a wooden flute on it.

Gideon went back outside. He heard a crow squalling in the fog, then wings flapping. He walked in that direction. Three more crows gave out hoarse rattling cries and took off from the ground.

He caught the taint of decomposing flesh and saw a long gray smudge. Horne's dog.

The crows had eaten the bitch's eyes. They had devoured the cheek flesh, exposing sharp white teeth in the jaws. Scavengers had opened the rib cage and consumed the innards. A big round hole blown through the ribs on both sides. Someone had shot the dog.

He stood listening, heard the crows' receding complaints and the rain ticking against the trees' new leaves.

He got back on Maude.

He visited farms and talked to Horne's neighbors. The people were champing at the bit, forestalled at plowing and planting by the cold and damp. Many of the residents in the Halfmoon Valley were Quakers, reputed to be abolitionists. Polite and convivial, they sat Gideon down, put food and drink before him, and talked a blue streak. They expressed sorrow and alarm at the fact that John Horne had gone missing. They said that the recluse bothered no one and often was not seen for weeks on end. No one knew why he had built his intricate, pointless wall.

Theories were offered: Horne had served in the second war against the British, and his mind had been shattered by the carnage he'd seen. He had lost his family in a pestilential plague in some city and withdrawn to this lightly settled place to mourn. The most outlandish story identified him as the inventor of a powerful incendiary, an improvement on Greek fire; after selling his abominable weapon to the army, he had given away his money and removed to his cabin in the woods, there to play his flute and think philosophical thoughts. Pointedly, or so it seemed to Gideon, no one suggested that John Horne was an escaped slave.

No one had any notion of who might have abducted him. And no one had seen or heard anything amiss on the night when Phineas Potter was run down and killed less than a mile from Horne's cabin.

$100 REWARD. Negro woman SOPHIA GORDON, about 24 years of age, rather small in size, of copper color, is tolerably good looking, has a low and soft manner of speech. She is believed to be among associates in Washington where she has been often hired.

Chapter 16

ON SATURDAY MORNING ALONZO ASKED: "YOU GOING TO WATCH them put that box of dead meat in the ground?"

"Alonzo," Gideon said, grimacing. Then: "Oh, forget it."

At midmorning he joined fifty or sixty others around the open grave with the coffin on the ground beside it. He had asked True if she wanted to attend Potter's funeral with him, but she had something else to do and wouldn't tell him what it was.

The sunny day offered a welcome change from yesterday's raw weather. Gideon spotted Lemuel Robinson, Potter's apprentice, a downcast expression on his face. Hosea Belknap, publisher of the *Colerain Democrat*, clasped a notebook under his arm; beside him was his thin, severe-looking wife. Horatio Foote stood off to one side. If they hadn't parted so stiffly earlier in the week, Gideon would have gone over and joined the headmaster. At the far edge of the gathering slouched the Cold Fish, cravat askew, jowls imperfectly shaved. The only black person Gideon noticed was Melchior Dorfman. The tinner did not look nervous or guilty but appeared pensive.

The minister read from *The Book of Common Prayer*.

"I am the resurrection and the life, saith the Lord: he that believeth in me, though he were dead, yet shall he live . . ."

As the familiar words droned on, Gideon thought of his little son David, lying in a different burial ground with True's kin. The boy had been so happy, so healthy. And then the influenza came.

His mind thus preoccupied, Gideon's eyes were drawn to a massive monument in the shape of an anvil, whose polished gray surface threw back the sun. That ostentatious hunk of granite was said to weigh seven tons; it had been freighted all the way from Vermont to mark the final resting place of the ironmaster Adonijah Thompson, who had left this world in 1835.

Gideon glanced in a different direction and saw the simple slate headstone of Judge Hiram Biddle, his mentor and friend, who had taken his own life as a result of crimes committed by the ironmaster in the near and distant past.

And, though he could not see it from here, Gideon knew that in the weedy reaches of the cemetery leaned the lichen-splotched marker of the Reverend Thomas McEwan, hanged some thirty years ago from a limb on the broad-spreading white oak near the jail—a grim public spectacle that people still talked about in Adamant and Colerain County.

So many bones under the ground. Lives abruptly or slowly, painfully ended. As the lives of the people clustered on this hill in the day's clear light, himself included, would someday be extinguished as well.

"... our Lord Jesus Christ, the love of God, and the fellowship of the Holy Ghost, be with us all evermore. Amen."

The minister began singing "Amazing Grace." Gideon joined in with the other mourners. The words, he knew, had been written by an English sea captain who had carried captives by the hundreds from Africa to America. What was his name? Newton, Gideon thought it was. The man had survived a wicked storm at sea and experienced a religious conversion, but still carried on in the slave trade for decades before finally disavowing it.

After the hymn ended, men fed out ropes and lowered Potter's coffin into the ground. A tall middle-aged man in a black suit picked up a spade and threw a shovelful of dirt into the grave, then put the spade down and brushed off his hands.

Hat in his own hands, Gideon approached a woman who lingered near the grave. She wore a black dress with leg-o'-mutton sleeves, and the brim of a black bonnet shaded her face. During the service the woman had linked her arm through that of the tall man who had sent the first symbolic clods thudding down on Potter's coffin.

"Pardon me," Gideon said. "Are you Philomena Hutchinson?"

"Yes." The woman pushed back the veil from her face.

Potter had been handsome. His sister was striking, with strong cheekbones, even features, and a flawless complexion. She held a black lace handkerchief in one hand but her eyes appeared dry.

"I am Gideon Stoltz, the county sheriff."

"Thank you for sending us the letter."

"I'm sorry I had to deliver such terrible news."

The tall man joined them, occasioning further introductions. It seemed to Gideon that Glenn Hutchinson wanted to get this over with, escape the scrutiny and sympathy, climb into the carriage parked at the edge of the cemetery and get home—get on with his life.

"As I said in my letter, I am investigating Mr. Potter's death as a homicide," Gideon said.

Glenn Hutchinson looked around as if to make sure no one was listening. "Considering Phineas's proclivities," he said, "I do not find that at all surprising."

Philomena Hutchinson's spine got straighter.

"My brother was a good and decent man," she said to Gideon. "I will not hear him spoken of as some sort of a degenerate. Phineas was high-minded in everything he said and did."

"I did not know Mr. Potter well," Gideon said. "I'm trying to build a picture of him. Do you know if he had any enemies?"

"I'm sure people disliked some of the things he put in his newspaper. But I don't know of anyone who would have wanted to kill him—for that or any other reason." Mrs. Hutchinson leveled a cool stare at her husband, then returned her gaze to Gideon.

"Sheriff Stoltz, can you tell me how he was killed? Don't spare the details."

"Your brother was run down by a wagon. It was going fast. Then someone made sure he was dead by hitting him on the head with a rock."

"Do you think he was conscious when they killed him?"

"I think he was either dead already from the wagon's impact or unconscious. It was a quick death."

She looked toward the grave, where the sexton and his helper worked with their shovels. "Do you have any idea who killed him?"

"Not yet. But I will find out." Gideon spoke with more confidence than he felt.

"In your letter you said he'd been robbed."

"His wallet was missing, and his pockets were turned inside out. His boots had been taken. If he rode to the place where he was killed, then someone made off with his horse. Mr. Potter owned a horse, correct?"

"A black gelding," Glenn Hutchinson said. "White socks on his left feet, front and back, and a white star. Phineas kept him on a farm near Adamant. Now and then he'd ride to Walkersville to see us."

"Whose farm?"

"It belongs to Ike Fye," Mrs. Hutchinson said. "Our mother's cousin."

Gideon had heard of Fye, a horse breeder; his place was south of town, just off the stage route. "Is Mr. Fye here today?"

Mrs. Hutchinson shook her head. "He couldn't leave his farm. We stopped and saw him on our way here."

"I see. What else can you tell me about your brother?"

"Phineas was passionate," she said. "About life, about learning. After he graduated from the Academy, he went to the university in Philadelphia. He always worked hard, and he excelled at everything he did. I was so proud of him. I loved him very much." Now the tears began to flow.

Gideon waited until she had composed herself. "The last time I saw him was at a speech by an abolitionist," he said. "This past Sunday evening, a few hours before he was killed. Do you think Mr. Potter's involvement in the anti-slavery movement could have led to his death?"

Glenn Hutchinson sniffed. "I think you should look for someone he approached. An assignation on the road at night for some immoral purpose."

For a moment Philomena Hutchinson looked as if she might slap her husband's face. Then she turned her back on him.

"For God's sake, Phil," Hutchinson said. "He's dead. The sheriff won't arrest a dead man for sodomy."

Gideon was shocked that Hutchinson would say such a thing. It made him wonder if the man bore a deep hatred toward his brother-in-law.

Before he could speculate further, Mrs. Hutchinson spoke: "Phineas was committed to fighting slavery. Deeply committed. As many of us are." Her voice was harsh. "Sheriff, would you capture a colored man or woman running for their life? Would you turn them over to a bounty hunter, to be beaten, branded, raped? To spend the rest of their life as someone's chattel? To be separated from their families, to know that their own children would be slaves, and their children's children?"

"Let's not get into politics," Mr. Hutchinson said.

"My husband is timid," Philomena Hutchinson said in a voice full of scorn. "He is also ashamed of my brother. Well, I'm not ashamed. Sheriff, I want you to find whoever killed Phineas. I want them arrested, tried, and convicted. And I want to watch them hang."

Mrs. Hutchinson opened her reticule and gave him a key. "To my brother's house," she said. "Find the truth if you can."

Gideon thanked the Hutchinsons for their time and bade them a safe journey home. He reckoned it would be a frosty trip in that carriage.

Turning away, he saw Hosea Belknap and his wife standing thirty feet off. He wondered if they'd heard any of the conversation.

Belknap had curly reddish hair and luxuriant sideburns. He looked about forty. A year ago, he had moved here from the South—Virginia, Gideon thought it was—and started the *Colerain Democrat* in direct competition with Potter's *Adamant Argus*.

"Sheriff, a moment of your time?" Belknap said.

Gideon stopped. "Of course."

"Let me introduce my wife," Belknap said. "Lenore works with me on the newspaper."

She was almost as tall as her husband. Under a wide-brimmed bonnet, her dark hair had been parted in the center and pulled back tightly. Her gaze, Gideon thought, seemed suspicious, guarded. Or some strange combination of frightened and belligerent.

"I'm sure you will recall that the *Democrat* endorsed your election as sheriff last autumn," Belknap said.

He had that leisurely Southern drawl: "Democrat" came out like "Dimocrayat."

"Yes. Thank you," Gideon said.

"Perhaps you saw the article we printed announcing Mr. Potter's death. We plan to publish a more extensive story next week. Other newspapers will pick it up. The murder hardly reflects well on our community, but it is important news when a member of the press is slain. Can you say what your investigation has revealed so far?"

"There's not much to tell. Potter was run over by a wagon traveling at a high rate of speed. Afterward, he was struck on the head with a rock. His wallet, boots, and horse were taken." He repeated Glenn Hutchinson's description of the gelding. Belknap wrote it down. "I don't know yet why Potter was on the Halfmoon Valley road. If anyone has information about the incident, or if they've seen his horse, they should come to the jail and tell me."

"We have spoken with a number of citizens," Belknap said. "None of them eyewitnesses, of course. We've learned nothing other than that Potter may have been involved—and I'm not saying he was—in hiding fugitives from servitude."

"We have spoken with white people," Mrs. Belknap said. "The negroes will not talk to us. Perhaps to protect one of their own."

Hosea Belknap said: "We understand that the tinner, Melchior Dorfman, is your prime suspect."

Gideon was instantly furious. He tried not to let it show. Alonzo, you are in deep *dreck*, he thought. "Mr. Dorfman is not a suspect," he said curtly. "There are no suspects yet."

"Sheriff, the negro is volatile and inclined to violence," Mrs. Belknap said. "You talk about a wagon running Potter down. The freight company hires colored men as drivers. You should look there as well."

"The black people in this county are no more volatile or violent than the whites," Gideon said. "Maybe less, because there are fewer of them and they don't want to get in trouble. Whoever killed Phineas Potter, I will bring them to justice, no matter what color their skin is."

"We will report to you anything that we believe relevant to your investigation," Belknap said. "We hope you'll do the same with us."

"I may report facts to you," Gideon said. "But I will not toss out dubious theories or gossip. I suggest you do the same."

Gideon left the cemetery. He decided to pay a visit to Ike Fye.

RUN AWAY from the Subscriber, a Negro Wench about 22 or 23 Years of Age, very black, about 6 Feet high, holds her Head pretty high when she speaks, and has a large Scar as long as One's Finger above her Breast. She has been seen with a Fellow named *Will*, who stole her from me in *Nansemond* County.

Chapter 17

THE MAN WHO CAME OUT OF THE BARN HAD JUG-HANDLE EARS with tufts of gray hair above them. Short and spare, with almost no hips or hind end so that his pants looked ready to fall down around his legs, which were bowed.

Gideon saw that Ike Fye's eyes were not on him but on his horse.

Fye walked up to Maude and placed a hand on her withers. "Sturdy, but I wouldn't call her cobby. Nice strong back, and I like the way she reaches under with her hind legs." He looked up at Gideon. "Covers the ground pretty good?"

"She does."

"You the one they call the Dutch Sheriff?"

"That's me," Gideon said, dismounting.

"Then she must be a Dutch horse." The man's tone teased rather than mocked, and his eyes twinkled.

"She comes from Lancaster County." Gideon heard himself pronounce it "cawnty," in true *Deitsch* fashion, and smiled. "I'm pretty sure the man who bred her was Dutch. His name was Lichtenberger."

The man stuck out a gnarled hand. The hand big for a small man. "Ike Fye," he said.

Gideon gripped it. "Gideon Stoltz."

Fye looked at Maude again. "You want her bred? I got a nice stud. Longer in the back than her, and a hand taller. He covers the ground good, too."

"That's not why I'm here."

Fye's face got sober. "I didn't reckon it was."

"Philomena Hutchinson told me that you took care of Phineas Potter's horse."

Fye nodded. "I should have gone to his funeral. But I have a mare that's about to foal. And, if I'm honest, I didn't want to see that boy go into the ground."

"I understand that Potter's horse is a black gelding with white feet on the left, front and back, and a white star."

"That's Barney," Fye said. "A good, solid riding horse."

"On the day Potter was killed, did he come here and get his horse?"

"He did. Couldn't stay and visit, had to get back to Adamant. There was a speech he wanted to hear."

"Did he say why he needed to ride out after the speech?"

"No. He didn't say a thing about what he was up to."

"Whoever killed Potter seems to have stolen his horse," Gideon said.

Fye's somber expression brightened. "Care to look at some horses?"

Gideon unsaddled Maude and put her in a dry lot. Fye hitched up his pants, then led them to a pasture. In it were ten mares and several foals. Three of the mares looked pregnant, one close to giving birth. A few of the horses lay on the ground resting, while others grazed or stood nuzzling one another. Fye slipped through the rail fence, and Gideon followed.

"I board a few horses, but most of these are mine. I breed, train, and sell them." Fye led Gideon through the herd, pointing out different mares and describing their temperaments and qualities under saddle.

Then he took Gideon to a different pasture.

A dozen geldings and, across a fence in his own pen, a dark bay stallion. The stallion whickered as the two men walked up. He appeared young but fully developed, well-built with a broad chest, a strong-looking topline, and a handsome arching neck. The horse looked oddly familiar to Gideon. The stallion put his nose in Fye's hand. "Hello, Buck," Fye said. "Sorry, but the gent don't want his mare bred."

"He's a beauty," Gideon said. "How old?"

"Five. Sired on my Jessie mare by Vagabond. I believe you know that horse."

Vagabond was the stallion owned by the old ironmaster, Adonijah Thompson. Pursued by Gideon on Maude, the ironmaster had purposely ridden his stallion over a cliff and into Panther Creek. Thompson drowned. Gideon found Vagabond standing in the shallows, his flanks gashed by the ironmaster's spurs, a front leg broken. Gideon had used his gun to end the stallion's suffering.

He didn't want to talk about killing the horse and was glad when Fye didn't bring it up. After a while the two men strolled back toward the barn.

"Did you know that Mr. Potter was helping fugitives from slavery get to freedom?" Gideon asked.

"No. But it don't surprise me. He was always a kind soul."

"What else can you tell me about him?"

"He wasn't much of a horseman. I think deep down he was afraid of horses, except for Barney. I taught Phineas how to ride him."

"Did he ever mention things he was writing about for his newspaper? Do you know if he was looking into any illegal activities?"

"I thought hiding slaves was against the law," Fye said with a shrug. "Phineas called me his uncle, but he didn't know me, not really, and I can't say I knew him very well, either. I don't know how he came to get killed. Maybe it was a robbery, like folks are saying. Maybe it was something else."

Fye's barn had stalls in its lower level, plenty of room for hay and grain in the mows above. The grounds were neatly kept, the outbuildings in good shape. Gideon saw a smithy and reckoned Fye did his own shoeing. Nearby stood a house.

"I don't like to pry," Gideon said.

"'Course you do. You're a sheriff." Fye's eyes danced.

"Is there a Mrs. Fye?"

"There used to be." Fye jutted his chin toward the slope behind the house. "She's under the sod. It's been twenty years. I get along. I got my horses and some cats." He added: "Will you stay for a cup of coffee?"

Gideon followed Fye into the house—one that had been built for a good-sized family.

As if divining his thoughts, Fye said: "Our young 'uns, the ones that lived, they scattered. Three boys are out west. The two girls got married and moved away."

"This place must be a lot of work for one man."

"Especially since that man is a year or two past his prime. I could use some help. But good help is hard to find."

Fye's coffee was hot and strong. The horse breeder filled a clay pipe with tobacco. He went to the fire and poked a live coal out of the ashes. He picked it up with his callused fingers, put the ember in his pipe's bowl, and drew on the pipe until smoke rose.

"You married?" he asked Gideon. "Any children?"

Gideon explained that he and his wife had had a baby son, carried off by the influenza epidemic more than a year ago.

"You should bring your wife here," Fye said. "I'd like to meet her."

"She rides. We have a gelding who takes good care of her. We'll come visit you someday."

He thanked Fye for the coffee and said he had to get back to town.

Ranaway my negro man named Simon, he *has been shot badly* in his back and right arm.

Chapter 18

WHEN TRUE ENTERED THE SMALL STONE BUILDING, THE GUNSMITH stopped his work and gaped at her. He probably hadn't had a woman in his shop ever before, she realized.

She didn't know the smith but suspected they were distantly related because his name was Bainey and she had Baineys on her ma's side.

"I want a gun," she said.

"Do you?" His tone was mocking.

Bainey was egg-bald, with a thick pelt of beard crowding his lips. He had massive forearms and large, strong-looking hands from hammering and filing and carving and whatever else someone who made and repaired guns did.

"It's a pistol I want," True said.

"Why is that?"

"To defend myself if need be."

The gunsmith folded his arms. "You are the sheriff's wife. Do you have his permission to buy a gun?"

She felt her face flush. "Why in the nation would I need anyone's permission to buy a gun?"

She had brought a large pack basket she'd just finished making. Inside it were several smaller baskets. She got them out and handed one to the smith. The baskets were pale and gave off the clean smell of the new-worked ash. "I can pay you with these baskets and some money." In a deerskin pouch hanging from a string around her neck were four dollars in banknotes she'd gotten from the dry goods man for her baskets, plus a gold piece her gram had given her after saying she had no need for cash money at her age. The coin had *1788* on it and a man who looked like a lordly mule with his big turned-down nose; Gram Burns said it was the King of Spain.

True told the gunsmith that before she married she was a Burns, and her ma's ma had been a Bainey. "You and I are kin, I reckon."

The smith unfolded his arms. "Well. I got a little boot pistol might do you." He rummaged in a drawer, laid the gun on his workbench. It was small and squat. Its wooden handle had a crack in it, and rust flecked its stubby barrel. "Made in Belgium."

"That's a flintlock. I want a percussion gun."

The smith lifted his eyebrows. "You know the difference between flintlock and percussion?"

"Of course I do. The flintlock has a piece of flint attached to the hammer that strikes the spark, and the percussion gun is a big improvement because it's . . . " Here she was less sure, but went on anyway: "It's a whole lot more reliable."

"Not as much chance of a hangfire," the smith said with a nod. "Shoots faster, too."

"That's why I want one."

"I have a real good percussion pistol. It will cost you a whale of a lot more than that Belgium gun, though."

He got out a polished wooden box and unlocked it with a brass key. He opened the lid. From a felt-lined central compartment he lifted a pistol.

It had two barrels, one on top of the other. Fernlike scrolls were engraved on the twin hammers and on the body of the gun. The down-curving wooden handle had a tapered piece of polished metal covering its butt. Two triggers, one in front of the other.

The smith handed her the pistol.

Right away it felt good in her hand, solid but not too heavy. On its upper barrel was engraved FORSYTH & CO., PATENT GUN MAKERS, LONDON.

"It's called a detonator," the gunsmith said. "Fifty-four caliber. I got it off a traveling dentist who needed the cash 'cause nobody was wanting their teeth pulled. I tried it out, and it shoots straight. You could take the head off a turkey with that little gun, if the turkey stood still long enough."

True raised the pistol, fixed her eye on a divot in the plaster on the far wall, and saw that she was staring straight down the upper barrel at it.

"Sold," she said. Immediately feeling foolish because she hadn't even asked the price.

Walking home, the box seemed to get heavier and heavier under her arm. The smith had taken her baskets and the banknotes and the gold piece, which he had practically pounced on when she laid it on his bench, and extracted from her a promise to weave a clothes hamper for his wife. True didn't know if it was a square deal or not, but she liked the pistol. It was a beautiful gun and just the right size. It made her feel secure; powerful, even.

Sections in the gun's box held various tools. The smith had shown her how to load and prime. The detonator used a fine-ground powder called fulminate to ignite the main powder charge and send the ball streaking down the barrel. He told her she needed to clean the gun soon after firing it, or else the residue from the combusted powder would corrode the metal. He had thrown in fifty lead balls and some gunpowder and a brass container of the fulminate, and said he could provide more when those ran out.

When Gideon got home that evening, a freshly baked molasses cake sat on the table. Beside the cake was a closed wooden box.

"Go ahead and open it," True said.

He lifted the lid.

"A detonator," True said. "That's what the gunsmith called it."

"Two barrels," Gideon said in a wondering tone. "Two shots." He lifted the pistol out of the box and aimed it at the window. Then he pivoted on his feet and aimed it at the door. "It points good."

"Will you help me learn to shoot it?"

"All right. Yes."

"How about tomorrow after church?"

One hundred dollars reward, for my negro Glasgow, and Kate, his wife. Glasgow is 24 years old—has *marks of the whip* on his back. Kate is 26—has a *scar* on her cheek, *and several marks of a whip.*

Chapter 19

———⦚⦚⦚———

LYING IN BED ALL DAY IN THE FANCY HOUSE, OTIS COULDN'T HELP hearing it in his mind: the shot that rang out after he raced off on that powerful uncontrolled horse and left Dan lying on the ground. Nor could he stop wondering if the people he'd stolen the horse from had shot Dan dead, or hanged him for a horse thief, or returned him to Red Rose and now he was back there striped from the whip or with an *R* branded on his cheek or wearing an iron collar around his neck with long prongs on it like Waller put on that other hand who ran away, after whipping his back raw and splashing brine all over it.

After Otis had abandoned Dan, after he got off the horse and sent the animal running for home, he'd resumed traveling afoot. Walking at night, hiding by day in brush or deep in the forest or tucked away beneath rock ledges on soft beds of old leaves and pine boughs. He stayed away from houses, which he located by seeing the tiny sparks of light flaring at their windows or, more often, hearing dogs barking. He swung out wide around towns.

He waded creeks, lugging a tree branch or whatever dry weathered board or junk wood he could find so that when the water got too deep he could float and paddle across.

Once he heard a hound giving tongue and a gun going off. His heart pounded against his ribs, and he burrowed deeper into the thicket where he lay; but nothing else happened, and finally he reckoned it was just someone out hunting rabbits.

Owls hooted and whinnied and caterwauled in the night, coons chittered, and wolves howled. Once he heard a long hoarse yowl that he judged might be from a panther. He hid behind a tree. He thought: I am very small. No flesh on these bones. Not even a mouthful. Presently the yowl sounded again, farther off.

He watched the moon wax and wane and sail across the sky. One night, the full moon became half covered as if a bloody hand lay on its face, while the stars blazed all around. The one star pointed at by the drinking gourd hung there shimmering and silvery, brighter than the rest.

One morning he opened his eyes to see a colored man digging onions in a field. He crept out of the tangle where he'd been resting. He coughed into his hand, and the man slowly raised up from his digging. The man came limping over, using his fork as a cane. An old man with cloudy eyes and a crinkly white beard. "You are a runaway," the man said: a statement, not a question. The old man got an onion out of his pouch and tossed it to him. The man told him he had passed over Mason and Dixon's line, and he was now in Pennsylvania. "You are free," the man said.

He didn't feel free. He felt hungry and parched and footsore and wearier and weaker than ever before in his life. Lonelier. And, free or not, he still felt skittish as a rat with a fyce dog hunting close in the tall grass.

The old man said he worked for a farmer, but he was not sure whether the farmer would like having a runaway on his land. The man shooed Otis back into the thicket and returned with buttered biscuits with ham inside and a jug of sweet tea. He lifted a crooked finger. "Black Town is over there," he said. "Some call it Little Africa. Maybe they'd help you. But watch out. The bounty hunters know about that place."

Otis stayed in the thicket and ate his biscuits. In the night he continued north. He followed the starlit road up the broad valley past farms and woodlots and through stretches of forest. Walking all night and traveling some ways into daylight before hiding. The air crisp, the trees showing fiery all around.

As he walked, his eyes raked the sides of the road, his mind always reckoning which way to run. When he heard a rider or a rig, he ducked. Next day he continued up the valley until mountains pinched in on both sides and the road bent left and climbed through a notch. Then down into the next valley, and he followed it north and east as well, for that was the way the valleys and the ridges and the roads all trended hereabouts.

Finally at dawn one day he found himself in a hollow with scrubby fields and weathered cabins and a gristmill and a tavern with a sign on a post showing a big white bird, painted shaky like the hand that had held the brush was attached to someone who was either crazy or drunk.

He felt used up from the walking and hiding and starving and shivering and fretting. He decided to stop and stay in this place for a while. Hoping that even if Waller had put a notice in a slew of newspapers, the people in this hollow might not have read it.

The place was called McDonough. Craddock, the man who owned the White Crow, put him to work grooming and feeding the horses of the tavern's guests, milking the cow, and doing work the white folks didn't prefer to do themselves, such as crawling up the chimney and scraping out the soot, cleaning spittoons and chamber pots, and digging out the privy.

Craddock let him stay in the barn among the cobwebs and stable litter. Worked him hard and never gave him a penny and even stole the second of the two silver half-dollars his mama had sent along with him: grinning and saying "Room and board" as he snatched the coin in his fist. Once Otis displeased Craddock by talking saucy, and the tavern keeper boxed his ears and said he might just ride over to Walkersville and see if there was a bill out for him, since he figured he had a runaway on his hands. But Craddock never did that. Nor did his stepson Thaddeus, the constable, though he held it over him, too. They had him on the jump all the time, fed him just enough scraps from the table to keep him alive.

He was in Pennsylvania. And he reckoned he was free: free labor for someone else.

He knew he should get moving again. Head for New York, which was above Pennsylvania, or maybe even Canada, a whole different country, and if he got that far he really would be free. Meanwhile he kept his eyes peeled for Waller or someone he might have sent. Though he had to admit that any of the travelers who came to the tavern could be a slave catcher.

He waited out the winter, sleeping at night under all the dusty mouse-chewed horse blankets he could find. When it was bitter cold, they let him sleep in the kitchen.

Then came the burning, which knocked everything cattywampus.

A woman had shown up on foot on a cold day at winter's end. A white woman, pretty to look at, though skinny and not much taller than himself.

Craddock turned the woman away since she didn't have money for lodging. Then changed his mind. He sent Otis to catch the woman before she walked off, tell her to come in the kitchen. And sent him off again right away to let Thaddeus know.

Later that night Otis woke to the horses stamping and whickering and kicking against their stalls. He bolted out of bed. The smell of smoke was thick. He spoke to the horses, stroked their necks and noses and ears, calmed them. He came out of the barn and saw the flames licking up from the tavern's windows and roof, and the woman, half-lit in the darkness so that it looked like she walked in little jerks, heading up into the notch.

He stood and watched as the flames got higher and the people in the tavern roused themselves and hurried out. Then Craddock had to run back inside to get his money, in a strongbox behind the bar in the serving room. The roof fell in, sparks swirling up like a golden whirlwind. The next morning they found him in the ruins. With his clothes burned off he looked like a turkey gobbler overrun by a brush fire, fat and charred, with blackened wattles on his neck and arms sticking up like wing stubs.

It satisfied him, seeing Craddock cooked like that. But the fire put him in a tight spot. With the tavern burned down, there might not be any work for him. He was scared that Thaddeus would turn him in for the reward that Waller surely was offering. He felt the man's baleful presence carrying north over the rippling ridges and the troughs of valleys that he had placed between himself and Red Rose.

He kept living in the barn, trying to stay on Thaddeus's good side, and every so often a traveler would lodge in one of the houses nearby, and he'd take care of the man's horse and Thaddeus would pocket whatever money changed hands. Thaddeus's ma, the widowed Mrs. Craddock, moved in with her son after the fire, and she fed Otis now and then.

Late that summer a sheriff rode in from the north. Otis would have hidden, but the sheriff caught him hunting for nails in the ashes of the tavern, a task Thaddeus had put him to. The sheriff asked where he could find Thaddeus. As he led the sheriff to the cabin, he reckoned it would end in a fight, Thaddeus being of that disposition. He didn't care. He wanted Thaddeus dead, and the sheriff, too, if it worked out that way, because then there would be two less white people in the world.

He hunkered down to watch.

The sheriff asked Thaddeus about a woman who had been found dead in the county where the sheriff came from. It turned out she was the pretty one that Thaddeus had his way with, who then set fire to the White Crow. Right quick Thaddeus took offense. He latched hold of the sheriff, aiming to turn him every which way but loose, but the sheriff grabbed a club out of his saddlebag and knocked one of Thaddeus's pins out from under him. Otis heard the hard thump and bone-snap. Thaddeus yelped and went down. Otis hoped the sheriff would beat Thaddeus's brains out, but all he did was pry information out of him.

The sheriff, being somewhat nicked up from the fight, went and soaked himself in the stream by the mill pond.

Where, for some reason unknown to him, Otis broke his rule about helping white people and warned the sheriff that Thaddeus's two brothers were on their way to serve him back. The sheriff had a rifle and a pistol, and Otis pointed out that he could hide in cover and shoot the Kirkwoods down. But the sheriff already had what he wanted, so he said he would leave. Otis told the sheriff to ride up through Nomans Notch, and he would send the Kirkwoods down the Mackeysville road in the other direction.

Before the sheriff left, Otis asked him about Adamant, the town where the sheriff was the law. The town where he'd heard a good many free colored folk lived.

He lasted out that fall and the winter that followed. Which meant he'd been in McDonough almost a year and a half, a lot longer than he had intended. He knew he should move on. Someone might have sent word about him to Red Rose. And anyway, he was always hungry, and with more and more work heaped on him since Thaddeus's broken leg was slow to heal and he was in a mood like a mean dog in a cage that people kept poking with sticks.

One night a Bible salesman stopped at a house in McDonough. Otis took care of the man's horse, then worked up the nerve to talk to him. He learned that the man was dead set against slavery. He had been to Adamant, where nobody in that heathen town wanted to buy his Bibles. However, he knew of a house where a fugitive could find shelter. The man told him how many houses to count on the street going north from the courthouse, and to look for a big stone house two and a half floors high, with one of the downstairs windows having only one shutter. Go around back and knock on the door three times. Then wait a bit and knock three more times.

Otis gathered what food he could lay his hands on, and in the night he made his way to the coach road that led north through the Seven Mountains to Adamant.

Two days later, just before dawn, he stood on the back stoop of the gray stone house. He knocked on the door three times. Waited. Knocked three times again. He heard someone coming. The sour-faced white woman opened the door and let him in. She marched him upstairs to this room, like she'd done it all before. The room he'd been locked up in ever since.

Six days, six knife marks on the chair leg.

Six days when he had the choice of standing at the window looking out at a tree's leaves, or at the birds, or lying in bed staring up at the ceiling.

Getting bored and more jittery each day.

Maybe the Bible man lied. He was a white man, after all. They lied as easy as they breathed. Maybe this was not a house of safety. Maybe the folks here were fixing to turn him in for the reward. He fretted that his mind was slip-sliding around like his mama's. He reckoned he had best get himself out of this comfortable, crazy-making trap of a place before it was too late.

Ranaway, a negro man named Squire—had on a chain locked with a house-lock, around his neck.

Chapter 20

———⚭———

"STAND SIDE ON TO WHATEVER YOU'RE SHOOTING AT." GIDEON DID not mention that in taking a sideways stance, True would offer an enemy as small a target as possible. He did not want to think about his wife shooting at anyone and, heaven forbid, getting shot at herself.

She wore an old homespun shirt and gray pants with faded blue stripes, the pant legs tucked into a pair of well-broken-in boots. Her long black hair was in a ponytail behind her head. She pushed up the brim of her dented slouch hat, still a touch big even after she'd padded the hatband. These items of apparel had belonged to True's grandfather, Ezekiel Burns, long dead. The pants, True had pointed out, made riding a horse easier than if she wore a dress. They didn't have a side-saddle, and, anyway, True thought that was a ridiculous awkward way to sit on a horse.

In her current getup, True hardly looked like a woman, Gideon thought, let alone a proper wife. Not that she seemed to care about the appearance she presented to the world—or what her husband might prefer.

At least she'd worn a dress to church that morning. Afterward, she had gone home and packed a lunch while he fetched the horses and got a gun for himself at the jail. Then they rode to an old ore digging, now used as a dump, where Gideon and Alonzo practiced shooting.

Maude and Jack stood a hundred yards off, hobbled and grazing.

True gave Gideon a questioning look.

"First you need to cock the gun," he said.

She narrowed her eyes. "I know that." Holding the pistol in her right hand, she used the heel of her left hand to notch back the hammer on the right side.

"Try shooting at that stump," Gideon said. It was a big enough target that she might hit it, which would build confidence and persuade True that she could learn to shoot if she practiced long enough.

"Line up the front and back sights on the target," he said. "Take a deep breath and let out about half of it. Then squeeze the trigger, slow and easy, so that it sort of surprises you when the gun goes off. And keep a tight hold on the grip." He laid his own pistol on the ground and plugged his ears with his fingers.

True aimed at the stump and tightened her index finger on the front trigger.

Crack! Smoke gouted from the barrel as the pistol bucked upward and a chunk of wood flew off the stump. Both horses gave little startled jumps and, as the shot echoed back and forth between the pale new-greening hills, returned to grazing.

True took five steps back. She cocked the second hammer, aimed, and squeezed the back trigger.

Crack! Another chip went whirring off the stump.

"Well done," Gideon said. Thinking: beginner's luck.

Now it was his turn. He would show True what a good shot he was. He set an old cracked jug on top of the stump, then picked up his pistol and went to the spot where True had stood when she fired her second barrel, and took five more steps back.

He cocked the hammer of his pistol, with its chunk of reddish flint. He raised the gun, controlled his breathing, and sighted on the jug. He squeezed the trigger. The hammer fell, the flint struck a spark off the frizzen, powder hissed in the pan for a long breathless moment before finally sending fire down the hole and igniting the charge: while he did his best to keep the sights from wobbling off the target.

Buh-room! Dirt kicked up beyond the stump. The jug sat there. As if mocking him.

Gideon saw how True avoided looking at him, trying, without complete success, to keep a smile off her face.

Wordlessly she reloaded and primed her pistol in the manner demonstrated to her by the gunsmith Bainey. She showed Gideon how the priming reservoir slid over the pan when the hammer was cocked, depositing the fulminate powder and covering it, then explained how it would snap out of the way when the trigger was pulled.

"An ingenious design," Gideon said. "And the workmanship couldn't be better."

"I like how it shoots," True said. "As soon as the hammer falls, the gun goes off."

"Not like a flint gun sometimes." Gideon looked ruefully at the one in his hand.

"See if you can hit the jug," he said. "But don't be too disappointed if you miss." He laid his pistol down again and covered his ears.

True cocked the detonator.

Crack! The top of the jug shattered.

Crack! Her second shot blew the jug's remains off the stump.

"You are good at this," Gideon said as True reloaded. "Maybe because you have such good eyesight." Often True would point out things he hadn't seen, like a drab little bird clinging to a tree or the shoe-button eye of a rabbit crouched in the brush. He reckoned she took to shooting so naturally because she had never picked up bad habits like jerking the trigger or flinching in anticipation of the recoil or the loud report.

For Gideon, the noise from firing a gun, especially a short-barreled one, was unpleasant at best and sometimes painful. His discomfort at shooting had gotten worse since his concussion after falling off Maude.

He began the laborious process of reloading his own gun, pouring powder down the barrel, following it with a cloth patch and a lead ball rammed home with the hickory rod. He replaced the rod in the ferrules beneath the barrel and primed the pan.

"I need something better to carry this detonator in than an old flour sack," True said.

"A purse?"

"I was thinking of a leather holster thing that I could tie to my saddle and maybe wear on a belt. I'll get Gaither Brown to make me something. Though he is a very low-quality man."

Gideon's part-time deputy Gaither Brown had a leatherworking shop near the jail. Gideon did not dispute True's judgment of the fellow.

He found some old bottles and lined them up on a log. He and True took turns shooting at them. True shattered three of the bottles. Gideon was not having a good day. With his last shot he finally broke one. He rubbed his temple with the inside of his wrist. His ears rang and his head ached and he was sweating all over. He fought off some mild dizziness by taking several deep breaths.

They sat down near the horses under a tree coming into leaf. True got out bread, cheese, and meat.

"Are you any closer to figuring out who killed Phineas Potter?" she asked.

"Not really. His sister didn't suspect anyone in particular of wanting to kill him. And Ike Fye, the man who kept Potter's horse, didn't have much to add."

"I keep my ears open when I'm in shops and at church," True said. "And you know our neighbor Mrs. Sayers is the world's own gossip, maybe even worse than Alonzo. I hear there's a group of folks in the county who hide runaway slaves, then help them get farther north or to the cities where they can pass as free."

"Was Potter in that group?"

"No one I talked to would say so, but that's the feeling I got." She went on: "People won't tell you about helping fugitives. They don't know if you'd look the other way or arrest them."

Gideon dodged the implied question. "Potter could have been on that road to meet a wagon bringing escaped slaves. But if he got run down by accident, the people who did it took things a lot further when they hit him over the head and then robbed him." Gideon brushed crumbs off his lap. "I have the key to his house. Let's take a look."

★★★

The dwelling, sided with weathered clapboards, stood on a back street. Inside, Gideon and True found a small kitchen and dining area and a sitting room with a great number of books on shelves. On the wall was a framed quotation: EDUCATION BEGINS THE GENTLEMAN, BUT READING, GOOD COMPANY, AND REFLECTION MUST FINISH HIM. It was attributed to someone named John Locke.

They climbed the stairs. The upper story was a single large room beneath the roof's pitch. At one end sat a bed and chest of drawers, at the other end a cluttered desk.

Gideon and True opened drawers in the desk. They examined receipts and old letters, including some from Potter's sister Philomena. The letters seemed to convey only mundane news, unless phrases like "the garden is bountiful this year" and "the roses are blooming beautifully" had other meanings. They found no diary or anything else of a personal nature.

True handed a paper to Gideon. "What do you make of this?"

On it were two words: "Barrens" and "Brodie."

The Barrens was a sprawl of land a dozen miles west of Adamant.

"Do you know anyone named Brodie?" Gideon asked. True shook her head.

Coming down the stairs, Gideon took notice of the floor. Hard pine, gold in color, and more elegant than the rest of the house. The boards, highly polished, looked like they'd been laid not long ago. True opened a closet door. Inside, a small carpet covered the floor. Several boxes of books sat on the rug. Gideon removed the boxes. True pulled the rug out of the way, then knelt and ran her hands over the floor.

She tapped her finger on a small square of wood, scarcely noticeable since its grain matched the flooring around it.

Using his penknife, Gideon teased the square out. Beneath it was a recessed iron ring. He lifted the ring and pulled. A trap door opened. Below the door was a ladder.

True found a sconce and lit a candle. Gideon went partway down the ladder, then took the sconce from True and continued on down with True following. They found themselves in a room fifteen feet wide by twenty feet long. Brick walls and a stone floor with a rug. A table and lamp. Stacked pallets and folded blankets in one corner.

"I wonder how many people he helped get to freedom," True said.

Ran away, a black woman, Betsey—had an *iron bar on her right leg*.

Chapter 21

⸺∞∞⸺

ON CALM NIGHTS, THE BARRENS' UNDULATING TERRAIN RADIATED heat to the sky while cold air drained in from the surrounding land. Frost could form in any month. The Barrens was also a flammable place, especially in dry weather, when fires started by lightning or by people swept through the grassy glades and pitch pines and bear oak and huckleberry stands.

A few roads and trails meandered through the area. Wolves and panthers prowled, and human predators—robbers and highwaymen—passed through and sometimes took up residence there.

Most of the farms that had been cut into the Barrens had failed and were now growing up in brush.

On one of those derelict farms, Liza Brodie went out the door of the ramshackle house into the chill dawn. She wore a threadbare linen frock beneath a brown woolen cloak. Her breath jetted out in clouds.

She was a big-boned woman with broad hips and large breasts. For thirty years she had worked in a brothel called Bodines in Greer County, south of the Seven Mountains. She had started out satisfying the sexual needs of drovers, wagoners, and farmhands. Then, as what little attractiveness she possessed diminished, she was put to cooking and cleaning and laundering, tasks that she found preferable to whoring. She had met William Jewell Jarrett and Gulliver Luck at the bawdy house years ago. Now she had quit that place and was determined never to go back.

She stood in the frozen grass, hacked up matter in her throat, and spat. She was visited with a sudden memory of her father, dead these many years and buried a few yards off. It was not a pleasant memory. She did not have many pleasant memories from her childhood or her youth. She shuffled over to her father's grave, marked with a chunk of pinkish sandstone, gathered her frock, and squatted. Farted as she pissed.

She looked at the corncrib. The big boss wanted the captives kept in the crib during the day so they could get some air, and in the upper floor of the house at night. He didn't want them in the crib overnight because they might figure out how to get loose. But with Jarrett and Luck gone all yesterday, Brodie had kept the captives locked inside the crib. She had checked it over carefully beforehand, and concluded there was no way they could escape.

She could hear them in there now, talking. She straightened, clumped back inside the house, and fetched food and water. She told the captives to move to the far end of the crib before she unlocked the padlock on the door and set the plates and jug inside on the ground.

"I can't manage you'uns by myself," she explained. "You will have to do your bidness in there till the boys get back."

After relocking the corncrib, she lit a fire under a large kettle in the yard. The kettle was filled with water fortified with chamber lye: piss. Clothing had soaked in the kettle overnight, her dress and petticoat, Jarrett's and Luck's much-mended shirts and undergarments, spare pants and socks.

When the wash had slow-boiled for an hour, Brodie snagged the clothes with a stick and transferred them to a wooden tub, its water clouded with soap. She stirred the clothes vigorously. Then she shifted them to a different tub filled with clean water. After rinsing them, she wrung them out and laid them on a plank. She picked up a flat wooden paddle and began beating the water out of the fabric. She took care not to break the buttons as she lifted the paddle and brought it down again and again, with a wet *smack*.

As she worked, she sang snatches from old hymns. Off-key utterances of "sins washed away" and "a place for me in heaven" rose with the steam and smoke. "Flee, oh flee, to Jesus' arms," she warbled. The only arms she'd known had been those of strange men with deep and sometimes twisted desires. And her father's arms, with hands that pummeled and punished.

She heard a horse nicker.

Presently the wagon trundled into the yard, Luck and Jarrett on the seat, a tarpaulin over the wagon's bed hummocked up in the middle.

Jarrett whooped and raised a jug.

"Two more!" he yelled.

Luck halted the team.

Jarrett got down, fumbled with knots and untied ropes, and pulled the tarpaulin off the wagon's bed.

A dark-skinned man and an equally dark boy, both bound and gagged, shrank back from the sudden light.

"This here is money!" Jarrett crowed.

"The Lord taketh whosoever he wishes," Luck said with a grin. "At which time, he alone appoints."

Jarrett sashayed over to Brodie. "Leave off with that warsh," he said. He put a hand at her ample waist, raised her other hand, and danced her in a circle. The small lively man laughed, while the ponderous heavy-footed woman shambled about and looked bemused. Then she planted her feet and cuffed Jarrett's hands aside.

"Where'd you get 'em?"

"Boss man located 'em. Living in a cabin over to Frogville."

Jarrett went to the wagon and untied the man's gag.

"We done nothing wrong!" the man blurted. "Been chopping wood for Mr. and Mrs. Olcott, that's all. They'll come looking for us!"

Jarrett tried to stuff the gag back in the man's mouth.

The man recoiled, shaking his head. "You can't do this!" he cried.

"Yes, we can," Jarrett said. He ambled over to where Brodie had been beating the laundry and picked up the paddle.

Ten dollars reward for my woman Siby, *very much scarred about the neck and ears by whipping.*

Chapter 22

————◦◦◦◦————

I N THE MORNING AT THE JAIL, GIDEON SHOWED ALONZO THE PAPER he and True had found on Potter's desk.

" 'Barrens,'" Alonzo read. " 'Brodie.' You know where the Barrens are at. Maybe someone named Brodie lives there. Or lived there, since few inhabit that dismal place anymore. Want me to ask around?"

"Yes." Gideon cleared his throat. "I spoke with Hosea and Lenore Belknap at Phineas Potter's funeral on Saturday. They said they'd heard that Melchior Dorfman is our main suspect in Potter's murder."

Alonzo looked at the floor.

"You shouldn't do that," Gideon said. "Blab things to people. Especially people who put out a newspaper."

"You reckon Dorfman did it, you as much as said so."

"I said or implied no such thing."

"Dorfman's got that fiery temper, which he showed it down in Hammertown going after those two Virginians. With us in between, thank you very much. And you saw him getting into it with Potter after the abolitionist's speech. That very night, Potter gets knocked on the head. Then we run into Dorfman on the Halfmoon Valley road when we go fetch the corpus."

"Probably just a coincidence," Gideon said. Though he didn't usually believe in coincidences. "Anyway, do not mention anything else about our investigation until we decide it should be made known."

Alonzo nodded assent.

"How well do you know the Belknaps?" Gideon asked.

"Lenore is Jack Riddle's baby sister. Jack is an old chum of mine. Their pa, Fat Reuben, he's got a brother in Virginia. Lenore went visiting there once and met Hosea, and they got hitched. Though what he sees in that dried-up beanpole I can't imagine."

Reuben Riddle was the banker who had stood up and shouted at the abolitionist speaker in the church, calling him an agitator and a fool. Riddle represented Colerain County in the state legislature.

"Do you know why the Belknaps came here?" Gideon asked.

"It had to do with that slave uprising in Virginia, when all those people got killed. Hosea and Lenore were in the middle of it. I don't know if their own slaves revolted or not. But Fat Reuben didn't want his little girl down there any longer. He owns property all over Adamant. He gave them that building on Decatur, and they moved here and started the *Democrat*."

"Which now conveniently has no competition," Gideon said, "since Phineas Potter is dead and the *Adamant Argus* has shut down. Though I do not necessarily suspect the Belknaps of murdering Potter. Let me repeat: I do not necessarily suspect the Belknaps of murdering Potter."

Alonzo smiled thinly.

"I'll go talk to them," Gideon said. "But first I need to see Melchior Dorfman. I doubt I'll get a very good reception."

★★★

Gideon found Dorfman opening up his shop. The tinner stiffened when he saw who had called out a greeting.

"I need to ask you some questions," Gideon said.

"I've got some for you, too." Dorfman went inside, and Gideon followed.

The tinner leaned against his work bench and crossed his arms. "You first."

"I saw you at Phineas Potter's funeral."

"That's not a question."

"Why did you go there?"

"To pay my respects."

"Even though the two of you didn't see eye to eye on certain matters?"

"We had our differences."

"I believe Potter hated slavery as much as you do."

Dorfman's eyes narrowed. "Hated slavery as much as a man who was once somebody's property?"

Gideon felt the blood rush to his face. "I only meant that he was a strong abolitionist. Very much opposed to slavery. At the funeral I spoke with his sister, and she said things that made me wonder if Potter was working to help get fugitives to safety. Maybe that's what got him killed."

"I can't say anything to that, Sheriff. Though I have to wonder how much Potter really cared for colored folks, since he couldn't bear the thought of you whites sharing this country with us lowly darkies."

"Maybe he thought black people would never get a fair shake here. That they'd do better in a land of their own."

Dorfman exhaled. "Let me build a fire and put some water on. If you're going to keep me from my work, we may as well drink some coffee."

Gideon found a stool and sat. *Ei yei yei,* how foolish he had sounded. Suggesting that Potter could have hated slavery to the same degree that a person of color did, especially a former slave—something he hadn't known about Dorfman.

What did he himself really know about slavery? Or the ways in which black people were scorned and threatened—sometimes even hurt or killed, just because of the color of their skin? To his shame, he realized he had never thought deeply about slavery. It was something that mostly went on in places farther south. And he didn't know many colored people well. No, he didn't know *any* colored people well. He saw them in town. He used the services they provided. A shave and a haircut, the livery hand currying Maude and tacking her up for him. He didn't know what a single black person really thought or believed, what they aspired to, what they'd endured. But judging from the few encounters he'd had with them, it seemed they were much the same as white folks, despite what others might say: He'd read that a personage no less revered than Thomas Jefferson, the country's third president, averred that negroes sweated and stank more than whites, needed less sleep, and lacked forethought and couldn't see danger unless it was right in front of them—well, Dorfman certainly saw the possibility of danger in Adamant and, with his friends, was preparing to resist it. Jefferson also wrote that male orangutans preferred negro females to those of their own kind. Gideon wondered how Jefferson could have known such a thing. Or had he said it to imply that blacks were less human than whites, to justify the fact that he himself kept people in bondage?

Jefferson had owned hundreds of slaves. He was rumored to have had children with one of them, a woman named Sally, who happened to be the half-sister of Jefferson's own wife Martha.

George Washington had owned slaves when he was president. So had James Madison and James Monroe, Virginians like Washington and Jefferson. Andrew Jackson had enslaved two hundred on his plantation in Tennessee. It was said that one of Jackson's servants, a man called Albert, ran away; when he was recaptured Jackson ordered that he be given a thousand lashes, and the whipping killed him.

Did that make Jackson a murderer?

A small number of blacks lived in the part of southeastern Pennsylvania where Gideon had grown up. In that heavily *Pennsylfawnisch Deitsch* area, he hadn't had much contact with them beyond seeing them in Lancaster on market days. He'd heard plenty of jokes about the *schwarzers*, though, which generally had them doing stupid or immoral things; he had even repeated some of those jokes himself because, at the time, he thought they were funny. There had been some cruel and violent incidents, too. He remembered hearing about a gang of white men, including the father of one of his friends, going to a disorderly house on Queen Street that specialized in colored girls. The men, drunk on wine, pulled down the house using poles and battering rams. The women came pouring out of the dwelling and fled for their lives, followed by catcalls and laughter as they flung themselves over a fence.

He watched as Dorfman prepared coffee. The tinner was a strong-looking man who held himself erect. He had a bald spot on the back of his head like a worn area on a carpet. Dorfman poured two steaming mugs, set one in front of Gideon, and resumed leaning against his workbench.

Dorfman sipped from his mug while regarding Gideon. "What do you see when you look at me?" he asked. "Someone worth cleaning your chimney or blacking your boots? Or maybe you see a tinner. Funny, how some folks call a tinsmith a 'whitesmith.'" He gave a forced laugh. "I don't know much about you, Stoltz, but let me tell you a bit about myself."

Gideon nodded.

"I grew up on a farm in Delaware. Our family had been enslaved in that state for over a hundred years. You might reckon that Dorfman is a German name, and you'd be right. I don't know when my people picked it up; the man who owned us was called Chapman.

"It was a small farm, vegetables and other truck. We raised chickens and turkeys for meat and eggs. Our family lived in a cabin out back of the Chapmans' house, which wasn't a mansion or a manor house, just a house like you'd see in the country around here.

"The Chapmans treated us pretty good. We were never beaten or whipped. We had Sundays and holidays off. Now and then they gave us money to buy things we needed.

"It seemed like every year the farm fell deeper in debt. Something had to give. So I was apprenticed to a tinsmith in Philadelphia—Mr. Chapman, he got paid for the seven years I was there. He rented me out like a mule." Dorfman paused. "He could have done worse. He could have listened to his wife and sold us to a slave dealer. Who would have chained us up with a couple dozen other folks and marched us south. Broke the family up, sold us to different farms or plantations in different states. We never would have seen each other again.

"I was twenty-one when I finished my apprenticeship. As part of the deal, I got manumitted—freed. They kept me on at the tin shop and paid me for my work. I saved my money, and after a while I was able to buy my parents from the Chapmans."

Dorfman paused. Perhaps, thought Gideon, to let it sink in: *"I was able to buy my parents."*

"They came to the city and lived in a house we rented," Dorfman went on. "My ma took in washing and did mending, and my pa worked on the docks. I met Sarah, and we got married. She was free-born; her family had lived in the city for years.

"Over time, we bought my brothers' and sisters' freedom, too. Things were going pretty well. Then one Fourth of July we put on our best clothes and went down to Independence Square to join everyone else and celebrate the holiday. You know, our nation's birthday.

"A gang of white boys had a different idea. They threw rocks at us and aimed sticks at our heads, said we had no business being there. I tell you, it hurt. Not just the sticks and stones, but seeing how those people hated us. It was all I could do not to grab a stick and beat one of them within an inch of his life. But the crowd would have killed us if we'd fought back."

Dorfman lifted his mug and drank.

Gideon did the same, realizing he had not yet taken a sip, so absorbed had he been by the tinner's tale. The coffee was strong and bitter.

"My parents are still there," Dorfman said. "I worry about them. Three years ago, mobs of whites went roaming around the city beating on colored folks. Last summer they sacked the African Presbyterian Church and burned down thirty colored homes. No one got killed, but it's just a matter of time."

Dorfman's eyes bored into Gideon's. "Sheriff, I pray that someone doesn't hurt or kill my ma or pa or one of my brothers or sisters or their children. I think about it a lot. And I hope nothing like that happens here. But tell me: What do you think the white folks in Adamant would do if a colored child tried to go to that academy up on the hill? Or if our businesses get too successful? Or one of us decides to run for office? I already told you how that election official tried to keep us colored men from voting last fall—when we helped get you reelected.

"Did you know that next week the legislature will be meeting in Harrisburg to write a new state constitution? What do you bet that once those politicians get done, colored men will have lost the right to vote?"

From reading the newspaper, Gideon knew that many prominent people in the state wanted to end negro suffrage—although he wondered whether the typical white citizen cared about it. Reuben Riddle, the banker that Alonzo called Fat Reuben, would be one of those politicians rewriting the state's constitution. It wouldn't surprise Gideon if Riddle favored denying colored men the vote.

"What brought you to Adamant?" Gideon asked.

"I got a letter from a friend. He said it was a good place to raise a family. Not as dangerous as the city, maybe. That you all needed a tin shop that offered good ware for fair prices. And he said a community of upright colored folks lived here." Dorfman finished his coffee and set the mug down. "And you, Sheriff? You aren't from these parts either."

"No. From Lancaster County."

"Why did you come to Adamant?"

"I wanted to see someplace new. I . . . I didn't want to farm. So I got on my horse and rode west, and this is where I ended up." Since he knew it would sound ridiculous, Gideon didn't add that the town's intriguing name, which he'd seen on a map, had been part of the draw.

"How did you get to be sheriff?" Dorfman asked. "Somehow you don't seem the type."

Gideon bristled. "What do you mean by that?"

"I'd have thought folks around here would want someone older, someone local. Someone who didn't talk like a . . ." Dorfman was unable to keep a smile off his lips "like a Dutchman."

"I got hired as a deputy at first," Gideon said. "When the sheriff died, the county said I should finish out his term. Then I got voted in last fall. I was surprised that I won. Maybe people think I'm doing a good job."

"Maybe you are doing a good job," Dorfman said, "or maybe not. What have you learned about John Horne? Or the man and woman who disappeared from that house in Hammertown?"

"That's partly why I came here today. To tell you that I talked to Annie Picard. I didn't find out anything other than those people's names, Amanda Jones and Felix Wiley. But I'm not finished. I plan to go back and question Picard again." He paused. "I also went to John Horne's cabin. I found his big gray dog. It was dead. Someone shot it."

Dorfman's face fell. "Then it's true. John's been kidnapped."

"Mr. Dorfman, the other night I saw you drinking in the Horse. Earlier you told me you never went to Hammertown."

Dorfman shrugged. "A little white lie. I admit that I enjoy a drink now and then. And a cigar."

A cigar box lay on the counter. Dorfman pointed at it. Gideon shook his head. Dorfman picked up a cigar, bit the end off, then lit up with a splint from the fire.

The tinner slitted his eyes against the smoke. "My friends and I, we were talking things over in that saloon. Speeches like that abolitionist gave, well, they are one thing. But strength is whole 'nother thing. And since the law does not exactly seem able to protect the colored people in this county, we've decided to form a vigilance committee. To watch out for ourselves, our wives and children. Sarah and I have a son, Paul, he's twelve, and another son, Silas, ten. Children are being snatched off the streets in the cities, men and women, too. Kidnapped and sold into slavery."

Dorfman's voice was harsh. "Do you know your Bible? Exodus 21, verse 16: 'He that stealeth a man, and selleth him, or if he be found in his hand, he shall surely be put to death.'"

"I disagree that the law isn't protecting the colored people here," Gideon said. "But Adamant has over a thousand people, and fifteen thousand live in this county. And there is one sheriff and two deputies to keep the peace. Well, one and a half deputies."

Dorfman blew out a cloud of smoke.

"I would like the names of the men who were with you in the Horse," Gideon said, "and in the street afterward, when you threatened those Southerners."

The tinner readily supplied names and occupations: Chalmers Smythe was a freighter, Joe Drew and Antoine McCray were carpenters. "That slave man," Dorfman said. "You should have arrested him when he pulled that pistol."

"I didn't want to make things worse. I'm holding his gun at the jail. And I am keeping an eye on him and his man Blaine. As far as I can tell, all they are doing is looking for that runaway—I've found nothing linking them to the disappearances of John Horne or the two people from Annie Picard's house. Or with Phineas Potter's death. However, I did find a cigar on the ground near Potter's body. A cigar like the one you threw down in the street after you told Waller he'd get turned into hash in hell. A cigar like the one you are smoking now."

Dorfman tapped cigar ash into his empty mug. "And that makes me your 'main suspect' in Potter's murder? Because I smoke? Or maybe it's the color of my skin. Use your brain, Stoltz. There are people who might want to get ahead of the law if they thought a black man had killed a white."

Gideon had concluded the same thing, that Alonzo naming Dorfman as a suspect in Potter's killing put the tinsmith in danger. How much danger, he didn't know.

"Let me tell you something else," Dorfman said. "Us colored men in town—we have guns, and know how to use them. We won't be peaceable if anyone threatens us. Or if we find out who's kidnapping our people."

Ranaway a negro man named Henry, *his left eye out*, **some scars from a** *dirk* **on and under his left arm, and** *much scarred* **with the whip.**

Chapter 23

—⟨∞⟩—

GIDEON TRUDGED TO THE COURTHOUSE SMARTING AFTER HIS conversation with Dorfman. He felt renewed anger at Alonzo for blabbing that the sheriff suspected the tinsmith of killing Phineas Potter. A wild notion came to him: fire Alonzo. But that would be stupid; for all his quirks and flaws, the man was a good deputy. If Gideon was honest with himself, he'd be lost without him. Dumpy, competent Alonzo Bell might even make a better sheriff than Gideon Stoltz. Who wasn't making much progress toward solving the crimes that had recently struck Colerain County.

Now Gideon hoped to learn about a person or persons called Brodie, the name on the paper he and True had found on Potter's desk.

The county's old courthouse had burned decades ago with the loss of all records, and Gideon was unsurprised when the clerk failed to find, among documents filed since then, a deed for a property owned by a Brodie, or anything showing that a Brodie had paid taxes, gotten married, registered a will, or died.

He went back to the jail. He brewed coffee. He sat at his desk and decided to make a list of potential suspects in Potter's killing and the presumed kidnappings—which might be separate crimes or might be linked.

He found an old paper that happened to be an 1827 notice for a runaway: "200 Dollars Reward. RAN AWAY from the subscriber living near Hagers-town, Washington Co., Md., a negro man named

JAMES PEMBROOK, about 21 years of age, five feet five inches high, very black, square & clumsily made, has a down look, prominent and reddish eyes, and mumbles or talks with his teeth closed, can read, and I believe write, is an excellent blacksmith, and pretty good rough carpenter; he received shortly before he absconded, a pretty severe cut from his ax on the inside of his right leg. Any person who will take him up and secure him in jail shall receive the above reward.—FRISBY TILGHMAN."

Gideon wondered if, ten years later, James Pembrook was still free. Just as he now found himself wondering whether Collins at the livery, Smythe the freighter, the carpenters Drew and McCray, or almost any other colored person in Adamant had run from slavery.

He turned the sheet over. He unstoppered an ink bottle, dipped his pen, and wrote:

Melchior Dorfman

He doubted that Dorfman had killed Potter. Still, the man had a lot of anger bottled up inside him. The tinner was brusque, prickly, perceptive. Gideon decided that he rather liked the man. Which, of course, didn't mean that Dorfman had not committed murder.

Beneath Dorfman's name he wrote:

Tazewell Waller (Franklin Blaine)

Annie Picard (Pierre)

Brodie???

He considered adding Potter's apprentice Lemuel Robinson but rejected the idea. Robinson had been too shaken up and appeared genuinely and deeply aggrieved at his master's death. If Robinson had killed Potter, he wouldn't have stuck around and continued working in the print shop.

He thought some more, then wrote:

Hosea and Lenore Belknap

★★★

Tramping down Decatur, approaching the office of the *Colerain Democrat*, Gideon recalled the newspaper's motto printed in each issue: *Too Much Government in the Land.*

Potter's death and the shuttering of the *Adamant Argus* meant the Belknaps' own paper would thrive. And could they have had something to do with the disappearances of those three people? Coming from Virginia, the Belknaps would have connections in that slave state. In no way did they seem to be the sort who would abduct people and sell them into bondage, but looks could deceive.

When Gideon went in the door, Hosea Belknap glanced up from the type case and smiled. Lenore Belknap, seated at a desk, gave Gideon a more guarded look.

The newspaperman set down his composing stick and came over with his hand out—then seemed to realize that an ink-stained handclasp wouldn't be appreciated, and rested his palms on the counter instead. Gideon noticed that Belknap's hands were small and soft looking, almost like a woman's.

"Good morning, Sheriff," Belknap said. "Some news for us regarding your investigation into Mr. Potter's death?"

"I'm afraid not. I was actually hoping that you could help me with a different matter."

"Certainly."

"Mr. Belknap, I don't know much about slavery. I understand that you came here from Virginia, and that you owned slaves there."

Belknap's expression immediately changed from accommodating to wary.

"You had a plantation, correct?" Gideon asked.

"Hardly. A farm, and not a very big one. Just under a hundred tillable acres."

"What did you grow?"

"Hay, corn, cotton. We had a nice orchard." Belknap seemed to relax a little. "We made and sold a very fine apple brandy, if I say so myself."

"And you worked your land with slaves?"

"With servants, yes. Most of them inherited from my parents. I assure you, Sheriff, our negroes were well treated. They were content. Never gave us a bit of trouble."

Gideon glanced at Lenore Belknap. He wondered if the sober expression on her face belied her husband's rosy tale.

"How many slaves did you own, Mr. Belknap?"

"The greatest number of servants under our ownership at any one time was, I believe . . . sixteen."

"Did you work alongside them?"

"We employed an overseer."

"He treated your slaves well?"

"He made sure they did their work. But yes, he treated them fairly." Belknap drummed his ink-smudged fingers on the countertop. "Sheriff, I'll be frank with you. I myself am not completely comfortable with the institution of servitude. Although I think you will agree with me when I call it a necessary evil. We may not want it, but we cannot end it. What would the negroes do? In Southampton County, where my family has lived for five generations, sixty-five hundred whites coexist with something like ten thousand blacks. Of these, perhaps eight thousand are servants; the rest are free.

"My father always said that servitude was the will of God. That's the older generation talking." Belknap's shoulders gave a hitch. "I'm not sure I believe that. But I can tell you that it's an economic necessity. It would not be possible for Southerners to manumit their servants. A prime field hand is worth five hundred dollars and up. In most cases, for an owner to free his bondsmen would mean financial ruin.

"And if those eight thousand servants in Southampton County were suddenly set free—well, I should not like to see the privation that would result. The same situation exists across the South. For the most part, the negroes do not own land. If they were freed, they would probably leave and come north in droves. Would you all want that to happen?"

Lenore Belknap got up from her chair and came and stood next to her husband. She wore her hair as she had on the day of Potter's funeral, pulled back tightly behind her head, straining her face.

"Please continue, Mr. Belknap," Gideon said.

"As the *Democrat* has pointed out in several editorials, the negroes are much better off in America than they were in Africa—a benighted continent, where barbarism, savagery, cannibalism, and other terrible and degrading things take place. Here, they help fuel the nation's growth. They're enlightened about Christian beliefs and shown a path to the one true religion that will lead them to salvation. Where we come from, they're allowed to attend church and hold their own praise meetings. Or they were, until," he hesitated, "certain events took place."

"And those events were . . . ?"

When Belknap failed to answer, Gideon looked at the man's wife. "Mrs. Belknap, I understand that you were born and raised in Adamant. Do you share your husband's views on slavery?"

"If anything, Hosea is too lenient," Lenore Belknap said. "I knew colored people here in Adamant. It wasn't a shock when I went and dwelt among them in Virginia. The ones down there—most of them are lazy and ignorant. Always ready with an excuse for why they can't do this, won't do that. And they can be wicked, ready to repay kindness and benevolence with violence."

"Kindness and benevolence," Gideon repeated. "I've heard slavery described with other words. Like cruelty and oppression."

"Don't listen to those oily tongued abolitionists," Lenore Belknap said. "They've never been down South. They've never gotten to know the negroes they claim to admire so."

"You mention violence. Can you tell me about that?"

"There's no need to discuss it, Lenore," Hosea Belknap said.

"It was that crazy Nat," his wife said. "One of their so-called preachers."

Gideon noticed that Lenore Belknap's eyes had gone slightly out of focus.

"Almost six years ago." Her voice was soft and contained. "Seems like it was only yesterday. The twenty-second of August, 1831. Early on a Monday morning. It was still dark when they started.

"Nat was so meek and polite that everyone thought he was harmless." Lenore Belknap shuddered. "Smart, I'll give him that. Nat Turner could read and write. And scheme and persuade. The other slaves looked up to him. He told them he saw signs in the heavens, that God spoke through him, saying that the blacks should rise up and kill the whites."

Lenore Belknap's eyes were opened wide, their irises ringed with white. She pointed a trembling finger at her face. "I saw him. With these eyes. A little knock-kneed man with whiskers on his chin. At the old Tom Moore place where he lived. It's the Travis place now, Joe Travis has his wheel shop there. *Had* his wheel shop. Sally told me that Tom used to whip Nat to keep him in line, but Joe, he was too softhearted, he would never do that.

"I was friends with Sally Travis; she married Joe after Tom died. We lived close, a few minutes' walk. Helped each other quilting, working in the garden, putting up food. Sally welcomed me even though I was a Yankee. Some nights I'd stay in their house, sleep on a daybed. In the evening we would sit on the porch, talking and watching the fireflies in the fields. Listening to the people down by their cabins, singing. Some of their songs were pretty. Some of them, if you listened to the words, they'd make your skin crawl."

Lenore Belknap swallowed. Her breathing had gone shallow. It was something Gideon understood. After he'd found his *memmi's* body, he couldn't control his breathing, his heart's crazed beating, or the way his limbs and his shoulders tensed. He saw strange things that he knew weren't there. He couldn't govern his mind, which would suddenly grab his body and carry it to places where he didn't want to go.

"Nat and his devils killed Sally and Joe." Lenore Belknap's voice was just above a whisper. "They were the first. Hacked to death in bed.

"That's how it started, with axes and knives and clubs. Later they got guns. Nat talked those ignorant, childish folks into being his weapons of death. They killed and they killed. Men, women, and children. Babies.

"By the grace of God, we were spared—Hosea, myself, and our two girls. After they butchered the Travises, Nat and his band went to the Turner place. Then the Whiteheads. The Porters. The sun came up. If they'd gone a little farther west, we'd be dead." She covered her mouth with her hands. "On and on they went, chopping people to death like they were chopping firewood."

"It's over and done with, Lenore," Hosea Belknap said.

"It could happen again," Lenore Belknap said. "It could happen anywhere in the South. It could happen here."

"That's enough," Hosea Belknap said. "You won't be able to sleep, you know how you get."

"Did your slaves join in the uprising?" Gideon asked.

"No," Hosea Belknap said. "Unfortunately, two of them lost their lives. That evening we decided to go to Cross Keys, where people were gathering, thinking we'd be safe there. Two of our boys—muttonheads, I suppose they were curious and got caught up in the excitement. Riding double on a mule. They went the opposite way and ran into a militia band."

"Curtis and Sam," Lenore Belknap said. "Two insolent, back-talking, lazy, balky boys. I hated the way they shuffled, walked slow whenever you told them to do anything. They went off to join Nat's gang, I know it sure as I'm born. It's a wonder they didn't kill us first. The militia strung them up. That was a loss to us. If they'd been arrested and put on trial, we would have saved nine hundred dollars. The state paid four fifty a head for each one they convicted and hanged."

"How many people died altogether?" Gideon asked.

"At least fifty-five," Hosea Belknap said, "perhaps as many as sixty. That's the whites. No one knows how many colored were killed. Possibly two hundred. You had militia and vigilantes coming in from all over southern Virginia and northern Carolina. Negroes were shot down or hanged or burned to death just because they were black. For weeks you'd see their heads on poles, their bodies rotting in trees. Then came the trials. And after that, the legal hangings."

"Did you go to any of the trials?"

"I attended Nat's court interrogation. Then Lenore and I both went to the trial itself. The courthouse was packed, as you can imagine. Newspapermen from all over. Afterward, I spoke with several of them. That was when I realized I could have a newspaper myself. I never really took to farming."

"Did Nat Turner say why he killed all those people?"

"There's a book, *The Confessions of Nat Turner*," Belknap said. "But the language in it is all wrong, fancy and polished, doesn't sound like Nat at all. Tom Gray wrote it; he's a lawyer. He made a pile of money off that book.

"Nat wanted revenge against all the whites who had enslaved him and his people," Belknap continued. "The negroes called him 'General Nat.' Mostly he let his troops do the killing."

The newspaperman's eyes looked sad. "Down there, a hanging is a public spectacle, not like up here, where you all hide it behind walls. The tree stood out in a field. There was a huge crowd, but I stood on a rock four or five perches away and had a good view. The sheriff put the noose around Nat's neck and threw the rope over a limb. Five men took hold of the other end." He hesitated. "You expect, in fact you desire, that the condemned man show regret. Or at least fear and distress. But Nat didn't weep or cry. He didn't struggle. He didn't do a thing. They hoisted him up, and it was like they were hanging a side of beef. He just hung there on the end of the rope like he was already dead."

Belknap let out a long breath. "I'm sure we have told you much more about those horrific events than you wished to hear." He glanced at his wife. "As you can see, the uprising left its mark on us."

"It drove us away," Lenore Belknap said. "We knew we could never feel safe again. Never be happy again. We'd always need to be watching out for the next time they rose up."

"You sold your farm?"

"We didn't get as much as we'd hoped," Hosea said. "Of course, with the way things were . . ."

"Fortunately, our servants brought a fair price," Lenore said.

"You sold them?"

"Of course," Lenore said.

"How did you do that?"

"Through one of the Richmond auction houses," Hosea said.

"When your slaves learned they were being sold, what did they do?"

"They begged not to be parted from their families. However, it was a financial decision. A necessity."

"Mr. Belknap, suppose someone kidnapped a black person here in Colerain County," Gideon said. "How would they go about selling them down South?"

Belknap's face took on the same wary aspect it had shown when Gideon first asked if he'd owned slaves. "Why do you ask?"

"Perhaps you've heard that several colored people have gone missing. One from west of town, and two here in Adamant."

"We've heard rumors."

"It's my responsibility to discover what happened to them. Just as I must learn who killed Phineas Potter. It might help me to know where you would take a person to sell them."

"Where *I* would take a person? Sir, are you implying . . . ?"

"No, I said that wrong. I'm not implying anything. Where would somebody, anybody, take a kidnapped person to sell them into slavery?"

"Sheriff, I can tell you that no reputable Southern auction house would sell a servant without a full and verifiable record of prior ownership. Imagine what would happen if they sold someone who was later proven to be stolen. Their reputation would be ruined."

"What about other businesses or people who don't work for what you call reputable auction houses? Are there people who deal in stolen slaves?"

Belknap removed a handkerchief from his waistcoat and wiped sweat from his upper lip.

Lenore Belknap said: "We would not know anyone like that. Sheriff Stoltz, you should stop badgering us. In fact, I think you should leave."

"I am not badgering you, ma'am, and I'm sorry if you think that I am."

"This newspaper supported you last fall for the election," Hosea said.

"I'm aware of that, and I am grateful. Nevertheless, I need to ask these questions. I have heard the term 'Georgia man' used to describe someone who takes slaves into the Deep South and sells them there. Do you know of any Georgia men?"

"Of course, such entrepreneurs exist," Hosea Belknap said. "They are also likely to be legitimate dealers; they just don't own a pen or a building where they can display and sell their merchandise. They have the ability and the expertise to safely transport servants over long distances. They have their reputations to consider, too. They would be liable for damages if a person bought a servant and then was forced to give them up because they'd been kidnapped."

"What about someone who doesn't care about their reputation or any laws?"

"I am not acquainted with any such individuals," Belknap said.

His wife went back to the desk where she had been working. Belknap returned to the type case and picked up his composing stick. He began slotting type into the stick, using his thumb to hold the line in place. "The next time we meet, Sheriff, I hope you will have done your job and arrested the scoundrel or scoundrels responsible for murdering Phineas Potter. Now good day to you, sir."

$50 REWARD. A negro man named Isaac, 22 years old, about 5 feet 10 or 11 inches high, dark complexion, well made, full face, speaks quick, and very correctly for a negro. *He was originally from New-York,* and no doubt will attempt to pass himself as free.

Chapter 24

———⊗∞⊗———

GIDEON HEADED TOWARD THE CENTER OF TOWN. HE SEEMED TO BE making people angry at him right and left. Well, a sheriff should solve crimes, not try to be popular.

He thought about Nat Turner's bloody rebellion and how its memory seared the Belknaps still. It had driven them to leave their farm, causing more trauma and grief as their own slaves were torn from their families and sold.

The more Gideon learned about slavery, the more repugnant it seemed. Calling it servitude—as Hosea Belknap daintily preferred— did not change the fact that slavery was a deeply cruel practice whose corrosive effects, Gideon realized, reached all the way into his own small corner of the world.

Payton's Tavern was on High Street just down from the Diamond. The place was of a much higher class than the watering holes in Hammertown. Gideon entered and found a table. When the waiter came, he asked for coffee, ham, biscuits, and gravy. After placing his order he realized he had drunk too much coffee already today—at home, at Dorfman's shop, at the jail. Nevertheless.

The tavern's coffee was black and strong. The food, when it arrived, was delicious, the biscuits warm and flaky, the ham with a subtle smoky taste, the gravy rich and tangy.

Payton's Tavern had belonged to the former sheriff of Colerain County, the man who had hired Gideon as his deputy four years ago.

Israel Payton had been gray-haired, slight of frame, and physically unprepossessing, yet he projected an air of quiet authority. He was patient and kind. His favorite saying was "Lord have mercy," which he seemed to utter every five minutes. Payton thought it important for a sheriff to be seen, and he rode all over the county, his travels often extending into the night. People reported finding him asleep, sitting in his saddle in the darkness while his horse grazed at the road's edge.

Payton had been childless and a widower. While sheriff, he turned over the running of his tavern to his brother Miles, who, upon Israel's sudden and unexpected death, inherited the business. As Gideon sat eating his lunch, Miles spotted him and came out from behind the bar.

"Sheriff Stoltz!" he called out while still halfway across the room. He grinned and pumped Gideon's hand. Miles had always been friendly toward Gideon, although he was otherwise unlike his brother: overweight, overbearing, and loud. After exchanging a few pleasantries, Gideon asked Miles if the name Brodie meant anything to him.

"Sounds vaguely familiar. Could be someone by that name lived around here, but I'm thinking it was a long time ago. Are they in some kind of trouble?"

"Might they have lived in the Barrens, or near there?"

Payton shrugged. "I couldn't say." Then: "Have you figured out who killed Phineas yet?"

As Gideon began cautiously explaining that he had made some progress, although he still had a lot to learn, he noticed that Miles had already lost interest: his eyes shifted around as he looked for some other patron who might offer more interesting palaver. "If you hear anything," Gideon said, "would you let me know? And if you remember anything about any Brodies . . ."

"I sure will." The tavern keeper hollered out a greeting to someone else and moved to a different table.

Gideon took another bite of ham: Miles Payton was a braying ass, but he served good food.

Israel Payton had taken a chance in hiring Gideon as his deputy, a twenty-year-old stranger and a Dutchman to boot. In the year that Gideon served under him, he'd learned a great deal from the older man. Unlike his abrasive brother, Payton had a way of subtly drawing a person out and getting them to reveal information. Gideon remembered how he had learned of Payton's death. He had just come back to the jail after delivering a summons. Gaither Brown ambled over from his leatherworking shop and said bluntly: "Israel fell over dead. A stroke of apoplexy." Then walked away as if nothing had changed.

Yet for Gideon, everything had changed. He felt shocked and bereft, abandoned. By then he was twenty-one, apparently old enough for the county commissioners to appoint him to finish out Payton's term. He might well have been the youngest sheriff in Pennsylvania—maybe he still was.

He finished his meal and let the waiter refill his coffee cup. Israel Payton had been elected sheriff three times. He had served two three-year terms—not consecutively, as the law forbade a sheriff from serving two terms in a row—and was a year into his third term when he died. In those seven years, Payton had never needed to deal with a murder: if he had, he would certainly have told Gideon about it. Whereas Gideon Stoltz, the raw, inexperienced Dutch Sheriff, had investigated no fewer than four killings in three years—now five killings, with Phineas Potter's slaying. Not to mention three recent disappearances of presumably kidnapped people. The phrase "Lord have mercy," delivered in Israel Payton's wry, quiet voice, whispered in his head.

Sheriff Payton had talked about motive, why people committed crimes, including murder. Payton liked to quote the Bible: "The love of money is the root of all evil." There were people who wanted money so badly they would extinguish another person's life to get it—even only a few dollars. You read about it in the newspaper all the time. Then there was envy. And lust and unrequited affection. The thought of lust as a motivation to kill made Gideon very uneasy, for that seemed to have been what had led some unknown man to murder his own *memmi*.

What had motivated the person or persons who killed Phineas Potter? Financial gain? Potter's wallet, boots, and horse had all been taken.

But robbers and highwaymen didn't drive wagons. They rode horses so they could swiftly flee the scenes of their crimes.

Had Potter's killing been motivated by lust? Glenn Hutchinson, Potter's brother-in-law, thought the newspaperman might have made unwanted advances to some other man, triggering an attack, a vicious blow to the head, an injury resulting in death.

Gideon nixed that theory: If Potter wanted to be intimate with another man, he would have done so in the privacy of his own home, not on a lonely road in the dead of the night. And there was no reason a wagon would have been involved.

Had someone killed Potter to keep him from uncovering a secret? Had the newspaperman gotten close to exposing an illegal activity when an evildoer chose to silence him? Could that crime be the kidnapping of black people?

Gideon considered the suspects whose names he had written on his list. Whoever killed Potter, whoever grabbed the two men and the woman, might be one and the same. They might be on his list, or they might not be. Or maybe there was no connection between the crimes.

He didn't know what his next step should be. All he could do was keep asking questions. He might not be as wise or subtle as Israel Payton, but he was persistent. *Obsenaat*, even. Stubborn.

He got up from the table and paid for his meal.

He noticed a picture tacked to the wall near the door. It looked like a page cut out of a magazine; it was just a typical tavern decoration. The image was a caricature of a black man wearing a seedy-looking jacket, heavily patched pantaloons, and a battered hat. One hand rested on an outshot hip, and the other was held up as if the man were snapping his fingers. The fellow had bulging eyes and an enormous mouth spread in a lascivious grin.

Gideon tore the picture off the wall. He crumpled it into a ball, dropped it on the floor, and left.

Ranaway, Bill—has *several* LARGE SCARS on his back from a *severe* whipping in *early* life.

Chapter 25

⎯⎯⊗⊗⊗⎯⎯

IN THE MORNING AFTER GIDEON HAD GONE TO WORK, TRUE GOT ready to ride. She had used most of the logs stored behind their house in making baskets and needed more ash wood. She wrote a note to Gideon and left it on the table.

She hadn't said anything to him about riding out, because she did not want him trying to talk her out of it or maybe even telling her she couldn't go. He wasn't the kind of husband who issued commands, but she didn't want to chance it. She reckoned she would not obey such an order anyway.

She put on the old pants and shirt and got the detonator out of its box. She wondered if she should load it, and concluded that it made no sense to carry a gun if it wasn't ready to shoot. She loaded both barrels, then placed the pistol in a cloth sack. She wrapped some leftover food in a sheet of newspaper and added that to the sack.

She and the red setter, Old Dick, walked through town attracting more than a few stares. True held her head up and stared back. At the livery stable she had the attendant saddle Jack.

True would never forget the first time she had worked up the nerve to ride the black gelding. It was last summer: she had been mired in depression, Gideon was off investigating a murder, and she realized she needed to get herself to her gram's cabin in Panther Valley before it was too late—before she did something bad, something that couldn't be undone. She felt a flush of shame at the thought that she had actually considered picking up a knife and—no, she wouldn't revisit that memory. But she had ridden Jack all the way to her gram's cabin in Panther Valley that day when her mind was a dark cloud playing tricks on her. He had gotten her there safely and she'd been riding him ever since.

Anyway, she didn't feel that way now. Instead, she felt eager and happy and free.

She put the sack with the detonator in one of the saddlebags and the food in the other. Then she got up on Jack. In her note, she had told Gideon that she would be riding to the ironworks in Panther. Having grown up there, she knew of a low area near the settlement where she might find some basket ash. Gram Burns had taught her to identify the trees, which often grew in swampy ground. If True located some suitable ones, she'd find out who owned them and see if they wanted to sell.

But instead of heading east toward the ironworks, she turned Jack west. Not knowing why, maybe just to see someplace different. A thrill of excitement coursed through her. She could do whatever she wanted with her time and with her horse. She rode through Hammertown, past Annie Picard's house, on into a mix of forested and farmed land.

Muncie Mountain carried along on her right, vanishing in haze in the distance. The trees cloaking the ridge were slowly leafing out, the greenery advancing like mold on leather from the base of the mountain toward its top.

Where the road dipped into low areas, True looked for basket ash: its slender form and corky grayish bark, its trunk free of branches for many feet from the ground up.

Jack walked steadily west on the Halfmoon Valley road with Old Dick trotting alongside.

True knew that if she went far enough the road would take her past the spot where Phineas Potter had been killed. Eventually, it would arrive at the north edge of the Barrens.

She met a man driving a cart. Wanting to help Gideon in his inquiries, she asked if the man knew of any Brodies living nearby. The man had never heard of anyone so named.

She met a peddler, a swarthy bearded fellow wearing an oddly shaped small-brimmed hat, hunched beneath a large bundle. He looked fearfully at Old Dick until True assured him the dog was friendly. Quickly the peddler slipped out from under his pack and opened it: Surely the miss or missus would like to buy some notions, pins and needles, a pair of scissors, a tortoiseshell comb? The man spoke rapidly and with a thick accent. A sharpening stone for the knives? The finest freshest black tea, just off the boat from China, did she want a sniff? He had some fabulous, excellent nutmegs—True broke in on his spiel and told him she didn't have any money with her. She asked him if, in his travels, he had ever met anyone named Brodie. The peddler began shoving his goods back into his pack. He shrugged his shoulders through the straps. He muttered something True couldn't make out, then spat toward the side of the road and stalked off.

True rode on. She didn't like the way the peddler had talked foreign at her and then spat. Maybe he had laid a curse on her. She considered turning around and going back to Adamant. But she hadn't found any ash trees yet.

A pair of crows harassed a raven, diving at it, pecking at its back, making the big bird squawk and stunt in its flight. Fleeing, the raven crossed in front of True. Ravens could foretell bad things about to happen. Again True considered returning to Adamant. But decided to keep going.

The sun climbed higher in the sky. The road descended into a wooded swale. From the soil, skunk cabbage pushed up their mottled maroon hoods. Above, the branches of trees wove together, shutting out the light: elms, sycamores, silver maples. No basket ash. Feeling peckish, True stopped Jack and dismounted. She unbuckled the rein on one side of his bridle and kept hold of its end, though she doubted the gelding would go anywhere. She smiled at the thought of how Jack used to yank the reins out of her hands, lower his head, and graze whenever he wanted to. He didn't do that anymore.

She got the food out of the saddlebag. A fallen tree trunk offered a seat. She ate, now and then tossing a crust or scrap to Old Dick.

Suddenly the dog spun around. The fur stood up all along his back, and a deep growl bubbled up from his throat.

A big woman stood twenty steps away. How had she gotten so close? The woman had a strange expression on her face; surly or angry. As if she'd caught True trespassing. The woman wore a dress with narrow green and red vertical stripes. No cap or bonnet. Crinkly brown hair with some gray in it. Something about the stripes on the woman's dress and her frizzy hair and the look on her square-jawed face sent a chill down True's spine.

The woman held a cloth sack in one hand and a short-bladed knife in her other hand. She took a few steps toward True and stopped.

Old Dick kept growling.

"You wouldn't sic your dog on me," the woman said.

"Settle, boy," True said.

The big woman edged closer. She was now a dozen steps away. "What are you doing here?" she asked.

"Looking for basket ash."

The woman held up her sack. "Me, I'm hunting spongies, poke salat, this an' that. Found some fiddleheads over yonder."

"Am I on your ground?" True asked.

"No, you ain't on my ground."

The woman took another step.

Old Dick bared his teeth and growled louder. He seemed to True to swell up half again as big as he really was.

The woman took a step back. "That dog wants to bite."

"Settle," True said again. Old Dick stopped growling for a moment but started in again. True said to the woman: "Do you live hereabouts?"

"I might."

"Do you know of anyone named Brodie?"

The woman's eyes narrowed: small eyes partly hidden by flesh. "Who wants to know?"

True decided not to give her real name. "Peg Bainey is my name."

"Why are you looking for the Brodies?"

True hesitated, then said, "My ma, she's got Brodies in her line back a ways." She embellished: "She said if I ever got out to the Barrens, or near there, I should ask around, see if any Brodies are living there yet."

The woman kept staring at True. She brought the knife that she held up to her face. She stuck out her lips and tapped the flat of the blade against them. Then said: "I don't know no one by that name."

True glanced at Jack. The gelding stood alert at the end of the rein. She looked at the saddlebag and considered how foolish it was to have brought a gun and then kept it buckled inside the bag. Not to mention riding somewhere different from where she'd told Gideon she was going in her note. But at least she had the dog.

Old Dick's growling sounded like water running deep underground.

True got up from the log. "I need to get home."

Old Dick was bristled up and growling steadily. "This dog, I don't know what's got into him," she said. "But if he takes against somebody, he can be a mean one. He won't listen to me then."

The big woman kept staring. It seemed to True that the woman inspected her with the same kind of devouring look that men sometimes gave her. She hated it. It made her feel like they were undressing her and running their filthy hands all over her body. The happy, carefree feeling that she'd started out with that morning was gone.

The big woman took a long look at Old Dick, as if thinking something through. Then she turned and started off, taking slow careful steps in the mucky terrain.

True fumbled the buckle open on the saddlebag, reached inside, and freed the detonator from its cloth sack. She left the pistol lying in the bottom of the bag where she could get it. She attached the rein end to Jack's bridle. All the while shooting glances over her shoulder at the woman in the red-and-green dress as she slowly moved off.

True got up on Jack and turned him around on the road and began riding toward home. Beyond the big woman she saw a black horse with its reins tied to a sapling. True touched Jack with her calves. The gelding tended to ignore such cues, but now he broke into a rocking-horse canter. Old Dick ran along with them.

True cantered the gelding out of the woods and into a stretch of open land, a field ready for the plow. The sun beat down on her shoulders. She stopped and looked back.

No sign of the woman or her horse.

Taken and committed to jail, a negro girl named Nancy, who is supposed to belong to Spencer P. Wright, of the State of Georgia. She is about 30 years of age, and is a LUNATIC. The owner is requested to come forward, prove property, pay charges, and take her away, or SHE WILL BE SOLD TO PAY HER JAIL FEES.

Chapter 26

———⊂⊃⊃⊂⊃———

GIDEON RAPPED ON THE DOOR OF THE LARGE STONE HOUSE. A woman answered and said: "Mr. Fish is not receiving visitors."

Gideon brushed past her. The sound of snoring led him to the parlor. It looked like the state's attorney had gone from bad to worse. He sat slumped in a chair, his head lolling back, stockinged feet up on a hassock. A tumbler sat on the floor on one side of the chair, an empty bottle on the other.

"Mr. Fish?" Gideon said.

Fish opened his eyes, lifted his head, and thumped both feet down on the floor. He struggled to sit up straight. Stared slack-mouthed at Gideon. "What . . . why are you . . . ?"

"I went to your office and you weren't there."

The whites of Fish's eyes were bloodshot, and his cheeks had a heavy growth of beard.

"Have you read the coroner's report yet?" Gideon asked.

Fish shook his head.

"I am looking at several potential suspects in Mr. Potter's death," Gideon continued. A ridiculously optimistic assessment of what he'd done so far, which was little more than writing down a few names on a piece of paper. "I also wanted to inform you that those colored people are still missing. John Horne appears to have been taken from his cabin in the Halfmoon Valley. I went there and found broken furniture and his dog shot dead. And the two people from the Picard house in Hammertown: I think it's likely they were kidnapped to be sold into slavery as well."

"Sounds like uninformed guesswork to me." Fish began to rise from the chair, then sat down again heavily. "You have no right being here," he snapped.

"I understand that you are grieving for Mr. Potter," Gideon said.

"What's that supposed to mean?"

"You and he were friends. His death has wounded you deeply."

"Phineas was . . . " a choking sound came from Fish's throat; he finished with four deliberate words: "a very fine man."

"Do you have any idea who killed him? Or why?"

"Do you not think I would have told you if I did?"

"His sister gave me a key to his house. I looked around there, including in his desk, hoping to find something that would explain why he was on the Halfmoon Valley road. A letter, an entry in a journal, something he'd written down, maybe about people he knew—acquaintances, enemies, friends."

Fish's eyes widened slightly. "And?"

"There was one thing. Potter, or at least I assume it was Potter, had written the words 'Brodie' and 'Barrens' on a piece of paper. Do you know anyone named Brodie?"

"I do not."

"I also found a secret room in his house, a cellar with a trap door. Potter must have sheltered runaway slaves there. Maybe that's what led to his death."

The state's attorney rubbed his face, then put his hands on the tops of his spindly legs. "I know of no one in this town or county hiding or otherwise aiding fugitives." Fish wrenched himself up out of the chair. "What are you doing, barging into my home and interrogating me?"

"I am not interrogating you, Mr. Fish. I'm asking for your help."

"You are the sheriff! Do your job!"

Anger flared in Gideon's mind. "The problem is that you are not doing your job. And your drunkenness and dissipation are keeping me from doing mine!"

He had come to Fish's house intending to ask questions in a patient, efficient way, like Sheriff Payton might have done, politely drawing information out of the man—now he had lost his temper. He had gone too far.

Fish donned the formal, emotionless mask that his face wore when he prepared to tear a witness apart in court. He enunciated his words carefully: "Keep in mind that you are a sheriff. A mere sheriff. An incompetent one, at that. You whine about needing help. I will be at my office tomorrow. I will read the autopsy report and see if anything stands out. You may consult with me then."

His eyes bored into Gideon's. "I will also decide how to deal with your insolence. Now get out of my house."

Gideon thought about apologizing, trying to repair the harm his outburst had caused. But he figured that would be impossible. He left the room. Fish's housekeeper gave him a smug look as she opened the outside door.

He emerged into slanting late-afternoon light. Above the town floated long rippling clouds, their bottoms pink, their tops gunmetal blue.

He put his head down and trudged toward home. True would be waiting for him. He would ask her how she'd spent her day, making baskets, or baking, or preparing the garden. Ordinary tasks that often seemed preferable to what he had to do as sheriff, questioning people who lied to him, scorned or feared or hated him, racking his brain trying to figure out who had committed some despicable act and why. He looked forward to an evening with his wife. Maybe he would share the stories he'd heard today from Dorfman and then from the Belknaps. He would tell True about his fruitless and perhaps damaging interview with the Cold Fish. It always seemed she could help him work things out, come up with ways to solve problems or simply shrug them off.

"Sheriff!"

He stopped and looked up. The Virginians stood one on each side of a tree next to the street. They both leaned against its trunk. Waller with his staring pale blue eyes, Blaine with his flamboyantly cocked hat and his expression that seemed suspicious and mocking at the same time.

Waller held a smoked-down cigar between two fingers. He took a drag on it, then threw it backhanded into the street. "Have you found Leo yet?"

Gideon shook his head.

"We've been looking around in this neighborhood," Waller said. "Someone may be hiding him in one of these fancy houses."

"Abolitionists are clever people," Blaine added.

"They'll hide a runaway down in the cellar," Waller said. "Or in the attic. In a hidey-hole tucked away next to a chimney or under a staircase."

"Why do you think someone around here is hiding fugitives?" Gideon asked.

"A little bird told me," Waller said.

"Who?"

Waller shrugged.

"I don't have time for this," Gideon said. "I have a murder to solve. And I need to find some people who very probably have been kidnapped."

"You have proven yourself unwilling to help me recover my property," Waller said. "You drag your feet. You claim that some Pennsylvania statute overrides the federal law—that's a bald-faced lie. The federal fugitive slave act is the law of the land." He added bitterly: "I'm not surprised. You are a damned Yankee."

Gideon strode past.

He asked himself again if Waller and Blaine might be part of a kidnapping ring. No, they would never draw this kind of attention to themselves. It didn't seem likely that they'd killed Potter, either. He wished the Virginians would give up searching for Leo, or Otis, or whoever he was, and leave Adamant. All they did was present a complication he didn't need.

He got home at dusk. Before entering the house, he spotted someone hurrying down the street. It took him a moment to realize it was True. Wearing her grandfather's outlandish trousers and hat and carrying a sack in her hand. With Old Dick beside her. When the setter saw Gideon, he came running, yipping and lashing his tail, and thrust his blocky muzzle into Gideon's hands.

"Where have you been, boy?" Gideon asked. Then he straightened and took True in his arms.

"I rode out on Jack," she said. "Looking for basket ash."

"Did you find any?"

"No. But I found something else. Let's go inside."

Gideon built a fire as True set out leftover corn pudding and sausage.

They sat at the table and ate. True pointed at a piece of folded paper. "I left you a note saying I was riding to Panther. Then I decided to go west instead. It was stupid of me. And dangerous."

"Where did you go?"

"The Halfmoon Valley. I asked people if they'd ever heard of anyone named Brodie. No one had." True drank some cider. "I met this woman. She was big and strong-looking, like she could whip a man in a fight. She had brown frizzy hair and wore a red-and-green-striped dress. The stripes were in this up-and-down pattern that almost made the dress shimmer. I was down off of Jack, eating lunch. I didn't see or hear the woman until she was close." True shuddered. "She had a knife. I don't know what she would have done if Old Dick hadn't been there. He made her keep her distance."

The setter, lying by the fire, thumped his tail on the floor at the sound of his name.

"Did you have your pistol?"

True gave a disgusted laugh. "In the bottom of my saddlebag. I asked the woman if she lived around there. She said 'I might.' Then I asked if she knew of any Brodies. She said not, but I don't believe her. Something about the way she answered."

"What was she doing?"

"Gathering food. She'd picked some fiddleheads and poke. The longer she stood there, the scareder I got. Old Dick growled at her, didn't you boy?"

Again the setter thumped his tail.

"Where did this happen?"

"Eight, maybe ten miles west of town."

"Not far from the Barrens."

"You told me that Phineas Potter had a black horse, and whoever killed him stole it."

"That's what I think happened."

"I had just gotten back up on Jack. The big woman was walking away, headed toward a horse standing off in the woods with its reins tied to a tree. A good-sized black horse. It threw its head up as I rode past."

"Potter's horse has white socks on his two left feet and a white star."

True shook her head. "I don't recall any white on the horse."

Gideon knew thieves could have blacked out white markings on a stolen horse with shoe polish or soot.

"Where exactly was this place?"

"Just past a field they were getting ready to plow. The road went down in a dip."

"I could look around there. But there are things I need to do first, people I need to talk to here in town. I want to go back to Hammertown."

"Not tonight." True reached across the table. She took one of Gideon's hands in hers. "Stay here with me, Gid."

Ranaway a negro man named Ned, *three of his fingers* are drawn into the palm of his hand by a *cut*, has a scar on the back of his neck nearly half round, done by a *knife*.

Chapter 27

— ⊶∞⊷ —

O TIS HAD SPENT THE DAY LOOKING OUT THE WINDOW. HE SAW birds chasing bugs in the treetops and squirrels jumping among the branches.

And, sometime after noon, a man walking slowly down the alley behind the house.

The first thing he spotted was the man's hat: brown, weathered, the brim cocked high on one side. The man had moseyed down the lane, turned and dallied back.

He wore high black boots polished to a shine. He looked like he was more accustomed to sitting a horse than strolling along on the ground. The man sidled up to the small carriage house behind the big stone house and looked in its entrance. Then he stepped back to the lane, loose-limbed and easy, studying the house as he went.

The man raised his face and stared at the window.

Otis pulled back. His stomach turned to ice.

A sharp-eyed white man with a yellow moustache and a chin beard and slave catcher written all over him.

He told himself the man couldn't have seen him, the window glass would have thrown back the light, blocking the man's gaze. But his heart still hammered in his breast.

Now, hours later, with darkness falling, he got up from the bed and peered out the window into the alley for the umpteenth time since he'd spotted the man.

No one there. Which didn't mean he wasn't close by.

He sat down in the chair. Clasped and unclasped his hands, used them to smooth the tops of his pant legs. His hands were sweaty, and he felt sweat running down his sides under his shirt.

He remembered back to the day he had come here. The sour-faced woman had taken him out of this room and led him down a flight of stairs to a different room. There she pointed at a big metal tub filled with water from which steam rose. She pointed at a stack of clothes, neatly folded, on the seat of a chair. Did she not know that he could understand her if she opened her mouth and talked?

She left the room.

He'd lingered in the bath. The first real bath he had taken in his life. Finally he got out and dried himself with a towel. He unfolded the clothes. They were not new, but they were of good quality. Shirt and trousers, both long enough in the arms and legs, unlike his old falling-apart duds. A leather belt with a brass buckle. Warm socks. Black shoes that didn't slide around on his feet or pinch his toes.

He was glad to be given these things. But why didn't someone come and talk to him, explain what was next? Nine days now. He had asked the sour-faced woman, asked her real polite, if he could talk to whoever was the boss of this place. She had looked at him like he was a bug she'd like to put her foot on and squash.

Now he got up from the chair and began pacing.

He hated being cooped up. He worried about someone turning him in. He hadn't come this far just to get taken back to Red Rose.

He tried the door. Locked, as usual.

He checked to see if the woman had left the key in the keyhole, thinking he might push it back through, then pull it in under the bottom of the door and see if he could work the lock from inside. But the woman had taken the key: he could see all the way through the hole into the hallway.

The next time she brought his food, he could shove past her, run down the stairs, and dash out of the house.

But if that man was watching, he could get snatched.

It would need to be at night. Deep in the night, when the slave catcher might not be around.

He would go out the window onto the roof. He looked out at the overlapping slates. The kind of dark gray stone they made grave markers out of. He could be a spider, creep across the slates, over to a rainspout and then slide down it. Or he could be a squirrel, and leap into a tree. The trees didn't stand very close to the house, but a branch on one of them poked down near the roof's edge.

He disliked being up high. Why couldn't he be down on the ground, with a horse to sweet-talk, and he'd get up on it and ride like the wind, the way he had done with that one after Dan fell off. He hoped Dan was somehow all right. But even as he hoped, he knew it was not so.

He tried to picture something good. In his mind's eye he saw a big field, with green grass waving in the breeze, and horses by the dozen, bays and duns and skewbalds and blacks and grays and sorrels and roans—all prancing and kicking up their heels and galloping across the field. He would go out among them and let himself be chosen by a horse. A horse to carry him on in life.

He lay back down on the bed and looked up at the ceiling.

Tonight.

★★★

The slates felt cold against his cheek. His nose picked up their sulfury rock scent and the clean smell of moss growing on them. His heart squelched against the roof's slant.

The house huge and silent beneath him.

Stars sparked between clouds in a sky black as a crow's wing.

He was scared. Afraid he might fall. He hoped he wouldn't piss his new pants.

He reached out toward the far end of the house with his right hand and foot, fingers and toes sliding across the slates and then stopping and waiting for the rest of his body to follow.

It refused.

He lay spread out on the unobliging slates.

A long stretch of the night had already passed. He had slept for some of it before waking up and putting on his clothes. He had raised the window sash as quietly as he could, climbed over the sill, found the roof with his bare feet, shifted sideways and lay down on his belly.

He reckoned he still had some hours before the birds began to sing and the sky got pink and the sun lit up the roof with him on it.

He took a deep breath and, trying not to think of the ground far below, forced his body to slide to the right. Scraping his cheek as he went.

Slung over his back, its drawstring around his neck, was the sack containing his new shoes and socks, his coat folded up tight, bread and cheese and meat from his supper, and the little compass his mama had gotten for him. He'd kept the sack ever since it was given to him by the man and woman who sheltered and fed and provisioned him somewhere down in Maryland before he came across the line onto the free soil of Pennsylvania.

Where he still was not free. Not free to roam around, or walk the streets of this town where any and all could see him, and catch him, and turn him in for the reward.

He extended his right hand and right foot again, and slid that way.

And again.

He came to the roof's edge. Gripped it with his right hand and slowly worked his way down the slates toward the bottom. The earth pulling at him like it meant to yank him out into thin air.

When his feet found the last row of slates, he went just a little farther and felt around with his toes. Below the slates there was no trough to catch the rain as it ran off the roof, which meant there would be no spout for him to slide down.

What to do?

Worm his way back across the roof and go in through the window and resume waiting in the little room?

Or get in a tree. He rose up on his forearms, turned his head and looked. One limb reached down crookedly toward the roof. In the darkness the limb appeared to be as thick as his leg where it branched off from another, larger limb; it got smaller, though, where it neared the roof, to not even the thickness of his wrist. An oak tree, he knew from studying it day after day, observing the pale gray-brown bark, the leaves with their rounded edges like somebody had carefully cut them out with scissors. The branches of oak trees were stout. Gathering firewood once, he'd tried to break an oak stick over his knee and nearly bust his leg instead.

He shrugged the sack off to one side and turned over onto his back. Knees up, the soles of his feet planted firmly on the slates. The branch a black line about eight feet out from the house.

Still on his back, he used his feet to push himself up the roof's slant. When he made it to the top, he hooked an arm over the peak and rose to a crouch. He looked all around. Adamant was a good-sized place, with plenty of streets and buildings. Dark hills cupped the town. In the starlight, his eyes caught a glinting twist of creek far below.

A dog barked somewhere. An owl laughed crazy-like. A dull *thump-thump* as a horse or cow kicked a stable wall.

The tree's limbs rose and fell in the faint breeze like a creature asleep and breathing. With his free hand, he positioned the sack on his back again. He rose on shaky legs, teetered, and got his balance. Fixing his eyes on the branch, he ran down the roof. When he got to the edge, he leaped out as far as he could.

★★★

For a long time he held on, hugging the branch that had cracked beneath him and bent down but had not broken.

He didn't want to put any more strain on the branch. And the *crack* it had made, and the rustling of the leaves, had been loud enough that someone could have heard. But he knew he had to move. Slowly he reached out his hand, gripped the branch higher up, and pulled himself upward. The branch cracked again. It sagged some more, but it held.

He clambered toward the tree's trunk. Once there, he gulped in breath. His hands were scraped and his face felt bruised. Wrapping his arms and legs around the trunk, he started shinnying downward. The trunk got thicker as he went. Where it met with another upward-extending trunk, he stopped in the fork and listened for a long time.

He heard nothing from the alley, the street, or the house. He decided he'd better have his shoes on in case he had to run.

He got his shoes and socks out of the sack and managed to put them on. He hung the sack's drawstring over his head again and went the rest of the way down.

As his feet touched the ground, something came at him out of the carriage house. It slammed into him, and he went down with weight on top of him and a hand over his mouth.

He couldn't open his mouth to bite, and his arms were pinned at his sides. A hard slap to the side of his head, and he saw stars and fought against dizziness as he felt a gag being forced into his mouth. He got his right hand free, reached into his pants pocket, and found the knife from his supper. He jammed it upward and felt it hit. He heard a muffled sound between a scream and a roar as he scrabbled to his feet and started to run.

He was brought up short when someone grabbed the sack on his back. The drawstring cut into his throat and yanked his head back. With his knife still clutched in his hand, he cut through the string and stumbled forward.

Then caught his balance and ran.

Ranaway from the subscriber, Ben. He ran off without any
known cause, and *I suppose he is aiming to go to his wife, who
was carried from the neighborhood last winter.*

Chapter 28

⸺◦◦◦◦⸺

GIDEON CLIMBED THE HILL TOWARD THE BIG STONE SCHOOL. Horatio Foote, headmaster, had sent a note asking him to come to the Academy for "an urgent matter."

A week had passed since Foote declined to answer Gideon's question about whether members of the county's anti-slavery society, to which the headmaster belonged, actively helped runaway slaves. He and Foote hadn't argued, but Gideon still chafed at the headmaster not trusting him enough to confide in him. He understood why: aiding fugitives from slavery was against federal law and could lead to a stiff fine or prison time.

Now, knocking on the entry door, he hoped the headmaster had some new information that could help him find out who had murdered Foote's former pupil Phineas Potter.

Nine days since the newspaperman's death, and people didn't seem to be talking about it anymore: a horrific, tragic event, to be sure, but life goes on, there were other things to think about, worry over. Gideon's own main worry was that he would not solve the crime.

The boy who answered the door said he should go straight up.

As he entered Foote's apartment, he was surprised to see that Foote was not alone. Flanking the headmaster were a short, plump, middle-aged woman in a brown dress and a pale cap, and a thin man of medium height wearing a gray coat whose color matched that of his hair. The man held a dark, broad-brimmed hat in his hands.

Foote said: "Sheriff Stoltz, I would like to introduce you to Ammon and Emily Olcott. They live near Frogville. They have something to tell you."

Gideon had once ridden through that curiously named hamlet in the western part of Colerain County. The Olcotts had made a considerable trip to get here. He wondered why they hadn't come to the jail to see him.

"We wish to report two missing persons," Ammon Olcott said.

"We believe they were kidnapped," his wife added.

"Our farm lies west of Frogville, near the county line," the man said. "God has given us a fine and fertile piece of land; we husband it, and we seek to make our home a place of peace and sanctuary where all are welcome. We are Friends, Quakers. We believe in helping our fellow man whenever we can."

Get to the point, thought Gideon.

"Yesterday, two people vanished from our farm," Olcott said, "a man named Benjamin, and his son, Thomas. Both are black. They were living in a cabin while putting up firewood. We go there several times a week to take them food and carry home the wood they've cut."

Emily Olcott looked intently at Gideon. "Horatio says that three other people have gone missing recently and that a kidnapping ring may be operating in the area. He also tells us you are a principled man. That we can trust you to do the right thing. Benjamin and Thomas are in flight from slavery." She stated that Benjamin was probably in his mid- to late-thirties, and Thomas might be thirteen or fourteen, then went on to describe them,

"Did you find any signs of violence or a struggle?" Gideon asked.

The Olcotts shook their heads.

"Tracks of horses, or a wagon, leading in some direction?"

"We drive a wagon ourselves," Ammon Olcott said, "and I didn't think to look for any other tracks."

"Is it possible that these people decided to leave on their own?"

"They would have told us," Emily said.

"When and how did Benjamin and Thomas come to your farm?"

The Olcotts exchanged glances. Then the woman turned toward Gideon and said: "We take full responsibility for sheltering them."

"We believe that God gives humans free will," her husband added, "and that slavery denies the negroes their own free will, negating their humanity. But they are people. And God calls on us to help them."

"If you tell me when and how these runaways came to you," Gideon said, "it might help me figure out who else knew about them and who might have taken them."

"A month ago, a man from Bedford County brought them," Emily Olcott said.

Bedford County was in south-central Pennsylvania just above the Maryland line.

"Like us, the man is a Friend," she continued. "He would not have betrayed them."

"How did they arrive?"

"In a wagon at night. We didn't know they were coming. That's often the way these things happen."

"Did anyone else learn that Benjamin and Thomas were on your farm?"

"The Olcotts told me," Foote said, "and I let some others know. People who might help get them to their next place of refuge." With an embarrassed look on his face, he said: "It was discussed at the last Anti-Slavery Society meeting."

"Who attended?"

The headmaster named Melchior and Sarah Dorfman, the barber George Watkins, Hack Latimer, and two farmers from the Halfmoon Valley. Also the minister of Adamant's Episcopal church, several merchants and craftsmen, a bank employee, the man who owned the tannery, and some of the men's wives.

"That's a lot of people," Gideon said.

"All of them trustworthy," Foote said. "All of them committed to ending slavery and helping fugitives gain their freedom."

"Could any of those people be hiding Benjamin and Thomas now?"

"If they were, we'd know it," Foote said.

Emily Olcott placed a hand on Gideon's arm.

"I sense that you possess an inward light. That you have a deep concern for others. We ask that you step outside of earthly law and follow God's law. Find Benjamin and Thomas and free them. We fear for their lives. And we feel a great guilt for having failed them."

Frogville was not far from the Barrens. Gideon asked if the Olcotts knew anyone out that way named Brodie. They did not. Foote didn't, either. Gideon promised to try to find the two missing people. There wasn't much else to say.

After the Olcotts left, Gideon noticed that the metal cage at the end of the room sat empty and with its door ajar. "Where's the wejack?"

Foote ran a hand over his mouth. "Last evening I saw him lying down and thought he had expired. I opened the door for a better look, and out he dashed.

"I enlisted several students, and we tried to catch him with a net. We failed. Possibly a good thing, since he might have bitten off any number of fingers. Finally we chased him down the stairs and out the door."

"I see. He did not look like a docile creature to me."

Foote shook his head sadly. "I never got to see him eat a porcupine. Or dissect him, and preserve the *os priapi* for further study. So be it. One question, and then I must return to teaching. Have you made any progress in finding out who killed Phineas?"

Gideon decided to be frank. "I don't have any real suspects yet."

"I'm sorry for how I acted last week," Foote said. "I should have trusted you not to interfere with those of us who oppose slavery.

You're in a difficult position, charged with enforcing an immoral law. But as I told the Olcotts, I believe you will do the right thing."

Walking back to the jail, Gideon wondered what he should do next. Talk with those members of the anti-slavery society that Foote had named? Ride to the Barrens to look for True's big menacing woman and try to locate anyone named Brodie?

Mrs. Olcott said she believed Gideon possessed "an inward light." It had been a compliment, of course. Religious people said poetic things like that all the time.

Someone else had once said that he "showed an inner light," or words to that effect. It had been a while ago; maybe several years. He thought hard but couldn't remember. Ever since his fall off Maude and his concussion, he'd had trouble dredging up certain memories. For some reason, it seemed important to puzzle this one out.

He had been on Maude, riding next to someone. Sheriff Payton? Alonzo? Neither of them would have said anything like that.

He stopped in the street. He closed his eyes and concentrated. Finally he shook his head and walked onward, irked that he couldn't remember.

$250 reward, for my negro man Jim—he is much marked with *shot* in his right thigh,—the shot entered on the outside, half way between the hip and knee joints.

Chapter 29

———◦⊰⊱◦———

Attending to paperwork at the jail, Gideon skimmed some of the fugitive notices that had come in the mail. Many were from Maryland, with others from Virginia and North Carolina and even states as far south as Georgia and Mississippi.

He read about women fleeing with their children. Men who were shoemakers, carpenters, ironworkers, blacksmiths, bakers, field hands. For some, their clothing was described. Or shackles and chains. Scars, because many had been wounded or maimed. Broken legs and ankles, hands or feet lacking fingers or toes, eyes missing—often it wasn't clear whether the injuries came from accidents or had been purposely inflicted. Brands, letters burned into faces or breasts. In some of the notices, the subscribers said their charges had "eloped without any cause or justification."

Gideon tried to imagine the courage and determination of these souls. The desperation. The fear of getting captured and sent back to the place they had fled; the punishment, the resentment, the pain. The rage. The wrongness of all of this cruelty and misery and suffering in the nation where he himself lived, worked, neighbored, voted, worshipped.

He sighed and leaned back in his chair.

Yesterday the *Colerain Democrat* had run an article on the murder of Phineas Potter, calling him "an esteemed journalist and the publisher of the *Adamant Argus*." Citing robbery as the probable motive, the story detailed the injuries Potter had sustained, documented by the coroner during an autopsy. It covered Potter's early life in Adamant and his academic achievements, and provided a brief history of his newspaper. It said nothing of his views on abolishing slavery or sending free people of color to Africa.

Gideon was relieved that the article mentioned nothing about Melchior Dorfman—or anyone else—being a suspect. It stated only that "Sheriff Stoltz is conducting an investigation."

★★★

Alonzo reported that a man had buttonholed him on the street and said he'd heard that someone else had spotted a mulatto woman, perhaps the whore Amanda, soliciting in an alley in Hammertown.

Pretty vague news. Nevertheless, that evening Gideon crossed through the covered bridge and entered Hammertown. He carried a club. He hadn't asked Alonzo, wanting to give his deputy the evening off. And he didn't want Gaither Brown's company. True hadn't been happy when he said he was going by himself.

Shouts and laughter and fiddle music rang out as laborers from the town and countryside roistered at the week's end, spending hard-earned wages on distractions from their grinding and harsh lives.

In the dimness, Gideon scanned faces. Most were white. A few were dark: A chimney sweep wearing sooty clothes. Two tannery workers, judging from the stench of rancid flesh and tannic acid that accompanied them. Gideon recognized Dorfman's friend, the freighter Chalmers Smythe, one of the group who had confronted Waller and Blaine more than a week ago; Smythe swaggered past toward the Horse.

Another familiar figure caught Gideon's eye: Hack Latimer. The rangy fellow went into the Broad Ax. Latimer had told Gideon that he was a reformed man, that he'd given up drinking, although True insisted that was a lie. Gideon would have liked to have a word with Latimer, but right now he was headed for a different establishment.

In the street, blacks and whites mingled with no apparent animosity. Gideon wondered how much ill will existed between the two races in Adamant. The colored people seemed peaceful, even amicable. But how friendly would they be if the numbers were reversed—if suddenly there were twenty dark faces for every pale one?

How many of these men had been enslaved earlier in their lives? Suffered abuses or injuries at the hands of whites? What sort of anger festered in their minds?

He mounted the stone steps to Annie Picard's house. Drapes covered the windows, and from inside came sounds of laughter and tinkling piano notes.

He rapped on the door with the butt of his club.

No answer. Gideon rapped again. Finally the door opened. The big butler Pierre stared out with his mismatched eyes. When he saw who it was, he blocked the entrance. He clenched his hands into fists whose knuckles were fretted with pale scars. His broad chest strained his vest.

"Go away," he rumbled.

"I need to talk with Madame Picard again," Gideon said.

"She is not available. Go away."

Gideon was tempted to prod the manservant out of the way with his club. But the big man stood above him and could easily shove him backward down the steps.

The Frenchman started to close the door, but Gideon stopped it with his boot and shoulder. "I will talk with her. Now."

Pierre glared with his hard-to-read eyes. The scar on his face was livid. After a long moment, he stepped aside, swept an outsized hand inward, and said, *"Entrez."*

The piano notes had stopped. The room glowed with whitish light from whale oil lamps and golden light from tapers in the brass candelabra. A fire flickered in the marble-cased fireplace. No one remained in the parlor. Patrons had gone upstairs or out the back while Pierre stalled him. It didn't matter to Gideon. It was Picard he wanted to talk to.

He waited for a good five minutes until the madam finally entered the room.

She wore a high-waisted purple gown with a bustle in back, a standing ruff of black lace at her dewlapped neck. A double string of pearls roped down over her ample bosom. Even dressed in such finery she reminded Gideon of a plump chicken.

"I have not located Amanda Jones or Felix Wiley," Gideon said. "They didn't leave on the stage like you told me earlier."

"Perhaps they departed in some other way."

"Or perhaps they were kidnapped."

Madame Picard shook her head as if that was impossible.

"Did you see them leave?" Gideon asked. "Watch them go out the door?"

She rubbed the slack skin of her chin. "I am trying to remember, but I cannot recall."

"You are a woman of business. A shrewd person, I'm told. I think you know exactly when and how they left."

She stayed silent.

"How much did you pay them at the time they left your service?"

"I am sure I was generous with them. But again, I cannot recall."

"Let me see your books."

A shrug. "That is not possible, as I do not keep detailed books. Sheriff, what is it that you want?"

"I want you to tell me exactly what became of those two people."

"I told you already. They returned to Philadelphia. They went back home."

"Who kidnapped them? How was it done?"

The butler Pierre stood by the fireplace. With a poker, he jabbed at the burning logs.

"I have tried to answer your questions to the best of my ability," Picard said. "Now I must request that you leave. Our guests do not appreciate your presence."

Gideon crossed to a table. He picked up a glass and sniffed its contents. "This is good whiskey. Not the mule kick they sell in the taverns. Where do you get it?"

"You behave rudely," Picard said.

"Are they still in this house? In the cellar, in chains? I'll need to look."

Madame Picard gestured to her manservant.

Pierre set the poker aside and got a candle. He led Gideon down some stairs into a stone cellar with crocks, barrels, crates. No chains or captives. After a cursory search, Gideon came back up. In the parlor Picard sat on a couch sipping wine from a long-stemmed glass.

"Perhaps I should look upstairs." Gideon had already decided against doing that—he was certain the man and woman were no longer here, and he did not want to encounter anyone he knew. There seemed to be no way to get Madame Picard to divulge any information.

Beside her he saw a brocade purse sitting on the couch. It hadn't been there earlier. When Picard saw him looking at it, she gave her head a slight nod.

"I prefer that you do not go upstairs," she said.

"I don't need to go there," Gideon said. "And I won't be bribed. But if I find out that you had anything to do with the disappearances of those people, I will arrest you and make sure that you are prosecuted to the fullest extent of the law. You could go to the penitentiary for many years." He waved a hand at the opulently furnished room. "You could lose all of this." He headed for the door.

Over the next two hours, Gideon visited the watering holes in Hammertown. He conversed with dozens of men and learned nothing about the disappearances. He talked to women strolling in the streets and dawdling in pairs at the mouths of alleys; only a few said they knew Amanda Jones, and none had seen her or Felix Wiley lately.

No one knew a thing about Phineas Potter's killing.

Gideon was talked-out, tired of breathing in tobacco smoke and smelling alcohol-laced breath. He felt depressed at the workers throwing away their wages, at men staggering down the street or passed out on the ground or leaning against buildings and vomiting.

He wondered what to do next. Almost two weeks had passed since Potter's murder. What an abhorrent word, *murder:* he said it under his breath, and the word itself frightened and revolted him. The years had flowed past, like the creek separating Hammertown from the rest of Adamant, but the memory of his *memmi's* lifeless body had not gone away. Rarely did it take over his mind these days, but he sensed that the image would be with him always, lurking at the edge of his thoughts.

He passed a darkened house. Between it and the next dwelling he heard a faint rustling. He stopped.

"Please." A woman's voice carried from between the two houses. He took a step toward it. *"Please!"* He brought the club up, took another step.

Something slipped down in front of his face and pulled back sharply. He dropped the club and shot his hands upward, his fingers clutching at the rope tightening around his neck, cutting off his breath. Something else came down over his head. He tried to yell but nothing came out. He was pushed hard from behind, forced ahead.

A blow crashed into his stomach, doubling him over. He dropped his hands to cover his midsection, felt the rope tighten again around his throat.

Another blow to his belly. Another. He sagged. Another hard, punishing blow. His knees buckled but he didn't go down, held up by the rope around his neck.

When the rope slackened, he fell to his knees. He heard a whooping sound and realized it was his own tormented lungs pulling in breath.

Another blow, delivered by an open hand against the side of his head. A voice came from the man in front: *"Mind your own business or next time you die."*

Strong hands gripped him by both arms, hauled him to his feet and hurried him ahead. Then he was tumbling through the air. He hit the creek headfirst, the frigid water engulfing him. He thrashed and managed to get the sack off his head.

When his face broke out of the cold flow, he gulped in a breath before being spun sideways and pulled under again, the water swirling him in a strange slow dance toward death.

Twenty five dollars reward for my man Isaac, he has a scar on his forehead caused by a *blow*, and one on his back made by *a shot from a pistol*.

Chapter 30

———∞∞∞———

THE CREEK SWEPT HIM UNDER THE BRIDGE TO WHERE STINKING tannery waste came sluicing out of a trough. Gideon bumped against the bank like a sodden log. He grabbed a protruding tree root, hung there for a while catching his breath, then hauled himself out. He lay on the bank panting and shivering. He turned over onto his back, his stomach a hot pulsing mash. Pain shot through his shoulders and back and down his arms.

He felt his gorge rise, flopped over onto his side, and vomited creek water and the remains of his supper.

They could have strangled him to death. Stabbed him. Picked up his own club and bashed in his skull.

But they hadn't meant to murder him.

Two men. Maybe more, but he thought just the two. And the woman or girl who was the bait. He hadn't seen any of them in the dark. The one who had held him from behind was big and strong. Annie Picard's manservant? But there'd been no French accent to the voice of the one in front, the one who delivered the blows before warning him to mind his own business. That voice was a low growl, harsh and nasal, with the accent he heard all over Colerain County.

He struggled to a sitting position, then lurched to his feet. As he stood there swaying, his legs spread apart, a wave of dizziness swept over him, and he put his head down and tried to breathe in deeply. Finally he got his balance and shoved his way through the brush, briars raking his legs. He emerged from the swale bordering the creek and stopped to rest. Then he staggered past a house and onto

Spring Street. One halting step at a time. At the intersection, he started up High Street. Moving more freely, although the pain was still intense and waves of nausea came and went.

He realized he had lost his hat when he tore the sack off his head in the creek. His new hat. It made him mad.

Adamant proper was quiet, only a few people out and about. Possibly they would think he was drunk; he hoped no one recognized him. He kept on in a slow shuffle, getting closer to home with each step.

True met him as he came through the door. Her eyes widened. "What happened?"

She helped him into a chair. He felt some of the tension let go in his shoulders and back.

"I'll heat up some water," she said. "Get out of those wet clothes."

She gave him a sponge bath, soaping and rinsing the abrasions on his neck. She mashed some plants and pressed them into the wounds, then loosely tied a strip of cloth around his neck to hold the poultice in place. "Plantain started coming up this week," she said. "Good thing I picked some."

She helped him into his sleeping gown and pulled a pair of thick wool stockings onto his feet. The setter Old Dick came and laid his head in Gideon's lap.

"Who did this?" she asked.

"I never saw them. I was down near the creek, headed for the bridge. A woman cried out, so I went to help. That's when they grabbed me. They put a rope around my neck and a sack over my head. It happened fast." He told True how they had beaten him, trying to leave nothing out, clarifying the attack for himself by describing it in detail.

"The one in front, after he finished working over my stomach, he hit me on the side of the head. He told me to mind my own business. Then they threw me in the creek."

"How does your head feel?"

"A little dizzy."

"I hope you are not concussed again." True laid her hand on his cheek. "I'll make some tea. Skullcap and ginseng. It will help your head."

She brewed tea from the dried leaves. She hunked some sugar out of the tub and sweetened the brew. Gideon didn't love the taste, but he drank the concoction anyway.

"What will you do now?" True asked. "I don't want you getting killed."

"I don't want to get killed either." He sat back in the chair. "The ones who attacked me—they must be behind the kidnappings."

"Or maybe they killed Phineas Potter," True said. "You must be very careful."

He nodded, closed his eyes.

"This place is getting more and more dangerous," True said. "I never heard of a murder when I was young. Or the sheriff getting beat up." She took Gideon's hand. "They say there's a financial panic, with banks collapsing all over the country. In the cities, folks are losing their jobs. They're going hungry, they can't pay their rent and their landlords are turning them out in the street. What if that happened here? It would make people even more desperate. More apt to rob and steal. And kill."

Gideon had read in the last issue of Potter's paper that cotton prices were plummeting in England, spelling tough times for America, because cotton was a major export. Cotton, the growing and harvesting of which were made possible by slavery.

"True, I just remembered something," he said. "We're supposed to go visit your kin tomorrow. I told the liveryman to have Jack harnessed to the wagon by eight."

"You're in no shape to go anywhere. You need to get a good night's sleep and then stay in bed tomorrow."

"I'm sorry we can't go." This was not a completely true statement. True's brothers had never held him in high regard.

"I'll go by myself," True said. "I'll get over to the livery before they put Jack in harness, and I'll ride him to Panther."

"Are you sure that's a good idea?"

"Unless you need me here. Then I'll stay." She gave her husband's hand a light squeeze. "Let's get you in bed."

Ranaway, negro boy KITT, 15 or 16 years old, *has a piece taken out of one of his ears.*

Chapter 31

—⊸∞⊶—

A GRIN SPLIT HER FATHER'S FACE AS TRUE RODE UP TO THE CABIN where she had been born and lived for eighteen years before marrying Gideon and moving to Adamant.

"Well," Davey Burns said, drawing out the word in a chuckle. "Looks like I got five boys. And here I was thinking I had four boys and a girl." He was a strong, sturdy man. As head collier, he supervised the cutting of timber and the making of charcoal, the fuel that fired the furnace and forge at Panther Ironworks.

"Where's your husband at?" True's father mimed looking all around. "I don't see him. All I see is a woman sitting on a horse who looks like she wears the pants in her family."

True got down off Jack. Wearing the faded comfortable old duds that had belonged to her pap, Davey Burns's father Ezekiel: pants, shirt, and battered hat.

"Gideon is under the weather," she said, hoping to let it go at that. At home this morning she'd applied a fresh poultice to Gideon's neck. He had promised to stay in bed, drink the tea she'd made, and rest.

She looked around at the familiar cabins, small peaked-roofed dwellings built of squared logs. Two dozen of them clustered around a grassy common with a roofed well at each end. The cabins' whitewashed walls were gray with soot. To the north stood the ironworks furnace with its pyramidal stone base and brick stack that sent smoke towering into the sky. She heard the furnace's low muffled roar along with the steady *thump-thump-thump* of the water-powered blowing tubs as they forced air into the hearth, melting the ore. She had grown up with those sounds in her ears and the iron-making's acrid scent in her nose.

On a nearby rise of land stood the stone house where the current ironmaster, Aaron Salter, lived. He had inherited the house and the ironworks from his uncle, the ferocious old high-horsed Adonijah Thompson. True's mother still worked in the "big house" as a servant, where True herself had been employed as a chore girl. She had some good memories from that part of her life, and others she would rather not recall.

All of the family earned their livings from the ironworks in one way or another. Her brother James was a founder: he directed the feeding of the furnace with charcoal, limestone, and ore and oversaw the periodic pours of molten iron into channels cut in the sand floor of the casting shed.

"Is Jimmy at the furnace today?" she asked her father.

"It's his day off. Him and Jackson and Jared are coming for dinner. They will miss seeing their Dutch brother-in-law." Davey Burns took his daughter in his arms and gave her a peck on the cheek. He tugged at her shirtsleeve. "Their wives will be here, too. Wearing proper garments for womenfolk."

True ignored the dig. "What about Jesse?"

"Maybe he'll show up, maybe he won't. You know how he is."

James, Jackson, Jared, and Jesse—the Jaybirds, as True had dubbed them when she was a girl—were all older than their sister. The first three were married and had children, so many that she could scarcely keep their names straight. Jesse, closest in age to True, was a bachelor. He rode around the county buying timber for the ironworks, for charcoal and construction.

"Before you were a collier, you did what Jesse does, right?" she said to her father. "Did you ever ride to the Barrens?"

"Too far to haul coal from there. In my day, we had enough forest here in this valley."

True asked if her father had ever met or heard of anyone named Brodie.

He shook his head. "No, sir." Winked at her.

True unsaddled Jack and put him in the fenced-in backyard. She followed her father into the cabin. True's mother, Abigail Burns, was cutting up vegetables for the stewpot. She put down her knife and hugged her daughter. "Where's Gideon?"

"He's not feeling well."

Davey Burns snorted. "Didn't want to put up with me and the boys and our tomfoolery."

"He's not afraid of you'uns," True said.

"He doesn't like us much, either," her father said.

"Is he sick?" True's mother asked with real concern.

"He's just under the weather," True said again. Knowing that at some point the news would reach Panther that the Dutch Sheriff had been set upon and beaten in Hammertown.

Her brothers and their wives and children arrived over the next hour. Talk and laughter filled the house. The children were embraced by their aunts and uncles and sent out to play. Davey Burns and his three eldest sons sat around the table, talking. True hoped her brother Jesse would show up; there were things she wanted to ask him.

She and her sisters-in-law helped her mother prepare dinner.

True knew she was different from these women. Her brothers' wives all had children; True's only child was dead. She listened to their chatter. But she didn't care about the fashionable dress and hat that the ironmaster's wife, Mrs. Salter, had just bought, or that Mr. So-and-So disciplined his missus with an apple switch. Stories about what this little niece or nephew had learned or said made her feel the hole in her heart left by David's death.

"Where's your hubby, where's that handsome Gideon at?" said Jim's wife Arlene.

"He's under the weather," True said yet again.

"You two planning on making me an auntie again anytime soon?" Arlene asked with a grin.

True looked away. It was nobody's business if or when they might have another child. She would not tell her sisters-in-law that she watched her period and counted days, wouldn't let Gideon near her when she was fertile. And that she chewed the seeds of wild carrot after they made love—all of this knowledge gotten from her gram. Because True was not disposed to bring another life into the world only to see it flit out again.

"If you won't tell us that," Arlene said, "maybe you will explain why you are wearing men's clothing."

The other sisters-in-law tittered. True's mother smiled and cut up a carrot, *chop chop chop*.

"The better to keep one leg on either side of a horse," True said.

"Are you trying to be a gentlewoman like Mrs. Salter, who goes out riding every day?"

"I would think she rides sidesaddle," True said.

"She does. On a fancy little mare."

"I reckon you don't ride, Arlene," True said.

"No, and nor should you. Not astride, anyway. Not if you want to have another baby."

"Who says I want to have another baby?"

Her sisters-in-law all looked askance.

True put down her knife and went over to the men. They'd gotten into a heated discussion about slavery. "It's the natural order of things," her brother Jim said.

"That's the truth," her father added. "Some folks are meant to be beneath other folks. Says so in the Bible."

"Like you and the rest of us are beneath Mr. Salter?" True's brother Jackson said.

"I wouldn't say that I'm beneath Mr. Salter," Davey Burns growled.

"Mr. Salter would say you are, Pa," Jackson replied. "He is a rich man and a smart man and wants everyone to know it."

"I hear that colored folks are not very smart," Jared Burns said. "That God didn't give them much in the way of brains."

To True this was amusing, since Jared was by far the simplest of the Burns brothers. Though he was good-hearted and always treated her kindly, unlike her brother Jesse. Who still hadn't shown up for this family gathering.

"You sure about that, Jare?" asked Jackson, a wicked smile on his lips. "That colored people are not too well-equipped with brains?"

Jared went on in an enthusiastic tone. "No, but they can dance! I saw one on stage once. His name was Jim Crow." Jared slapped the tops of his thighs. "You should've seen him! There was even a boy come out and danced right alongside of him. He did the very same dance! It was like a little mirror image of him, you might say."

"Jare, we were all at that show," James said. "At the theater in Adamant. You, Jack, Jesse, me, and Pa. We rode there in an ore wagon, remember? Speaking of Jesse, where is that rounder?"

"Hey, Jare," Jackson said. "That Jim Crow? He was a white man with bootblack on his face. You are about half dumb if you think he was really colored."

"Don't be ignorant to your brother," Davey Burns said to Jackson. He swiveled toward the cabin's door, which had just opened. "Well, look what the cat drug in. Your ears burning, Jesse? Where you been?"

"Probably just got out of bed," Jim Burns piped up.

"I bet his latest wench kicked him out on the floor," Jackson said. "Hello, little brother."

Jesse Burns was not little. He was the tallest of the Jaybirds, a broad-shouldered man with a heavy brow. Years ago, smallpox had pitted his face—a visage weathered brown from all the time he spent outdoors. Jesse wore a beard. True thought it likely her brother found it hard to shave that marred face. She reckoned that Jesse's character was marred, too: he had deviled her without cease from the time they were young.

"Hello, True," Jesse said to her in a falsely hearty voice. Grinned as he pointedly inspected her clothes. "Let's you and me get down on the floor and wrassle. How 'bout it? You being a strong fellow and a man-killer, I am plumb scairt of you, but I will chance a contest of strength."

"Quit your yammering, Jesse," True said.

"Do you have your gun with you?" Jesse looked around at his father and the rest of the Jaybirds. "True got himself a gun. I have it on good authority."

In fact, True had brought the detonator. It was in the bag attached to her saddle, which was on the . . .

Dear God, she thought, and rushed out of the cabin.

She let out a sigh of relief when she found the bag still buckled shut, the saddle resting on the top rail of the fence. She cursed herself for leaving the pistol unattended. She heard her nieces and nephews on the common, calling out and laughing as they played with the children of other families on the ironworks.

She got out the detonator and carried it inside.

"It's loaded," she said. The Jaybirds and her father all had to handle it, and remark on the two barrels, one on top of the other.

"What will you do with this shooter?" Jesse hefted the pistol and looked down its top barrel at a spot on the wall.

"Protect me and mine," True said.

He grinned at her. Handed the gun back butt first.

★★★

After the meal, after the chitchat and cleaning up, she went outside to where her father and brothers loitered by the fence.

"Come out to join the rest of the fellers, did you?" Davey Burns held out a plug of tobacco. "Care for some chaw?"

True shook her head and put the detonator back in the saddlebag. A film of ash from the furnace lay on the saddle's seat; she wiped it off with her hand. She looked at Jesse. She wanted to talk to him, but not with the others around. Anyway, she could never really talk when her brothers and their pa were jawing; it was like they didn't hear her.

Jesse's roan stood saddled with his reins looped over the fence. A bad-tempered hammerheaded gelding that True knew to keep a healthy distance from. Jesse cinched the girth tight, pulling his hand away quickly when the horse snaked his head around to bite.

"Where you headed, Jesse?" True asked.

"Down the road a piece." Jesse as snide and unhelpful as ever.

"Can I ride with you?"

"I ain't going to Adamant."

"I don't care where you're going."

"Then I don't care if you ride with me or not."

True bridled and saddled Jack, and she and Jesse mounted and said goodbye to the men, then rode off down the blue-tinged road, its surface made of slag, refuse from the ironmaking process.

"Why didn't that Dutch husband of yours come today?" Jesse asked. "I want a real answer, Sis, not a lie."

True decided she might as well speak the truth, since Jesse would hear it soon enough. "He got beat up last night in Hammertown."

"Huh. Snooping around where he ain't wanted."

"He is the sheriff of this county, as you well know. He was looking for clues to whoever murdered Phineas Potter. And for information on the colored people who've gone missing. At least five of them so far."

"I heard about that," Jesse said. "And there's a two-hundred-dollar reward out for a young'un escaped from down South, who may be in this county. I'd sure like to catch that little devil and turn him in for the bounty."

True rolled her eyes. Jesse was a hopeless case.

He looked over at her. "How bad did they beat him?"

"Bad enough. One of them put a rope around his neck from behind and the other worked him over from the front. They had a sack on his head so he couldn't see."

"They mark his pretty face? Put out an eye, maybe?"

She shuddered. "No. Not that."

"He wouldn't come back from something like that. He's soft. It would break him, losing an eye."

"You don't know him," True said. "Gideon is brave, and he is tough."

Jesse scoffed. "Tough enough to get beat up in Hammertown."

"He was asking around in all the saloons and at Annie Picard's house. Someone wants him to stop asking. He saw Hack Latimer down there, though Hack swore he'd stopped drinking."

"That damned Hack."

"I thought he was your friend."

"He is. Sort of. He owes me money. Seems like he has owed me money since Christ was a corporal."

True couldn't help laughing.

"Hack owes everybody," Jesse went on. "You'd think I would have learned by now not to trust him. I told you we had a gold eagle riding on Gideon for the election. Well, Hack never paid. Then I ran into him at a horse race, and he wanted to bet double or nothing. I knew the two horses, and I was pretty sure which one would win, so I picked that one and he took the other. After the race, he owed me two eagles. I am not sure I will ever see that money."

The blue road threw back the sunlight in little sparkles and made a crunching sound beneath the horses' hooves. True had no idea where Jesse lived these days, or where he was going now.

"There's something I need to ask you," she said.

"Ask away. It don't mean I'll answer."

"You ride all over the place." In addition to prospecting for wood for the ironworks, Jesse also found farms for people looking to buy land. Rumor had it that he trafficked in illegal whiskey and might even be involved in shoving worthless notes from defunct banks. "Have you been in the Barrens?" True asked.

"Now and then."

"Did you ever come across anyone there named Brodie?"

Jesse thought for a bit, then shook his head.

The road pinched in between two cut banks. Jack got too close to Jesse's gelding, and the roan swung his big blunt head around and bared his teeth. Jack quickly stopped and backed up.

When they got out in the open, Jesse waited for True to catch up.

"I don't know of any Brodies in the Barrens," he said, "but the place where they ran that horse race at, there's a woman by that name works there."

"Where?"

"Potlicker Flats. South of here. A place called Bodines, a little ways off the stage road. The sort of house our old ma wouldn't want her favorite son to frequent. Nor even set foot in." Jesse grinned at her. "An establishment along the lines of Annie Picard's."

"A woman named Brodie works there?"

"Works or worked there. I haven't seen her in a while."

"Tell me about her."

"Liza Brodie. Which you might call her a brute, sort of an ancient whore. She's their washerwoman. I heard her say once that she grew up on a farm west of Adamant."

The Barrens lay west of Adamant.

"This Brodie woman, is she ugly?"

"Well, she ain't no oil painting, that's for sure. Big jaw on her like a man. Her hair is frizzy-like. Snakes or bats or a flock of birds could roost in it."

"What color hair?"

"Shit-brindle brown."

"How big is she?"

"Big as me, almost. I wouldn't tangle with her. And she'd break you in half, little brother." A taunting smile. "You know what they

208 • • *Lay This Body Down*

were going to call you if you were a boy? Another 'J' name. Jehoshaphat. You want to be a man, wearing pants like that and Pap's old hat, then I think I will call you Jehoshaphat. Maybe Fatty for short."

"Ma and Pa never would've named me that."

"Don't be so sure."

They rode on. Still headed away from Adamant. True knew she should stop and turn around.

Jesse had said he'd bet with Hack on the horse race at the Bodines place where this Liza Brodie worked. True was recalling the black horse Liza Brodie had the day she'd met her—for surely it was the same woman. She was thinking fast, ideas flickering through her brain. "Would Hack know this Brodie woman?"

"Maybe. Prob'ly."

"Does Hack ever go down South? Or have any connections there?"

"Why do you want to know?"

"Because I do."

"He's got an uncle in Annapolis, Maryland. Judah Lovegood; Hack is named after him. This uncle has a big plantation where he grows tobacco. Hack lived there for a while when he was young. He used to brag about it, how him and his cousins would go out gambling and drinking and racing horses and generally cutting up."

"This uncle has slaves?"

"By the score. Hack said he used to trifle with the girls." Jesse grinned. "I hear Hack went and joined the anti-slavery society in Adamant. Now that's a hoot. You think Hack cares about black people? He couldn't give a tinker's cuss about anybody but himself."

True stopped Jack. "Jesse, I need to turn around."

"All right, Jehoshaphat. I'll be seeing you."

Jesse walked his roan horse down the road.

Fifty dollars reward, for the negro Jim Blake—has a *piece cut out of each ear*, and the middle finger of the left hand *cut off* to the second joint.

Chapter 32

⸺⬦⬦⬦⸺

GIDEON WOKE FROM A NAP. SUNSHINE AND MILD AIR STREAMED IN through the open window. The house was quiet. True had been gone for hours.

He took a testing breath. The dull ache in his ribs flared and made him groan. The abrasions on his neck burned. His shoulders and back throbbed. The tea True had left for him hadn't blunted his headache.

He had spent a restless night. After dosing himself with the tea, he was up several times to relieve himself. He had lain awake, unable to get the attack in Hammertown out of his mind. When he finally slept, he dreamed he was falling down a well. He fell a long way, banging and scraping against rocks in the wall before hitting the water. He went under but managed to right himself and get his head above the surface. Treading water, he looked up and saw a star blazing in the night sky at the top of the shaft. The water in which he was immersed chilled him to the bone. Water tainted with death: of thousands upon millions of lives, animal and human, extinguished and decomposed to a foul essence and drained into this hole in the ground. In his dream he tried to keep his mouth above the fetid liquid, but it kept pulling him down. His arms and legs thrashed, and he felt his body weakening and going numb. He would drown here and add his own polluted self to the miasma. As he slipped beneath the surface, he saw the star wink out.

Now, lying in bed, he shivered at the memory and drew the quilt around him.

True must have gotten to Panther by now. What would her family make of her, wearing men's clothing and riding there by herself? Of course they would conclude that he was a poor husband, to let his wife dress like that and go out unprotected into the world. He knew he shouldn't care what they thought. He was just glad that True was back to living, back to being herself. After they had lost David, it had grieved him to see her lying in bed for days on end, sunk in despair. He had worried they might never be together again.

Which would have been a shame, because True was strong and smart and he loved her and depended on her far more than he often admitted, either to her or to himself.

He closed his eyes and tried to sleep, but his mind wouldn't settle.

Phineas Potter had been killed two weeks ago today. Gideon still had no real sense of who had murdered the newspaperman. He wondered if the answer was right in front of him. Was he craning his neck and looking over the killer, or around him? Had he forgotten some chance remark he'd heard? Failed to recognize some key detail, some important piece of evidence?

In his mind's eye suddenly appeared a vision of the stranger he had seen in the Broad Ax: the short, dark-complected hook-nosed man, sitting by himself at a table, who had stolen out of the saloon when Gideon's back was turned.

He now remembered when and where he had seen the man. As though the new blow to his head had dislodged a memory that the old concussion had buried.

Four years ago, after he had defied his father, left their farm in Lancaster County, ridden west on Maude, and traveled into the lightly settled back country toward the intriguingly named town of Adamant.

Crossing through the Seven Mountains, he had fallen in with a talkative person whom he had thought of ever since as the Tattered Man. The fellow wore ragged clothing, rode a big mule. He claimed to be a preacher; he brandished a Bible and said Gideon showed an "inner light." Yes, it had been the Tattered Man, he'd been the one who had said that. The fellow offered to accompany him to Adamant, show him the way. He'd led Gideon down a faint trail, nattering as they went.

Then the hook-nosed man appeared in front of them, his gray horse stepping out of the brush, while another bandit, also mounted and carrying a long sword, boxed them in from behind. The Tattered Man rode forward on his mule: it touched noses with the hook-nosed man's gray, whimpered in the way that mules sometimes did. Gideon knew he was trapped. A steep slope angled up on his right, an even steeper one fell away to the left, both heavily wooded. He made the split-second decision that he would not let these men rob and kill him. He touched Maude with his calves. Sensing his fear, she sprang forward and threaded the gap between the Tattered Man's mule and the hook-nosed man's horse, with Gideon's knees banging into the men's legs. As he galloped off down the trail, he heard their gunshots—thank God they'd done no more damage than taking the tip off Maude's ear.

Before the ambush, the Tattered Man had warned him about an outlaw named William Jewell Jarrett. When Hook-Nose blocked their way, the Tattered Man had said: "Speak of the devil, and his horns appear."

William Jewell Jarrett was Hook-Nose, the same man who had slipped out of the Broad Ax that night. Either Jarrett had recognized Gideon as his earlier escaped victim, or he simply saw him as a lawman wearing a badge. Either way, Gideon knew that the man was up to no good.

He remembered back again to that day in the Seven Mountains. After escaping from the bandits, he had left the trail, gotten off Maude, and sat down against a tree to rest; weary and wrung out after his long travels and his brush with death, he had fallen asleep. Wakening later, fearing the highwaymen might still be looking for him, he rode ahead cautiously and came up on the Tattered Man from behind. The man looked drunk; he wobbled sitting on his mule. When Gideon kicked him out of the saddle, he hit the ground hard. Stupidly, Gideon dismounted to see whether the fellow was badly hurt. The Tattered Man suddenly revived, got his hands around Gideon's neck, and tried to strangle him. Gideon had clubbed the brigand in the side of the head using the man's own pistol. To this day, he didn't know if that hard blow had killed the man, or if he'd survived.

Now, lying in bed at home, Gideon drew in a deep breath. Pain radiated outward from his stomach and ribs.

But he was damned if he would stay in bed.

He got up and dressed, pushed his feet into boots. He found his old hat, once dark brown and now the color of weak tea, with a hole in the crown chewed by a mouse. It made him mad all over again, losing his new hat in the creek last night.

Outside, he visited the backhouse, then unchained Old Dick. With the dog beside him, he started toward the center of town.

At first his steps were halting, full of aches and pains. Maybe this was how he'd feel when he got old. If he lived that long.

Folks were out for Sunday strolls; others spaded gardens or fed chickens or chopped wood. Many more undoubtedly were worshipping in the churches. At the Diamond, Gideon turned down High Street. The hitch in his stride was almost gone, the pain in his stomach lessened.

True wouldn't be keen on him going out, but she needn't know of it.

He would go to Hammertown. Find where he'd been attacked and look around for anything that might reveal his assailants' identity. Could one of them have been Hook-Nose, the highwayman William Jewell Jarrett? Jarrett was not a big man, and Gideon was sure that at least one and possibly both of his assailants had been as tall as he was.

The slope leveled out. Spring Creek flowed from left to right. Its ripples reflected the sun, curls of light bouncing off the green water and quivering on the bridge's stone abutments. His eyes didn't like the glare. He appreciated the shade as he and Old Dick crossed through the covered bridge.

Hammertown looked slightly less woebegone on this fresh day.

He came to where four houses squatted side by side between the street and the creek. He looked down each alleyway between them. He stopped at the one from which he thought the woman had called, down which his attackers had rushed him before throwing him into the creek. Entering the space, he looked around.

"What the hell are you doing?" screeched a woman from out front.

Gideon left the alley. "I am the sheriff," he said. "I am investigating an assault. Were you here last night?"

The woman went back inside her house and slammed the door.

He searched through all three alleys and found nothing important.

He and Old Dick went farther into Hammertown. None of the drunks who had cluttered the streets last night were still present. A man with an eye patch curried a swaybacked horse. Some children threw rocks at a cat that went skittering off. Gideon kept Old Dick at heel to keep him from joining in the fun.

They came to where most of the tippling houses stood. All of them closed on this Sabbath day.

Beside one of the saloons, Old Dick's nostrils flared. The dog dropped his head and swung it from side to side as he tested the ground. He sniffed his way into an opening between two buildings.

Cracked weathered boards leaned against a half-demolished box. Sodden clumps of rags, broken jugs, a shoe missing its sole. Old Dick, his tail wagging, sniffed his way through the rubbish to the box.

A boy rabbited out the far side. He shot a look over his shoulder and raced down the alley. A thin lad, hatless, his skin medium brown in color. Clutching something in his hand.

Gideon spoke to Old Dick, and the dog came back.

Sore and gimpy, Gideon couldn't have outrun the lad even if he'd wanted to. He recognized him, though. The same young fellow who had helped him out of that jam last August in Greer County. The thirteen-year-old runaway with the two-hundred-dollar reward on his head put there by the Virginian Tazewell Waller.

A brushy field lay beyond the alley. The boy went partway out into the field and stopped. He turned around and stared. Gideon wondered if the boy would recognize him as the man he had helped last summer, the Colerain County sheriff. Who had the power to help him. Or to end his run for freedom.

They stood looking at each other.

Gideon saw that the boy held a knife in his hand: held it up so that it could be seen. Gideon raised his own hand, palm outward.

After a while the boy lowered the knife. He slowly lifted his other hand and returned the greeting.

Ran away, Laman, an old negro man, grey, has *only one eye.*

Chapter 33

⁂

"I WON'T LET 'EM TAKE US BACK," MUTTERED BENJAMIN.
Next to him, on the floor in the cramped upper room in the old house, Felix Wiley wagged his head.

"You are a fool," Wiley said. He used the same tone a parent might employ when instructing a child. "They are not sending you and your boy back to wherever it is you ran from."

"What do you mean?"

"I heard them talking. They're taking us to Maryland, to a Georgia man there. He will chain us up with a bunch of others, and by the time we are done with that long walk, we will be in Georgia or Alabama or Mississippi. Cotton land."

"I won't let them." Benjamin's voice had gone weak.

His son Thomas sat on his other side, arms clasped around his knees, forehead pressed into his arms.

"Where are you from?" Wiley said.

"North Carolina."

Wiley raised his eyebrows. "You got quite a ways, then. How'd you manage that?"

"We got helped by a preacher down there. Then passed from one family to another coming north. White people, mostly. We are bound for Canada."

"No. You are going way down South." Wiley looked at Thomas. "Where's this boy's ma?"

"She wouldn't run. Said it was too risky."

"She was right. How'd they catch you?"

"We were working for some white people, cutting firewood. Not far from here."

"They turn you in?"

"I don't think so. Those two men, they just showed up. They had guns . . ." His voice trailed off.

On Wiley's other side sat Amanda Jones. "Maybe there's something we can do, baby," she said to Wiley. "To get ourselves free."

"That big ugly bitch, she will blow you in half with that scattergun if you try anything," Wiley said. "She ain't right in the head. Those two white men, they ain't right, either."

At the far end of the line sat John Horne in his uniform coat.

"You, bluecoat," Benjamin said.

Horne shifted his eyes and said nothing.

"You been a soldier? You got any idea how we can get out of this fix?"

"Save your breath," Wiley said. "He ain't said a word since we got here."

From downstairs came the sound of voices. The words were not discernible. The voices rose and fell in a querulous way.

"How long have you been here?" Benjamin asked Wiley.

"Must be three weeks."

"How did they catch you?"

Wiley worked his mouth like he'd swallowed something foul. "Makes no difference how they caught us. We are here, you and your boy are here, that bump-on-a-log in the blue coat is here. And all of us, we are headed south."

★★★

"We should leave right now," William Jewell Jarrett said. "Load up the merchandise and head for Maryland. I don't see no reason to wait any longer."

"He wants two more." Liza Brodie sat at the head of the table. "He says his lucky number is seven. And he says two more will make it worth our while to carry them all south."

"*Seven*," Jarrett said disgustedly. He reached for the jug, put it to his mouth. The knob in his neck bobbed. He lowered the jug and wiped his lips. "*Seven*."

"I have never been to Maryland," Gulliver Luck said mildly. "I'd like to go take a look-see. They say that travel broadens the mind."

"My mind is broad enough," Jarrett said.

"The Lord moves in mysterious ways," Luck replied.

"So does the big boss," said Jarrett. "Anyway, we don't need your versifying, Gullie."

"Whoso despiseth the word shall be destroyed."

Jarrett snorted. "Will you shut up if I pass the jug?"

"I might."

Jarrett shoved the vessel across the table.

"The three of us are doing all the work," Jarrett said. "The big boss, he ain't doing a thing."

"He is locating the merchandise," Brodie said. "Anyway, he is smarter than both of you'uns put together."

Jarrett waited for Luck to finish drinking, then got the jug back. He took a nip. "We catch 'em." He tilted the jug again. "We guard 'em." Another slug of applejack. "And I want paid."

"The harvest is plenteous, but the laborers are few," Luck said.

"There you go again with that Bible yap. You ask me, it's time the laborers get some of the harvest." Jarrett smiled, his eyes narrowing, his brows forming a dark vee above them. "Use of the merchandise while it is in our possession."

A grin spread across Luck's face.

"Way I see it, she is just a whore," Jarrett added.

Brodie frowned.

Jarrett caught the big woman's expression. "Meaning no disrespect. I am referring to that little colored piece."

Luck's grin exposed the brown pegs of his teeth. "A sporting lady. She is surely skilled in amorous congress."

Jarrett looked at Brodie. "I know you like to watch."

She shrugged.

"Give me the keys."

Brodie got the keys out of her apron and tossed them onto the table.

One hundred dollars reward for a negro fellow Pompey, 40 years old, he is *branded* on the *left jaw*.

Chapter 34

———— ⊶⊷ ————

COMING IN FROM THE CHILL, TRUE MET WITH FRAGRANCE AND warmth. A pot simmered on the fire. Gideon came up to her, and she wrapped her arms around him carefully and held him for a while.

She pulled back and looked at him. "How are you feeling?"

"Better."

"I have something to tell you."

"I have something to tell you, too. Sit down, you must be tired after that ride."

They settled into chairs. True's eyes were bright. "I talked to Jesse. He knows a woman named Liza Brodie. A washerwoman at a disorderly house on the other side of the mountains. A place called Bodines near Potlicker Flats."

"The stage road goes through there."

"This woman grew up in Colerain County, on a farm west of Adamant. In the Barrens. Jesse described her, and she has to be the big woman I met when I was out looking for basket ash. She had that black horse with her, maybe Potter's."

Gideon felt excitement rising within him.

"Jesse was at this Bodines place for a horse race," True said, "and he won a bet with Hack Latimer that Hack never paid. Jesse says Hack might know this Liza Brodie. And it turns out that Hack has an uncle down in Maryland, with a big plantation; Hack lived there for a while. Jesse said Hack was wild back then. He still is, and crookeder than a ram's horn. He owes Jesse money. From what you heard in Hammertown, he owes a lot of people money."

"Which gives him a strong motive to kidnap people and sell them to repair his finances," Gideon said. "Take them to that uncle in Maryland."

"Or to some other shady character he met down there."

"Honey, you are a wonder." Gideon took True's hand. "Now I'll tell you what I found: the runaway boy those Virginians are chasing."

"You did? Where?"

"In Hammertown. I felt better, so I decided to check on the place where I got attacked. I didn't find anything. But then I went in among the saloons. I had Old Dick with me. He took up a scent and found the boy hiding in a wooden box in an alley."

"Dear God. How long has that child been there?"

"I don't know. I only talked to him for a short while."

"You didn't bring him home?"

"It was broad daylight, I was afraid someone would see him. I told him to get back in the box, and I'd come and get him after dark." Gideon paused. "The federal law says I must turn him over to his master. But I won't do that. I will enforce the Pennsylvania law instead, the 1826 one. That man Waller, he doesn't have the right papers. He needs an affidavit, so that he can get a warrant and—"

True laid a finger on Gideon's lips. "I don't need to know any of that. It's simple. No one has the right to own another person." She stood. "Let's get moving. It'll be dark by the time we get there."

True changed out of her riding clothes into a dress and shawl and bonnet so she wouldn't attract any more attention than necessary. They took Old Dick.

They exchanged greetings with a few other pedestrians as they made their way down High Street in the twilight. They crossed the bridge over Spring Creek. Hammertown lay shuttered and silent. At the alley's opening, the setter began wagging his tail. Gideon and True looked all around, at the street, the saloons, the few small windows like squinting eyes in the mean houses. When they were satisfied that no one was watching, they entered the alley. They found the boy in the box, asleep, covered with an old blanket.

"Otis," Gideon said softly.

The lad stirred and murmured.

True knelt, laid her wrist against his forehead.

"He's burning up."

"Wake up, Otis," Gideon said.

The boy opened his eyes. He startled momentarily, then eased back.

Old Dick stuck his nose in the boy's face. Otis put his hand on the dog's head, stroked a feathered ear.

"Let's get you up," Gideon said.

True had brought along her grandfather's hat and a coat her brothers had outgrown and passed down to her. She held the coat out, and Otis reached one arm into it, then the other arm.

The hat sank down on the boy's head, which helped obscure his face.

Leaving, they stood at the mouth of the alley for a while. They heard and saw nothing. As they made their way to the bridge, Gideon saw that the boy's steps were faltering.

"How do you feel?"

"All right," Otis replied. "Where are we going?"

"To our house," True said.

They crossed through the bridge. Then Spring Street, High Street to the Diamond, south on Franklin toward home. Twenty minutes of plodding.

A figure emerged from a side street. Gideon stepped forward, placing himself between the newcomer and Otis; out of the corner of his eye he saw True do the same. The man walked toward them unsteadily.

Old Dick started growling.

The man stopped.

"Who is it?" Gideon said.

"It's me. Gaither."

Gideon made out the unpleasant face and portly form of his part-time deputy Gaither Brown.

"What are you doing out tonight?" Gideon asked.

"What you always tell me to do. Patrolling the town. Making sure all is well."

The smell of liquor strong on Brown's breath.

"There's no need for you to be out tonight," Gideon said. "The town is quiet. Locked up tight."

"Tight as a bull's ass in fly time." Brown guffawed. He looked at True as if to see how she might respond to his quip.

"Gaither Brown, you are a shining example of manhood," True said.

Brown craned his neck, trying to look past her. "Who's that?"

"You've been drinking," Gideon said.

The deputy's eyes reflected twin shards of light from some hidden source. Prying eyes, canny eyes. It came to Gideon how little he liked or trusted the man.

He took Brown's elbow. "I'll walk a ways with you." He steered Brown toward the jail.

True turned toward home. Otis took a few steps, then stumbled.

Gaither Brown halted and stared.

"Let's keep going," Gideon said.

"Who's that?" Brown said again.

"A young fellow lives a few doors down from us."

"What's wrong with him?"

"Taken sick. Come on, Gaither."

Brown lumbered along beside Gideon.

"That wife of yours," he said. "I didn't like her saying that—about me being a shining sample of manhood or some such."

"Don't let it bother you."

"Why do you let her run her mouth like that? She's your wife, man. You know what they say, a woman, a dog, and a walnut tree, the harder you beat 'em, the better they be."

"Is that what you do to your wife, Gaither?"

"A little correction now and then is not a bad thing."

Gideon walked with Gaither as far as the jail and thanked him for keeping an eye on the town. Then he turned and strode toward home.

Ran away from the subscriber, his man Joe. He visits the city occasionally, where he has been harbored by his *mother* and *sister*. I will give one hundred dollars for proof sufficient to *convict his harborers*.

Chapter 35

❧

BEFORE ENTERING THE HOUSE, OTIS HAD TO USE THE PRIVY. AFTER-ward, True had him wash his hands thoroughly. Then she sat him down at the table and served him a bowl of soup. As he ate, she watched him closely. His eyes appeared lackluster. Now and then he shivered.

"How do you feel?" True asked.

"My head hurts." He took another spoonful of soup. "I get hot and cold sometimes. Right now I'm cold."

True fetched a quilt and arranged it over his shoulders. "Does your stomach hurt?"

"Yes'm."

"Do you have the runs?"

"Yes'm."

"Is there blood when you go?"

He shook his head.

True felt relieved. "How long have you been sick?"

"Since the day before yesterday."

The door opened, and Otis flinched. When he saw who it was, he relaxed.

"Hello, Otis," Gideon said.

"The man we saw. Will he turn me in?"

"I don't think he got a good look at you. Anyway, I'm the sheriff. That man is just a deputy. And I am not going to hand you over to anyone."

Gideon took off his coat and hat and sat down across from Otis. He waited until the lad had finished eating.

"Can I ask you some questions?" Gideon said.

Otis nodded.

"How long have you been in Adamant?"

"A couple of weeks."

"In that alley the whole time?"

"No, sir. First I was in a big house. In a little room way up high."

"Do you know whose house it was?"

He shook his head. "All I know is they are supposed to help the people who run."

Gideon asked where the house was, and Otis told him as accurately as he could.

"How did you learn about the house?"

"I heard about it from a man who came to that other place, where you fought with Thaddeus."

He meant the settlement called McDonough, where Gideon had first laid eyes on Otis last summer.

"In that big house, nobody told me anything," Otis continued. "I was there for nine days. I started getting afraid they'd turn me in and I'd get sent back. The room where I was, it had a window. I looked out it one day and saw this man. He went past real slow, looking all around. I reckoned he was a slave catcher."

"So you decided to leave," Gideon said. "Did you just walk out the door? They let you go, just like that?"

"I went out the window and down the roof. It was at night. I jumped into a tree and climbed down." He shivered again. "They almost caught me, but I got away."

"And you've been hiding in that alley ever since?"

Otis nodded. "A colored man came in there to dump some trash. He's a cook in one of the saloons. He brought me food and that blanket."

"What about water?" True asked.

"He left a jug. When it got empty, I'd fill it in the creek." The boy squirmed in the chair, then stood up, the quilt sliding off him. "I have to go again."

While Otis used the privy, Gideon stood guard. He had told the boy he would not hand him over to anyone, and that was a promise he meant to keep. He had a notion of which house the boy had sheltered in earlier, and, if he was right, it was an astonishing thing. He wondered what they should do next. Maybe he could talk to Headmaster Foote and see if the anti-slavery people could take the lad and move him on north, assuming Otis wasn't too sick to travel. But those folks hadn't done a good job of protecting the man and boy who had gone missing from the Olcotts' farm in Frogville. And he could not go back to the safe house where he'd been, since the Virginians knew of it.

Back inside, True had Otis wash his hands again and sit in the chair. "I need to make some medicine for you," she told him, wrapping him in the quilt. "It should get you feeling better again."

She collected a knife, a sack, and a lantern. Gideon asked quietly if she knew what illness the boy had.

"It's probably from the creek water. Could be dysentery."

Gideon knew that people sometimes died from dysentery.

"I shouldn't be long. Try to get more soup in him. Warm water, too, as much as he'll drink; put a little salt and sugar in it. Fill the small kettle with fresh water and set it on the fire. I'll be back as soon as I can."

After True left, Otis ate more soup and drank a little water. Then he lay back in the chair and dozed.

When True returned, she took a bunch of roots from her sack and placed them on the washbench. "Dewberry, from that empty lot down the street," she told her husband. She put a handful of bitter-smelling shavings next to the roots. "Cherry bark." After washing and separating the roots, she used twine to bind them and the bark together into an oblong packet. She put the packet in the kettle simmering over the fire.

Later she woke Otis and had him drink some of the preparation. Gideon took him out to the privy again, and then True put him in their bed. "I'll sit up with him," she said.

Gideon lay down near the fire between two blankets. The floor was hard, and his ribs and back complained. His mind was reeling with thoughts. But weary as he was, he soon fell asleep.

Ran away, the mulatto wench Mary—has a cut on the left arm, a scar on the shoulder, and two upper teeth missing.

Chapter 36

———⊷———

IN THE NIGHT, TRUE DOSED OTIS SEVERAL TIMES WITH THE MEDICINAL tea. When he needed to use the privy, she stood outside with Old Dick by her side and the detonator in her hand.

By morning the boy's fever had come down. He was sleeping soundly as Gideon and True ate breakfast. Gideon nodded toward the bedroom. "If you can take care of him, I want to ride to the Barrens later today."

"Are you sure you're well enough to ride?"

"I'm fine." Gideon was far from fine, and he reckoned True knew it, too. He did not look forward to getting on a horse, but it was his duty. And he was fired up after learning from True about a woman named Brodie who had grown up west of Adamant. "I won't be back tonight, so I'll find someplace to stay. Will you be all right with Otis?"

"I hope so."

"He shouldn't use the privy during the daytime; someone could see him. The pot will have to do."

She nodded. "I'm not sure how safe it is to keep him here."

"Right now I can't think of anyplace where he'd be safer."

True took Gideon's hand. "Promise me you'll be careful. That big woman scares me."

Gideon promised. Then he kissed True and left.

Walking up the street, his body ached with each step, and drawing a full breath sent pain rippling through his torso. He decided that those hurts were bearable.

Waller and Blaine were standing in front of the jail. He felt a chill of fear that somehow they'd learned he and True were hiding Otis.

When he unlocked the door and went in, the Virginians followed him.

He hung up his coat and his disreputable old hat and sat down behind his desk. He regarded the men: Waller with his thick body and aggressive stance, Blaine with his neatly kept moustache and chin beard and the rakish tilt to his hat.

Waller brought his face close to Gideon's. "Where's Leo?"

Gideon looked into Waller's pale blue eyes. "I have no news for you." It wasn't exactly a lie; he knew the boy not as Leo but as Otis. Anyway, he would prevaricate if he had to.

"You have done nothing to locate my servant," Waller said.

"I am busy with a murder investigation."

Waller stepped back. "Show him," he said to Blaine.

Blaine shrugged off his coat. He undid the top three buttons of his shirt and gingerly pushed it down.

A white cloth was tied around his upper arm, spotted with dried blood.

"Leo did that," Waller said.

"I heard him jump off the roof of a house we were watching at night," said Blaine. "I grabbed him. The little bastard had a knife."

Blaine's use of the word *bastard*, followed by a slightly apologetic look at his employer, confirmed for Gideon what he'd suspected all along.

"A bad wound, Mr. Blaine?" he asked.

"Bad enough. Been most of a week, and it keeps opening up when I move my arm too much."

"I take it you were not able to hold him."

Blaine scowled and began buttoning his shirt.

"Mr. Blaine, you have just admitted to me that you set upon some young fellow in the dark," Gideon said. "What you did could be viewed as an assault. It sounds like the lad acted in self-defense."

Waller's face went red. "I demand that you find Leo and lock him in a cell. Call what Mr. Blaine did assault, if it makes you happy. I will cover any fine, and we'll take the boy off your hands and get out of your town for good."

Gideon picked up a goose quill. He got out his penknife and opened the blade. He used the knife to carefully trim the shaft's end. "You say this happened almost a week ago. Why did you wait so long to tell me?"

Neither Waller nor Blaine answered.

"I think I know." Gideon looked up. "You hoped someone would catch him and bring him to you for the reward. Then you could put him on a horse and get him across the state line. Illegally."

"Do your job, Sheriff," Waller said.

"I am doing my job. And part of my job is to instruct you to obey the law as it exists in Pennsylvania. I told you already, but I'll say it again. To recapture someone who has run from slavery, you must first secure an affidavit from your home state. It must have the name of the person on it, his age, and an accurate description. It must be issued and legally authorized by an official in Virginia. Then you can use that affidavit to apply for a warrant here in Pennsylvania."

Gideon turned the quill in his fingers, examining its chisel-shaped end. "This state's fugitive slave law says that anyone who carries off a colored person without following the procedure I just explained can face a felony kidnapping charge. My advice to you is to go home and forget about Leo."

Waller slammed his hands down on Gideon's desk. "This is petti-fogging nonsense! You call yourself a sheriff, yet you ignore the law of the land. You are either incompetent, or a coward, or a blasted abolitionist, or all three. And you talk out of both sides of your mouth. Self-defense? If you cared about lawful self-defense, you would give me back my pistol, which you took from me that night when I sought to defend myself from those riotous villains!" He held out his hand. "Give me my gun."

Gideon waited before speaking. "I will return your pistol when you and Mr. Blaine leave Colerain County. Come to the jail mounted on your horses, with a receipt showing that you have checked out of the hotel, and swear an oath that you are going back to Virginia. Then I'll return your firearm."

He unstoppered the bottle in his desk's inkwell and got out a piece of paper. "I have work to do," he said.

Waller spun on his heel and stalked out, Blaine following.

Right after they exited, Alonzo came in through the door.

"The Virginians do not look happy," he said.

"No. They are displeased."

"I was having coffee with Gaither," Alonzo said. "He told me he saw you and your wife last night. You had a boy with you. Gaither says the lad was sick. Some kind of contagion we should be worried about?"

Gideon was glad Alonzo hadn't come in a moment earlier and made this statement in front of the Virginians. "Nothing to be concerned about."

"Who is the boy?"

Gideon wondered just how much Gaither had seen. Before he could decide how to answer, a young man came in and handed him a folded piece of paper. The fellow stood there until Gideon found a coin and gave it to him.

"I have not had a chance to tell you," Gideon said to Alonzo, "but I was attacked in Hammertown on Saturday night."

"Holy Moses. They do that to your neck?"

Gideon's fingers rose to touch the wound. "They put a rope around my neck and a sack over my head. They said to stop my investigation or I'll end up dead. Well, I won't stop."

He unfolded the paper the boy had delivered and read what was written on it in a neat lawyerly hand.

"The Cold Fish wants to see me." He rooted around in his desk and found an old kerchief. Tying it around his neck, he told Alonzo that after meeting with the state's attorney he planned to ride to the Barrens. "I hope to find out if any Brodies live there."

★★★

In his office, seated behind his desk, Alvin Fish maintained a position of remote authority much as Gideon had done when dealing with the Virginians.

"Give me a detailed report on your investigation," the attorney said. His clothes were neat and clean, his face shaven. He cupped his chin in his hand and slowly tapped his lips with a bony finger as he stared at Gideon and waited for a reply.

"I may have made some progress in learning about the kidnapped people," Gideon said. "Their abductions may be—"

Fish made an abrupt cutting gesture with his hand. "What have you learned about Phineas's murder?"

"I am trying to tell you that there may be a connection between his killing and the disappearances."

When Fish did not respond, Gideon continued: "Potter was involved in helping fugitives. I already told you about the secret cellar in his house. I think he was also investigating the kidnappings of those people. Depending on what he found, he might have come to you or me. Or maybe he planned to reveal the crimes in his newspaper.

"I mentioned finding on his desk a piece of paper with the words 'Brodie' and 'Barrens.' I have learned that a woman named Liza Brodie grew up on a farm in the Barrens. She's been involved in prostitution in Greer County, where she could have met all kinds of unsavory characters. I have a witness who may have seen this woman with Potter's horse."

"Who is your witness?"

Gideon didn't want to admit it, but finally said: "My wife."

Fish sat back and let his hands fall on his desk.

"She was out riding near the Barrens," Gideon said. "She saw a woman who answers to this Liza Brodie's description. The woman had a black horse. I plan to look for the farm and find out if anything illegal is taking place there."

"Your *wife*," Fish said. "Who may have seen some *woman* with a *horse*. Sheriff Stoltz, I cannot begin to tell you how weary I am of your vague statements, none of which disguise your lack of progress toward solving the Potter case. This has always been your method, to fumble about hoping your inept actions finally lead you to uncovering something concrete."

"Mr. Fish, since I became sheriff I have brought three killers to justice. Shall I name them for you?"

"That is not necessary." Fish's voice dripped with scorn. "From what you have just told me, I can draw no other conclusion than that you have made essentially no progress in apprehending Potter's killer or killers. They are still out there, still at large, ready to kill again. You do not deserve to draw a sheriff's pay."

Gideon felt a scalding anger. A week ago, Fish had abused him in this same manner. Gideon had answered back, and Fish had threatened to discipline him for insubordination. It had hung over his head ever since.

And two days ago, on Saturday night, carrying out his duty, he had taken his investigation to Hammertown and been assaulted—choked, beaten, almost drowned. He could easily have been killed.

He wouldn't take this. The Cold Fish might be his superior, but he would not be *beyuust* like this, he would serve the *baschdard* back.

Phineas Potter's brother-in-law had implied that Potter engaged in sodomy. It was a felony punishable by five years in prison. Not to mention the scandal that would accompany being accused of such a practice.

Fish was Potter's friend. His bosom friend. Potter's death had clearly left the state's attorney shaken. I will accuse him, Gideon thought. Threaten him with exposure.

He locked eyes with Fish. He tried to decide how to frame his accusation. Gideon heard a clock ticking somewhere in the room. He continued to stare. Fish blinked and lowered his eyes.

Gideon turned and went out, leaving the door open behind him.

Ranaway, Bill—has a scar over one eye, also one on his leg, from *the bite of a dog*—has a *burn on his buttock, from a piece of hot iron in the shape of a T*.

Chapter 37

⟨⟩

H E STALKED DOWN THE HILL. FISH HATED HIM AND WOULD RATHER insult him than make any attempt to work with him. He hated the Cold Fish right back.

He tried to tamp down his anger, knowing it wouldn't help him think. He needed to keep collecting facts, continue building a picture of what might have happened, both to Potter and the missing people. At some point, maybe all the bits and pieces of information would fall into place. Although what he had found so far was pretty thin stuff, mostly hearsay and rumors and questionable connections, like True's meeting a big ugly woman with a black horse.

No wonder Fish had been unimpressed. Still, Gideon couldn't forgive the state's attorney's spite.

At the sawmill, Hack Latimer was out in the yard standing among stacks of lumber and writing in a small book.

Gideon came up on him from behind. "Mr. Latimer?"

Latimer spun around.

Deep-set eyes, hidden in shadow. Gideon saw those eyes widen. They lowered from Gideon's own eyes to the kerchief around his neck, then rose up again.

"Were you in Hammertown on Saturday night?" Gideon asked.

Latimer took the pencil he'd been using and, with his right hand, stuck it up between his temple and his hatband, where it lodged in place.

Gideon studied Latimer's hand. The knuckles appeared unmarked. Still, they might not have been bruised or scraped if the hand, balled into a fist and maybe even wearing a glove, had been driven into someone's unprotected belly again and again.

He waited for an answer. If Latimer lied about being in Hammertown, it could mean he'd been one of Gideon's assailants.

"Yes, I was there."

"Drinking, gambling . . . ?"

Latimer shrugged. "Both legal pastimes, last I checked."

"You told me earlier that you had stopped drinking."

A rueful expression. "The spirit is willing, but the flesh is weak."

"I saw you going into the Broad Ax. Did you meet anyone there?"

"No one in particular."

"Did you visit any other establishments?"

"One or two."

"How about Annie Picard's house?"

"No, sir. Not there."

"Did you get into any fights?"

Latimer smiled. "I gave up on the rough-and-tumble years ago."

Gideon changed his line of inquiry. "You belong to the anti-slavery society. Were you aware that two fugitives, a father and son, were working for a couple named Olcott near Frogville?"

The smile left Latimer's face. "Yes. And if you know, too, that means there are some loose lips in the society. It's not something the law should know about—unless, Sheriff, you are sympathetic to the cause and want to help fugitives get to freedom."

"Did you know that the father and son have both gone missing?"

Latimer looked surprised. "I hadn't heard that. Maybe they went on north." He indicated the stacked lumber. "I should finish tallying these boards."

"One more question. Do you know a woman named Liza Brodie?"

Gideon thought he saw Latimer's eyes narrow slightly and their pupils contract. But with Latimer's hat brim shading his face, Gideon couldn't be sure.

The sawmill man shook his head. "I can't place the name."

"What about a tavern called Bodines? In Potlicker Flats."

"I've been there a time or two."

"I understand this Liza Brodie works there."

"Then I never met her. Or if I did, I never got her name. Why are you looking for this woman?"

"Just part of my investigation."

Latimer extracted the pencil from between his hatband and the side of his head. "I hear Mel Dorfman is a suspect in Potter's killing."

"You hear wrong."

Latimer twirled the pencil with his fingers. "These disappearances, kidnappings, maybe. In the cities it's often the coloreds who do the dirty work. Hired by whites. A colored fellow comes in from outside and makes friends with the local negroes. He gets them liquored up, or drugs them, lures them to a place where they can be caught. Then they're taken south and sold." He shook his head. "I don't reckon Mel would do a wicked thing like that. But maybe someone else."

"Do you have anyone in mind?"

"I heard that a fellow from Philadelphia might be up to such tricks. He was at Annie Picard's for a while. Felix Wiley is his name. Could be he's the one behind those disappearances."

"Where did you hear that?"

"In Hammertown. Though I can't recall who told me."

"Thanks for the information. I will leave you to your work."

Latimer nodded and returned to tallying.

★★★

As Maude ambled west in her easy traveling gait, Gideon wondered if the mixed-race man Felix Wiley could be involved in a kidnapping racket. It might be the truth. Or another rumor. Or skillful misdirection on Hack Latimer's part. He found it hard to read the sawmill man, and, like True, he didn't trust him.

A big black-and-white woodpecker banged out a tattoo against a hollow tree. Small birds flitted in the shadows like barely apprehended thoughts. Once Maude startled at a loud rustling sound and a fleeing blur—hogs, put out in the woods to forage and gone wild.

At the place where Phineas Potter was killed, Gideon stopped. He sat, feeling Maude breathing in and out beneath him, and let his unfocused vision play back and forth over the land. Could he feel a ghostly presence in this place where a person had been brutally killed? His thoughts flew back to his family's farmhouse. Sometimes he had felt it there: the sense of a lingering spirit, coupled with a feeling of guilt because he had not been able to save his mother, and because he himself still lived.

Nothing seemed to talk to him at the murder site. The day was slipping past, so he clucked to Maude and rode on.

They passed a new-plowed field, the soil glistening in the sun and giving off a rich earthy scent. The road dipped into a swale. He entered the forest gloom and found what might be the low damp area where True said she'd encountered the big woman. No one was present—not that he'd expected to find anyone there.

A mile farther along, two men were chopping down trees near a recently built cabin. They were new to Colerain County and didn't know anyone named Brodie. They directed Gideon to a crossroads store and postal station another mile west.

The road went up a slight grade and entered into light again, an expanse of cleared land where newly sown timothy grass sprouted among the stumps.

The sun, red and slightly flattened, lowered in the west. Gideon looked across the roll of the Barrens. A pale blue ridge extended along the southern horizon five miles off, floating above a layer of haze or smoke: Tussey Mountain, the first in the complex of ridges known as the Seven Mountains. The breeze brought the smell of burning vegetation.

At the crossroads store he wrapped Maude's reins around a rail and went inside. The store was well-stocked: sacks of coffee, tea, sugar, salt, barrels of molasses and flour. Eggs, firkins of butter, and hanging joints of meat suggested that local people traded there for credit.

Behind the counter stood a balding man in his middle years with a long scrawny neck above a high collar. Gideon gave the man his name and said he was the county sheriff.

"Stoltz!" The storekeeper's squawky voice made the name sound like a bird's cry. "I heard a Dutchman got made sheriff over us. Now in the door he comes."

"Not 'made sheriff,'" Gideon said. "Elected. Last fall."

"Elected, then." The man stuck out his hand. "Andrew McGurk. You just walked into McGurk's Store. Been here going on fifty years."

"Maybe you can help me. I am looking for a farm owned by people named Brodie. Do you know of it?"

The storekeeper went to the door and pointed. "Thataway. South. The old Brodie place. I can't tell you exactly where it's at, but my pa will know."

"May I speak with him?"

"Sure. You gotta watch out, though." Without further explanation, McGurk took off his apron. "I may as well close for the day. You'll be needing a place to stay; you don't want to be out in the Barrens at night. A pallet and blankets do you all right? Now put your horse away. Oats and hay in the barn. Then come around to the house."

When Gideon entered the storekeeper's home, he smelled food cooking and realized how hungry he was.

"Set yourself down," McGurk instructed. A bossy fellow. But the blessing he gave was short, and the food good and plentiful: pork, cornmeal mush, and pickles, served by McGurk's plump wife. While Gideon and McGurk supped, she prepared a plate of food and took it out of the room.

Gideon asked McGurk if he had heard anything about Phineas Potter's death.

"Only that he got run over on the road and brained with a rock. Do you know who did it?"

"Not yet. What can you tell me about the Brodies?"

"They left here, must be forty years ago, 'round the time I was born. They lived on droughty land not much good for farming, like most of the Barrens. Or the Plains, as some call it."

"I smelled smoke out there," Gideon said. "It seemed to be coming from that direction."

"People set fires in the Barrens every spring. Makes the blueberry bushes put out more berries the year following. When it's dry like this, if a wind springs up those fires can burn for miles."

"Where did the Brodies go when they left?"

"They went west; Ohio, I think. Outrunning their debts. I will take you to see my pa directly. He's dying. Been dying for a good six months. I wish he'd get it over with, and I reckon he wishes the same."

Presently McGurk led Gideon down a hallway. They entered a room with a bed and its occupant, a washstand, a chair with a hole in its seat and a slop jar underneath. The odor was bad. McGurk's wife had just finished feeding the old man. She mopped his loose pink mouth with a cloth and left.

McGurk addressed his father in a loud voice. "This is the sheriff! Fellow name of Stoltz! He wants to know about the Brodies! I told him you know where their farm is at!"

The old man's milky eyes searched for Gideon. His toothless gums wobbled. Gideon got closer and leaned in to hear. The man shot out his hand, grabbed the back of Gideon's arm, and pinched the flesh hard through the shirtsleeve.

"*Oii!*" Gideon blurted. He pulled back and shot a reproachful glance at the son.

"I told you, gotta watch out for him," the storekeeper said.

"Brodies," the dying man said in a crowing voice. "You run into them briar-hoppers, tell 'em to pay up. Twelve dollars and thirty-two cents they owe me."

Gideon rubbed his arm. "Where do they live?"

"Who?"

"The Brodies!" the younger McGurk said.

"Oh, them. Take the Tar Kiln road south. Go a couple of miles. You will come to a big ledge of rocks on the left. Carry on another three, four furlongs till you get to a big pine. Stands there all by itself, unless someone chopped it down or it got burned up or shivered by lightning. I ain't been down that road in years.

"What do you want with the Brodies?" the old man demanded. "They were bad, every one of them. The pa, he was big and quick with his fists. He terrorized a lot of folks for years. Then he died. Under suspicious circumstances. The old woman and her boys pulled up stakes and went west."

"Your son said they left here forty years ago," Gideon said.

"Who?"

"The Brodies!" the junior McGurk yelled again.

"Yep. So they did."

"I am looking for a woman named Liza Brodie," Gideon said. "Forty years ago she would have been a girl."

The cloudy eyes blinked. "Little Liza. They'd come to the store, and her pa would tie a rope around her neck and snub t'other end to a tree so she wouldn't wander off. She'd set there in the dirt and sing. Hymns, I suspect, though you could hardly make out a word from all the gibberish."

"Do you know what became of her?"

"She grew up. Turned into a wanton jezebel. I think her ma sold her down Greer County way."

Gideon sighed. He looked at the younger McGurk. "Have you seen a big woman around here lately? A big tall woman with frizzy hair?"

"No one like that."

"How about a short man with somewhat dark or olive-colored skin and a hooked nose?"

"That one I have seen. Came in the store two weeks ago, him and another jasper. They bought a good deal of food and drink. Cleaned me out of applejack."

"Did they tell you their names?"

"They did not."

"Did you see which way they went when they left?"

"They had a wagon. They took the Tar Kiln road headed south."

"They owe me," the old man cried, suddenly sitting up in bed. "The Brodies, the damn Brodies, they never pay their debts." He turned his skull-like face and milky eyes toward Gideon. "You collect that twelve dollars and thirty-two cents, and I will give you half. No banknotes, mind. Silver and gold."

Gideon promised he would try.

Stolen, a negro man named Winter—has a *notch* cut out of the left ear, and the mark of *four or five buck shot* on his legs.

Chapter 38

⸺⸺∞⸺⸺

A SOUND JARRED GIDEON AWAKE. IT TOOK HIM A WHILE TO remember where he was, in a house on the edge of the Barrens.

He lay in the dark listening. A sharp wail broke the stillness: the old man dying in the room down the hall. Gideon heard someone go clumping across the floor, then low voices.

He changed position. The hay or straw or whatever had been used to stuff the pallet was lumpy and smelled of mold.

His mind shifted, as it often did, to considerations of the evil that lurked all around.

Phineas Potter had fought evil by helping fugitives gain their freedom. But it had crushed him, in the form of a wagon pulled by galloping horses driven by some uncaring soul.

The people who'd been kidnapped: snared by evil.

Tazewell Waller, in his single-minded pursuit, driven to commit the evil act of carrying his own son back into bondage.

It seemed that Liza Brodie had been formed by evil and might now be serving as its instrument.

Gideon knew he wouldn't get back to sleep. He rose, dressed in the dark, and left money on the kitchen table.

He saddled Maude in the light of a quarter moon and rode her south on the Tar Kiln road.

So much had happened lately that he could barely organize all the events in his mind. At the moment, one thing stood out: the slave hunter Franklin Blaine saying of Otis, "I heard him jump off the roof of a house we were watching." The Virginian had grabbed Otis and gotten his arm sliced. That was a week ago, right around the time when Gideon had run into Waller and Blaine on the street near the Cold Fish's house. Waller had said they suspected someone in that high-toned neighborhood of hiding fugitive slaves.

Otis had talked about the "big fancy house" not far from the courthouse, where he'd been stashed in an upstairs room, and kept waiting, uninformed about how the people in that house might help him.

Gideon recalled how nervous Fish had been the night Gideon showed up unexpectedly to inform him of Potter's death. When he answered the door, the state's attorney had held a pistol in his hand. Otis could have been in an attic room in Fish's house then. Later, with Fish so shattered by the death of Phineas Potter, the state's attorney might have left the lad ignored.

Could Fish be illegally harboring fugitives?

Potter did it; maybe the two of them were in it together.

Was the Cold Fish kinder and more humane than Gideon had ever imagined?

He startled at a raspy screeching bark. He knew it for a fox, but the sound still raised the hairs on the back of his neck.

The sky glowed faintly in the east. The sinking moon gradually became pallid, and the blue dome of the sky clarified overhead. The beauty of the dawn almost persuaded Gideon that he was on a pleasure jaunt and not a mission in search of evil.

He had come armed with a pistol, a carbine, a knife sheathed in his boot, and a club sticking out of a saddlebag.

He passed the rock formation the old man had mentioned: twenty feet tall, blotched with moss and scabbed with dull green lichen. When he arrived at the tall pine, the rising sun cast an orange light on the tree's green crown.

Across the road, a narrow track led west. Hoof prints and the parallel lines of wagon wheels marked its surface.

It would be the height of stupidity to ride brazenly down the track and blunder into a dangerous situation. He could ride back to

Adamant and organize a posse, then return tomorrow. Or he could sneak ahead on foot, make sure this road led to the Brodie place, and try to learn if captives were being held there. It would help him know the lay of the land, and what they'd be facing if he came back with a posse.

He dismounted and led Maude off the road through patchy woods. In a grassy glade, he hobbled the mare.

He slipped the carbine out of its scabbard and checked the pistol in his belt. He picked his way back through the scrub toward the offshoot road until he spotted the narrow track; he turned and went parallel to it, headed west, twenty paces off to the side, avoiding twigs that might snap and treading quietly on patches of moss and rotten leaves.

Through the trees he glimpsed a small, weather-beaten house. He worked his way closer and stopped fifty yards off.

Smoke curled from the house's chimney. Nearby stood a log corncrib and a dilapidated barn. A wagon with its tongue resting on the ground.

Beyond the corncrib the land dropped off gradually. Gideon made out a horse's upraised head and the dark horizontal line of its back: a black horse, staring at him, its ears pricked. Another horse, a gray, walked out from where it had been standing behind the black. It stared at him, too.

Slowly he lowered himself down behind a clump of shrubs. His nerves were on edge. He was all set to run if the horses alerted anyone in the house. But after a while, they stopped paying attention to him.

A half hour passed. The horses wandered to an area where he couldn't see them. He sat with the carbine in his lap. He shifted forward onto his knees and straightened slightly to work a kink out of his back.

The farmhouse door opened, and Gideon eased himself back down. He got as low as he could behind the brush while staying able to see.

Out of the house stepped a big frizzy-haired woman in a striped dress, holding a double-barreled shotgun. The woman looked all around. She turned back to the house and motioned with the gun's barrels.

People came out through the doorway: a young woman and a man, a man and a boy, and a man in a blue uniform coat, chained together in a line. Behind the captives came the hook-nosed man, William Jewell Jarrett. And then his partner, the Tattered Man. Both men had pistols in their hands.

During the next few minutes, Gideon watched as the captives were obliged to expose themselves and urinate and defecate on the ground. In their humiliation, Gideon thought they must feel like animals under their captors' gaze.

The captives filed into the corncrib. The Tattered Man secured the door with a padlock, then he, Brodie, and Jarrett headed back to the house. They went inside and shut the door.

It didn't look like they were preparing to take their captives south anytime soon. Gideon could ride back to Adamant, raise a posse, return tomorrow, and free the people and arrest the kidnappers.

A blow between his shoulder blades drove him into the ground. He landed face down on top of the carbine. A knee dug painfully into his spine.

Something hard pressed against the back of his head.

"Move a muscle and I blow your brains out."

The man hallooed. There came an answering call. A moment later, footfalls approached from behind.

"Well, holy hell," a second voice said. "Look what you caught, Bill."

The man holding the pistol against Gideon's skull said: "Put your hands behind your back."

Gideon did so, and the second man tied his hands together, cinching the rope tight around his wrists.

A few seconds later a hard blow smashed into his side. The kick knocked the air out of his lungs. He lay writhing and gasping on the ground. The boot nudged his shoulder, turned him over. He looked up at Jarrett and the Tattered Man.

Jarrett's hand moved to his belt, then darted toward Gideon's face. Gideon recoiled as the blade slashed his cheek. Hot blood spurted.

The Tattered Man laid a hand on his partner's arm. "Hold off on that, Billy Boy."

"Why? He ain't leaving here alive."

"Let the big boss decide how to settle his hash." The Tattered Man grinned, showing broken brown teeth. "Maybe hang him nice and slow. Or shoot him in the guts. Or drownd him."

"I don't see no crick or pond, Gullie," Jarrett said.

"Watering trough!" The Tattered Man let out a whinnying laugh.

Jarrett suddenly crouched and thrust with the knife again. Gideon tried to roll away. The blade blurred past his face. Jarrett laughed and straightened. "You are a dead man," he said.

They got him to his feet. The Tattered Man picked up the carbine. Jarrett took the pistol from Gideon's belt and tucked it into his own belt. Then he reached down and got the knife from Gideon's boot. He used its tip to prick Gideon in the side. When Gideon shrank away, Jarrett laughed.

"You ain't so smart," the Tattered Man said. "We seen the light flash off your gun. Billy here, he out the back door and circled around behind you. You were easy to catch."

Gideon felt blood running down his face. It dripped onto his shirt. In his ribs, pain throbbed where he'd been kicked.

They marched him to where the captives had relieved themselves earlier, then pushed him down to his knees. Out of the house came the big woman. She hustled up to him, thumbed back the hammers of the shotgun, and pointed the weapon at his face.

"Who are you?" she yelled.

He felt himself shaking all over.

"Start talking," Jarrett said. He brandished his knife.

"Stoltz, Gideon Stoltz. I am the county sheriff."

The big woman snugged her cheek against the shotgun's stock. Her eyes like small dry pebbles. Her right eye stared down the rib between the two barrels.

Gideon shut his own eyes. He would never see True again.

But no shot came, no sudden crashing blow extinguished his senses. He opened his eyes. The woman had lowered the shotgun. Had the fact that he was a sheriff kept her from pulling the trigger?

"You dumb Dutch bastard," Jarrett said. "I seen you in the Broad Ax with your fat-ass deputy. Didn't know who I was, did you? No, and I didn't know you then, either. Look here, Gully. He's the one we damn near got in the Seven Mountains a few years back."

"And they went and made him sheriff." Luck gave his whinnying laugh again. "I guess no one else wanted the job."

"We had you at a stand that time, till you bust out with your horse," Jarrett said. He looked around. "Where's your horse at?"

Gideon didn't answer.

The Tattered Man kicked him in the stomach. Fire exploded in his gut as he fell onto his side. "That's for thumping me that time in the Seven Mountains," the man said. He reached down and grabbed the kerchief covering the wounds on Gideon's neck. He wrenched it back and forth, then slung Gideon back down.

Gideon tried to ignore the pain. His mind whirled. If they found Maude's tracks, they could figure out where he had left her. But he would not tell them where she was, not even if he had to die here and now. Lying helpless on the ground, he tried to keep alive a hope that somehow he could get free, reach Maude, and flee.

Tears ran down his face, making the gash in his cheek sting. He didn't want to weep, but he couldn't help it. The tears were for True, for his *memmi,* for all the cruelties people visited on one another, the misery they forced others to bear. He felt detached from the act of shedding tears in front of these hard men, the big woman, the people in the crib.

Jarrett, the Tattered Man, and Brodie walked away like he was a pile of trash.

Ran away, the mulatto boy Quash—considerably marked on
the back and other places with the lash.

Chapter 39

⊸⧟⊷

TRUE FILLED TWO PLATES WITH FRIED MUSH AND EGGS AND BACON
and toasted bread, set the plates on the table, and sat down
across from Otis. The lad tied into his breakfast. He must be a healthy
young man, she thought, for her potion to have cured him that fast.

She welcomed a conversation but didn't know how to start one.
She had never talked with a black person before in her life.

When Otis finally slowed down with knife and fork, he said:
"Where did he go?"

"Gideon? He went looking for some people."

"Who?"

"Bad people."

"Won't have to look far to find folks like that."

"He's also searching for some people he thinks were kidnapped.
To be taken south and sold into slavery. It's against the law in
Pennsylvania."

"What will he do with me?"

"I guess that depends on what *you* want to do."

Otis returned to his meal, finishing the food and scraping the
plate clean.

"Ma'am," he said, "I have been running for a long time."

"So I've heard."

"I'm not being saucy, ma'am. You have helped me. Gideon has
helped me. But I want to be with other people like me. Colored
people."

True thought for a bit. "You might be less likely to get noticed
that way."

"Waller, he's here. The one who owned me."

She saw how the fear tightened the lad's face and made his narrow shoulders clench.

"They almost caught me, ma'am. They might get me the next time."

She rose and put more food on his plate. "Call me True," she said. "That's my name. You call me True, and I'll call you Otis."

"All right, ma'am. True. That's a name I never heard before."

"I don't know anyone else with that name, either. But I like it. It's a sight better than, oh, Jehoshaphat, wouldn't you say?"

Otis grinned, then went back to eating.

"Gideon says you are from Virginia, Otis," True said.

"Yes'm. True."

"Where are you going?"

"North. Maybe Canada. They can't get you once you cross that line."

"I hope you make it. Meantime, you must stay hidden."

"You mean, stay inside the house."

"For the time being, yes. I'll be honest, I don't know how safe you are here. That deputy last night, the one who was drunk, he could have seen you, though I don't think he did. And there's a regular busybody lives next door, always sticking her nose over the fence." True paused. "I know of a man and woman who might take you in. The man is a tinsmith. The woman is a teacher. They have two boys about your age."

"Colored folks?"

"Yes."

"When can I go there?"

"I could talk to the woman later today. But now I need to go get water."

"Can that dog come inside?"

"Of course."

When she went out she looked all around, trying not to be conspicuous about it, and could see no one watching the house. She let Old Dick off his chain and brought him inside. Otis got down on the floor and petted the red setter and made a fuss over him; Old Dick lashed his tail and licked the boy's face. True got Otis to promise that he would bar the door, and she went out again.

She carried a bucket in each hand. She wished Gideon were here; she would rather he made the decision to move Otis.

Maybe the Dorfmans would take him. True had never met Sarah Dorfman, had only seen her on the street. She knew she would be taking a chance by moving Otis, but she had a bad feeling about keeping him at their house—a jangly persistent feeling that he was in danger.

She had a bad feeling about Gideon, too. Was it the second sight? She couldn't picture where her husband was at that moment, but she had the strong sense that it was a bad place.

She was relieved to find no one else at the well. She sent the bucket down and cranked it back up and poured water into her own buckets. She did this three times. When her buckets were full, she leaned over the stone housing and looked down. The water shimmered twenty feet below. Gradually, it calmed. Its surface reflected the pale blur of her face. She thought in a general way about Gideon. She tried to open her mind, make it receptive to anything that might let itself be known. But nothing appeared.

She feared that someone had hurt him again. Then she feared anew for Otis, worrying that she shouldn't have left him alone.

She hurried back, the buckets knocking against her legs, water sloshing. She rapped on the door. She looked around. Nosy Tish was in her garden. Of course the old biddy could see her knocking on her own door and would know that someone else was inside the house.

Tish waved and called out: "Oh, True, honey!" True kept her head down and pretended she hadn't heard.

When the door opened, she hustled inside. She set the buckets down, slammed the door, and put the bar back in place.

She saw the fear freezing Otis's face.

Four hours later, standing on the Dorfmans' stoop, she tried to figure out what to say. Otis had asked her so many times through the morning and early afternoon that finally she had gone out again and walked up the hill to the tinner's house.

She cleared her throat, smoothed the front of her dress. Lifted her hand and knocked.

The woman who opened the door wore a calico dress like the one True had on. Graying hair showed beneath the woman's cap. She was shorter than True, and slight of build, but her stare and the way she held herself made True feel like Sarah Dorfman was the taller of the two women.

"Yes?"

"Mrs. Dorfman, I am True Stoltz. My husband is the sheriff, Gideon Stoltz. I need to talk to you."

Sarah Dorfman had wide-set eyes, high cheekbones, and a broad mouth. Some deep lines in that face. Her skin was a light tan color, scarcely darker than True's at summer's end. True found herself wondering if the woman thought of herself as colored, then realized it was unlikely that a single white person in Adamant thought of her as anything else.

Behind her a gaggle of dark faces peered out at the strange white woman standing on the stoop.

Sarah Dorfman spoke to one of the taller children. "Take them to the classroom. Have them work on their spelling."

True wished the woman would invite her inside. But that didn't happen. True looked around. She saw no one who might see or overhear. Though that didn't mean they weren't watching.

"There's this boy," she began, not really knowing what to say. "He ran north from Virginia. Gideon found him, down in Hammertown, hiding in an alley. He's at our house now. He goes by the name of Otis. He was sick, but he's better now, out of bed and his appetite is good. Gideon isn't here, he rode out yesterday doing his job as sheriff. And two men from Virginia are in town, hunting for Otis. They put up those posters with the big reward." She was unsure how to go on. Then spoke the plain truth: "I fear that they or someone else might take Otis out of our house."

"I see," Mrs. Dorfman said. "You are afraid that you and your husband will get found out for illegally harboring a runaway, and he'll lose his job."

True felt flummoxed. It wasn't what she'd meant at all. She felt her face burning.

"Mrs. Dorfman, one of my husband's deputies ran into us when we were taking Otis home last night. He might have seen him, I don't know if he did or not. And I have this nosy neighbor. I reckon she knows we've got someone in our house."

Sarah Dorfman crossed her arms.

"Can he come here?" True asked. "I could bring him after dark."

Sarah Dorfman shook her head. "You don't know a thing about us. You don't know what we might do with that boy. Maybe turn him in for the reward. Two hundred dollars would do us a lot of good."

"My husband trusts Mr. Dorfman."

"Trusts him?" Sarah Dorfman snorted. "Ma'am, you don't know what it's like to live in this place. Being afraid that your neighbors are planning to burn you out, or maybe make you crawl in the street, or that they'll snatch one of your children and sell them into slavery."

"Please," True said. "If you won't take him, maybe you know of some other family that will. Otis says he wants to be with his own people."

"You are asking too much." Sarah Dorfman glared at True.

True drew herself up. "I am afraid for that boy," she said fiercely.

For a while, neither woman spoke. Sarah Dorfman wagged her head. Her mouth twisted. True knew it wasn't a smile.

"I will ask my husband," the woman said. "I am not promising anything. If he decides we can help, we'll get word to you."

Was committed to jail, a negro boy—had on a large neck iron with a huge pair of horns and a large bar or band of iron on his left leg.

Chapter 40

⸺∞⸺

GIDEON CAME AWAKE AND SAW THE CORNCRIB LOOMING BEFORE him. Had he fainted? Slept? The sun was high in the sky, maybe even angling down toward the horizon.

He took a tentative breath and felt searing pain in his ribs. He hurt all over. The rope binding his wrists was tight. He twisted his hands one way and then the other, and the rope cut into his wrists.

At least they hadn't killed him. Yet. Maybe they were working themselves up to it now inside the house while tipping a jug. Jarrett's knife, a rope over a limb, a pistol ball through his guts? Fear washed over him, and he began to tremble. He almost wished the big woman had pulled the trigger this morning and ended it all in an instant.

He looked up. The sky was a deep blue, with small gauzy clouds sailing across it. He tried to let the fear drain out of him into the ground. He needed to think. This morning, right after they'd caught him, the Tattered Man had said something to Jarrett about a "big boss." Had he meant the big woman, Liza Brodie, or was someone else leading this kidnapping gang?

If the big boss wasn't here yet, and if they were waiting for that person to decide what should be done with him, then maybe he had some time left. Time to get free and escape.

"Looks like he woke up."

The voice came from the corncrib. A man's voice, high-pitched and whiny. "He doesn't look like a sheriff."

"He's young." This second voice deeper than the first.

Gideon's eyes caught a shadowy movement in a gap between two logs.

"If he is a sheriff, he ain't much good at it," the whiny voice said.

Gideon turned his head and looked at the house. The door was shut. Near it, a small dirty window. Anyone looking out that window could see him. He looked back at the corncrib. He didn't see a protruding nail or a jagged hunk of metal that he might use to saw through the rope binding his wrists. The crib's corner posts had been set on flat stones stacked from the ground up. Maybe he could fray the rope against one of the stones.

The stones didn't look like they had sharp edges.

"Sheriff." A woman's voice. He was certain it was Amanda Jones.

"Yes," Gideon answered.

"Can you get over here? There's some room between the logs in front of me. I could reach through and maybe untie you."

Gideon looked at the house again. All they could do was come out and kill him.

Slowly he rolled toward the corncrib.

"This way," she said.

"Mandy, don't." It was the first voice Gideon had heard, the whiny one. "They see you, those men will come out and hurt us."

"You think they didn't hurt me already?" the woman said.

Gideon rolled again. Tried not to think about what he might be rolling through. He bumped against the corncrib. He lay mostly on his back. Looking up, he saw the edge of the shake roof against the sky.

"Can you get up?" Amanda Jones said.

He struggled to a sitting position with his back against the wall.

"Higher. About halfway to standing."

"Mandy, you'll get us in trouble," the whiny voice said.

"I got to try this. Or they will take us south. And I'll never get home again."

Gideon braced his feet on the ground and pushed upward, his back scraping against the logs.

"That's good. Now move your hands a bit to your left."

He did so. His calves and hamstrings strained. He felt her fingers touch the back of one of his hands, then move quickly to the knot.

"Mandy, I will holler," the whiny voice said. "I don't want them finding out we helped him and then beating on us."

"Felix, you want to get beat on out in a cotton field?" Amanda Jones gave an exasperated huff. "This rope is tight."

"I said I'll holler!"

Then the deeper voice Gideon had heard earlier: "You do that, I will kill you. I will kill you some night when they are taking us south."

Silence.

Amanda Jones's fingers kept working.

Gideon looked at the house. The dirty window. The plank door still shut.

A minute passed. The backs of his legs started cramping. He tried to breathe easy, relax his legs and shoulders and back.

He felt the rope slacken.

"Got it," Amanda Jones said.

He slumped to a sitting position, the rope loose around his wrists. Tried to move his fingers, but they were numb. He separated his hands and brought them into his lap and got the rope all the way off.

He was free.

He could run, if his legs cooperated. Though maybe that wouldn't be the smart thing to do. He flexed his hands and worked some feeling back into his fingers. Stretched out his legs, reached down and kneaded the backs of his thighs. Thinking.

He turned his head. "I'll come back for you. I promise."

He wound the rope around his hand: he wouldn't leave it near the crib to let Brodie and the two men know who'd freed him. And he thought of a way he could use it.

He got to his feet, his heart racing. He found his old battered hat and put it on his head. He willed himself not to go too fast.

Down the slope he went, to the dirt lot bounded by a stake-and-rider fence. Inside the fence were a tall mule, which he recognized as belonging to the Tattered Man from that encounter four years ago in the Seven Mountains; a gray, Jarrett's mount; two strong-looking bays, which must be the wagon horses; and a black gelding with two white feet on the left and a white star on his forehead: Potter's gelding Barney.

Carefully he removed the lower rails from between a pair of uprights and set them aside. He slipped in under the top rail. He murmured to the horses and the mule. They were not skittish. He went up to Barney and quietly spoke his name, stroked his neck for a while and then gently snugged the rope around it near his withers. He took both ends in one hand.

Using the rope, he led Barney to the spot where he had taken down the rails. With his free hand, he eased the remaining rail out and set it to one side. Still holding onto the rope, he guided Barney back into the lot. He moved the black gelding around behind the other horses and the mule. He made a clucking sound.

The gray walked out of the lot and started grazing.

Gideon took hold of Barney's mane, made a little jump, and hauled himself up onto the gelding's back. Pain bloomed in his ribs but he ignored it. He got properly astride Barney and felt the horse elevate beneath him at having someone strange on his bare back, and then he sensed the horse getting charged up as the two big bays ambled out through the opening in the fence. Gideon slipped the rope free from Barney's neck and coiled it loosely in one hand while gripping Barney's mane with his other hand. He clasped his legs around the horse's barrel and used them and the turning of his hips to point the gelding toward the back end of the laggard mule, and he walked Barney forward, chivying the mule out through the gap in the fence.

He rode through the gap and aimed the gelding between the corncrib and the house. He took the looped rope, leaned over, and slapped it down on the mule's rump. The mule snorted and bolted and Barney surged ahead as the mule and the horses all scattered.

The door to the house flew open, and the Tattered Man came rushing out. Gideon was glad that it was not Liza Brodie with her pebble eyes and her scattergun. He drove Barney at the Tattered Man, who threw himself backward.

Barney dug in with his hooves and got up on the offshoot road. Gideon turned him east and galloped.

Ran away, negro Ben, has a scar on his right hand, his thumb and fore finger being injured by being *shot* last fall, a part of *the bone came out*, he also has one or two *large scars* on his back and hips.

Chapter 41

———— ⚬◆⚬ ————

G IDEON RODE MAUDE STRAIGHT TO ADAMANT. HE HAD NO SPARE bridle or halter for Barney, and the rope that had bound his hands was too short to secure the gelding, but the horse followed anyway.

At nightfall, when Gideon reached the boardinghouse where Alonzo lived, he wanted to get hold of Barney but the gelding was already trotting off, headed for Ike Fye's farm.

When Gideon got down off Maude, his legs felt dead. He wanted to go home, but he needed to set things in motion first. He rapped on the boardinghouse door. The woman who answered recoiled— from the blood all over his face and shirt, he knew. He got Alonzo out on the porch and told his deputy that he had found the old Brodie place, with the five people held captive there. The kidnappers, four of them, knew he was aware of their activities and likely would depart with their captives soon.

"Take Maude to the livery. Get me a fresh horse. That chestnut I sometimes ride."

"This is not something we can do by ourselves," Alonzo said.

"No. We need more men. Get Gaither. And some others."

They went over names and came up with eight: all capable riders with good horses and guns. "We'll meet at the jail at midnight," Gideon said. "I will deputize everyone then."

"What the devil happened out there?"

"I'll tell you later."

He set off for home, walking as fast as his bruised body allowed. He wanted to eat some food, get cleaned up, maybe lie down and rest. He tried to ignore the weariness and pain. In a few hours he would have to get back on a horse and do it all again.

The door to his house was barred. He knocked and called out: "True, it's me."

She let him in. Otis was wearing the old coat True had given him, and True held the detonator in her hand.

"What's going on?" Gideon asked.

She put the weapon on the table. "Thank heavens it's you." She took him by the shoulders, looked at his face. "You're hurt bad."

"Not too bad."

"Get your shirt off," True said to her husband, "and sit down in that chair. Otis, build up the fire and put some water on." She fetched soap and clean rags. She laid her hand on Gideon's jaw, turned his face and studied the wound in the candlelight.

Gideon explained that he had found the Brodie homestead and verified that a gang was holding the five people who had disappeared; he identified the kidnappers as Liza Brodie, William Jewell Jarrett, the scoundrel he knew as the Tattered Man, and someone they called "the big boss," whom he had not seen.

"Which one cut you?"

"Jarrett."

"That knife almost took out your eye."

As she cleaned the wound, True told Gideon how worried she had been, about him and whether someone had learned that Otis was hiding in their house and passed that information on to Waller and Blaine. She said that Melchior and Sarah Dorfman had sent one of their sons saying they would take him. "He'll be safer there," she said. "And he wants to go."

She cleaned off Gideon's face and neck. "Lean your head back." To Otis: "Bring the candle closer." True cleaned the knife wound with soap and water, then dribbled whiskey into it.

Gideon clenched his jaw. True blotted up fresh blood with a clean cloth and dabbed the gash with a salve she used whenever she or Gideon cut themselves. Then she held the tip of a needle in the fire and threaded a whiskey-soaked thread through its eye. She sewed the wound shut, biting off the thread after each stitch. "You will carry a scar."

Putting on a clean shirt, Gideon told True about his plan to return to the Brodie homestead with a posse and rescue the captives before the gang left.

"I'm going with you," she said.

"No."

"You take him to the Dorfmans." She jerked her chin toward Otis. "I'm off to the livery to get Jack."

"I forbid it."

"Listen to me. You say Alonzo is putting a posse together. First of all, Gaither Brown is worthless. Those men you named? You think they'll risk their lives for colored people?" She glanced at Otis, then back at Gideon. "You need me. I can ride, and I can shoot."

She went into the bedroom. When she came out three minutes later she had on her old trousers and shirt. She put on a coat and settled her grandfather's slightly oversized hat on her head. She picked up the detonator. "I'll meet you here or at the Dorfmans' or in between. Be careful taking Otis there. Someone may be lying in wait."

"I don't have a gun." Gideon looked down. "They took mine."

True handed him the detonator, then unbarred the door and went out.

★★★

Gideon and Otis climbed the hill. Gideon kept his hand on True's gun in his pocket as he scanned the houses and the empty lots in between.

Otis stayed close. "I want to go along with you all," he said.

"You can stay with the Dorfmans. They'll take care of you."

"Take me with you. I can help." Otis was puzzled at this new way of thinking: courting danger to help someone else. His habit had been to look out for himself and no one else.

Striding along, Gideon considered how the villains must now be feverishly preparing to leave with their captives. If the posse got there after they departed, they would pursue them: the wagon would be slow and probably could be overtaken. Assuming they could figure out which way it went. No, much better to get to the farm before the wagon left.

They came to the Dorfmans' house. Melchior opened the door at Gideon's knock. He gestured for Otis and Gideon to step inside. Sarah Dorfman stood nearby, as did a younger man: Gideon recognized the freighter Chalmers Smythe.

"Thank you for agreeing to take Otis," Gideon said to Dorfman. "I will leave him with you now."

"What happened to your face?" Dorfman asked.

"I found out where those people are being held. One of the kidnappers did it."

"Where are they?"

"West of here, on an old farm. Your friend John Horne is there, and four others." Gideon turned toward the door. "I need to go. I have a posse to swear in."

"I'll go with you," Dorfman said.

"No," Sarah Dorfman said. "The sheriff has his own men."

"Sarah, those people need help. I must go." Dorfman looked at Gideon. "That is, if the sheriff of Colerain County will allow a colored man to do his part as a citizen."

"Count me in, too," Chalmers Smythe said.

Gideon remembered Dorfman saying that the colored men in town had formed a vigilance committee, that they had guns and knew how to use them. He weighed what True had said: Alonzo would be hard-pressed to recruit very many men to the posse. If the kidnappers were confronted by a large group of armed men—and, well, one woman, because he didn't know how he could keep that wife of his from going, too—then maybe they would lay down their guns. If not, more weapons on the side of the law would be an undeniable advantage.

Sarah Dorfman took her husband's arm. "Melchior. Think of your sons. Think of me. How would I manage . . ." Dorfman gently removed his wife's hand and took both her hands in his. He looked at her for a long moment, then kissed her hands and kissed her gently on the lips. He let go and turned to Gideon.

"We are meeting at the jail at midnight," Gideon said. "I welcome your help."

"I want to go, too," Otis said. "I can ride. I can hold horses for you."

Smythe looked Otis up and down. "He's a jockey, this one, I'd swear it. I can get you a mount, young fella. Sheriff?"

Gideon knew that if Otis went with them, all the posse members would then know of his presence. But if he left the boy here without Melchior Dorfman to protect him, and if Waller and Blaine found out . . .

"Let me go with you," Otis said again.

On impulse, Gideon nodded.

Ran away, George, he has a *sword cut* lately received on his left arm.

Chapter 42

———◆◆◆———

THEY WALKED THEIR HORSES WEST UNDER STARS IN THE SKY LIKE chips of old ice, their brilliance washed out by the moon.

At the jail, Gideon had been disheartened: other than Gaither Brown, Alonzo had recruited exactly one man.

Posse comitatus. Sheriff Payton had told him it was Latin for "the power of the county." It signified the body of men a sheriff could call into service to aid and support him in executing the law. In theory, Gideon could have drafted any adult male, handed him a gun, put him on a horse, and said, "You are a deputy, follow me." In practice, he could no more make a man ride out armed and risk his life than he could cause a pig to fly.

Gideon and Alonzo rode in front. Then Gaither Brown, and beside him the sole white male volunteer, a pudgy man in his twenties named Avery Dotson. Dotson clerked in a hardware store. He belonged to the Adamant Guards, a semi-organized troop of a couple dozen men who got together to smoke and tipple and play cards and occasionally sharpen their eyes and test their firearms by shooting mark. As Alonzo had reported quietly to Gideon, everyone else he asked had flatly refused.

Behind Brown and Dotson rode True Burns Stoltz on the gelding Jack. With her slim build and in her present masculine garb, she would not be identified as a female by any but the most discerning eye.

Next to True rode Otis Johnson, and behind them were Melchior Dorfman and Chalmers Smythe.

Gideon glanced at Dotson. The man had looked jittery from the moment he arrived at the jail and didn't see any of his friends. His apprehension had increased steadily. Dotson communicated his fearfulness to his horse, which had spooked several times, with Dotson hauling inexpertly on the reins before finally getting the horse back under control and pointed in the right direction.

Gideon let out a long breath and looked ahead at the shadowy road. In his lap he cradled a rifle, and in his belt was a pistol.

He kept wondering who the fourth kidnapper, the one in charge of the gang, would be. He thought it was probably Hack Latimer, with his many debts and his Southern connections. But he was far from certain.

He had come up with a plan. Not much of a plan, he had to admit to himself. He was banking on the kidnappers not having left the farm yet. They would have needed to round up the horses he scattered yesterday. And the Tattered Man had talked about having to consult with the "big boss"; if that was Latimer, the Tattered Man or Jarrett would have had to ride to Adamant to fetch him and then ride back to the Brodie place.

Gideon believed the offshoot road extended no farther west than the old farm, so when the gang departed they would have to drive their wagon east before turning onto the Tar Kiln road. Gideon decided that if they did not meet the kidnappers on the way, or see fresh wagon tracks, the posse would stop at the rock formation where the offshoot road branched off. There they would dismount and leave Otis with the horses. The party would continue on foot to the Brodie farm, where he hoped to catch the kidnappers by surprise.

★★★

True watched Gaither Brown. The man kept getting out a flask and raising it to his lips. Some of his remarks, directed at Avery Dotson, came back to her: "You tell me why I should . . . county don't pay me enough . . . he can't make me do this, nobody can." Several times she came close to telling Gaither to shut his mouth and keep his bottle in his coat, but she knew he wouldn't attend to her remarks so she said nothing.

She listened to the night: The breeze quietly seething in the trees. Frogs in a distant pool calling like little stones chinked together. The deep booming hoots of a horned owl.

She felt the air cool on her face, heard saddle leather creaking and the footfalls and exhalations of the horses, smelled leaves moldering on the forest floor. She felt completely and vividly alive, even knowing she might be dead in a few hours. Anger flared in her breast toward the man who had cut Gideon. Anger at all of those people for what they had done and were still doing to the ones they'd abducted. She felt fear, too, thinking about the violent men and the big powerful woman with her mannish stare and her strange shimmery dress.

Off to the side in the scrub timber, something glowed like foxfire. True turned her head to look, and it vanished. When she directed her eyes forward again, she could detect the pale glow at the edge of her vision. It traveled with them, ghosting along just above the ground, in among the trees.

She knew what it was. Last summer, riding Jack to her gram's cabin in the Panther Valley, weak and sick in her soul, her mind barely able to hold on to reality, True had met another rider: a gaunt old man on a small horse. The man's hair the same pale gray as his mount. The man had stopped at a wide place in the road and let her ride up. He took off his hat and held it against his breast. His shirt pinned shut with the long straight needles off a thornbush. He looked into her eyes. His own eyes, pale as old denim, were whimsical and knowing. He said to her: "You are a wildwood flower. A precious bloom waiting to be plucked."

Later she'd asked her gram who the old man was. Gram Burns had replied in a vague way, saying only, "Everyone comes to know him by and by."

272 •• *Lay This Body Down*

She reckoned she was the only one in this ragtag posse who could see the pale rider accompanying them as they walked their horses steadily west on the Halfmoon Valley road. The only one who knew what he portended.

★★★

Otis did not much like the gelding the freighter Chalmers Smythe had given him. The horse, a sorrel, was not smooth in his movements; he threw in a little hitch with his right hind leg every now and then, probably from stiffness caused by an old injury. He was not a young horse, either, and was set in his ways, and so crooked from misusing himself that when Otis attempted to ride him straight the horse grumpily tried to get out of the containment of his rider's legs and reins, throwing his head around and crabbing sideways to avoid stepping under himself with that stiff right hind.

However, Otis could ride him. He could ride nearly anything if he needed to. Once he rode a goat through a thorn patch on a dare. He reckoned he could even ride a camel. He had seen a picture of one, a long-faced hairy thing on stilt legs with two hillocks on its back, its rider sitting on a little saddle between them. His mama showed him the picture in a book in the study in the big house.

He thought about Waller. Who, he reckoned, was his pa. Not that it made Otis want to be anywhere near him. If anything, it made him want to kill the man. For using his mama, for making her brain slide around like it was loose sometimes inside her head. For wanting to steal his own hard-won freedom and haul him back to Red Rose.

Otis remained surprised that he had volunteered to go with these people and help some folks he didn't know and hadn't met. He wondered how it would end. If it all went to hell, he planned to get on the fastest horse and gallop north, all the way to Canada this time.

★★★

The posse came to the crossroads, where McGurk's Store and house were dark.

Gaither Brown got down off his horse. He landed flat-footed and staggered a step or two. "I made up my mind. I will rest here for a while, and then I am headed back to town."

"You are a coward, Gaither Brown," True said. "A yellow-belly and a drunk."

"Sheriff, your wife speaks very impolite," Gaither said. "You should teach her a lesson."

"Get back on your horse, Gaither," Gideon said. Though he wondered what good the fool would be, inebriated as he was.

"You think I'm about to risk my neck for a bunch of darkies, you got another think coming," Gaither said.

Melchior Dorfman sat on his horse and looked down like thunder at Gaither Brown.

Chalmers Smythe spat on the ground.

"Gaither, I am done with you," Gideon said.

"I do not give a good god-damn," Gaither said.

Gideon desired to lift his rifle and bring its barrel down hard on Brown's head. Instead he looked at the other riders. "Let's go," he said. He turned Maude south on the Tar Kiln road.

After a while he looked back and saw that Avery Dotson was no longer with them.

Reducing the posse to four men, one half-grown boy, and a headstrong mettlesome woman.

Ranaway from the plantation of James Surgette, the following negroes, Randal, *has one ear cropped*, Bob, *has lost one eye*, Kentucky Tom, *has one jaw broken*.

Chapter 43

—∞∞∞—

THE STRENGTHENING DAWN SURPASSED THE SINKING MOON'S SHINE. A breeze rose in the north and gradually freshened. The posse, on foot, advanced west on the offshoot road. No new wagon tracks marked its surface.

With his concentration focused ahead—on what they would find at the old farm, and what they would do once they got there—Gideon was not aware of Otis Johnson following fifty paces behind. The boy had hobbled the horses, decided to come watch.

The road left the woods and entered a brushy field. Gideon's hands tightened on his rifle's stock. He glanced at True striding beside him. She looked his way, made brief eye contact, looked forward again.

The rising sun warmed their backs. Their shadows bobbed in front of them.

The road rounded a bend. Gideon saw the weathered house and the corncrib and the dilapidated barn and the wagon with the captives in it, all in sharp detail. Every board and bolt in the wagon, every buckle on the harness, the horses' pricked ears and raised heads and flared nostrils. The wide eyes of the boy staring out at them from the wagon bed.

The Tattered Man was bent over, harnessing the horses. William Jewell Jarrett stood off to one side with a pistol in each hand.

"Let's go," Gideon said.

They started jogging.

They got within range before Jarrett looked up, lifting an arm to block the low rays of the sun.

"You are under arrest!" Gideon shouted.

As planned, the posse spread out and leveled their guns.

Gideon did not see Liza Brodie or anyone who might be the big boss. Then Hack Latimer straightened up on the far side of the wagon with a pistol in his hand.

Liza Brodie ran out of the house carrying the shotgun.

"Put your guns down!" Gideon yelled.

Brodie thumbed back her shotgun's hammers and swept the buttstock to her shoulder. Before she could pull the trigger, Melchior Dorfman fired. His rifle's ball tore a furrow down her left arm and shattered her elbow. The impact knocked the woman sideways. As she fell, her shotgun's right barrel discharged with a loud *boom* and its heavy buckshot tore up the ground in front of the house.

Using his left forearm, Jarrett cocked the pistol in his right hand and aimed it. Gideon heard the *crack* and the ball screeching past his head. Another *crack* to his right from True's detonator, and Jarrett yelped and fell.

John Horne leaned out of the wagon, lowered his hands on both sides of Latimer's head, then crossed his hands and tightened the chain between them, jerking Latimer's head back. Latimer reached up with his free hand and clawed at the chain cutting off his breath.

The team of horses reared, their steel-shod hooves catching the light. Chalmers Smythe ran and grabbed one of the lines. Otis Johnson dashed in and caught the horses' bridles and was lifted off the ground as the team reared again.

The Tattered Man grabbed the second, unfired pistol from the wounded Jarrett's hand and brought it to bear. His shot went wild as Gideon fired. The Tattered Man cried out "Godawmighty!" and sat down heavily, then collapsed onto his back.

Gideon ran toward Hack Latimer. Latimer's face was beet red, and his shoulders jerked. Gideon did not want Latimer choked to death: the man must answer for his crimes in court.

Before Gideon could get there, Latimer directed his pistol above and behind his head and pulled the trigger. The ball tore through the underside of John Horne's jaw and exited from the top of his head.

Others in the wagon screamed.

Gideon slammed Latimer in the face with his rifle's butt, and the sawmill man went down.

Brodie got up on one knee, her left arm dangling uselessly, her right hand clenching the shotgun against her side. True tried to aim the detonator at Brodie but her hand shook wildly. She thought about rushing in and holding the gun against the woman's head and pulling the trigger, but before she could move, Brodie's shotgun went off.

A deep rending *boom,* and Melchior Dorfman was bowled over backward.

Brodie dropped the shotgun, lurched to her feet, and went stumbling off past the corncrib.

True pointed the detonator at Brodie, yanked the trigger, and missed.

Jarrett, bleeding from a wound in his side, picked himself up and followed the big woman as she lumbered into the brush.

Pale smoke hung in the air. The smell of burnt gunpowder bit at Gideon's nose. He ran to Melchior Dorfman and went to his knees.

Dorfman's eyes found Gideon's. "My boys," he said. "Sarah, tell her . . . " He coughed, and blood came out of his mouth.

"Lieber Gott," Gideon said.

Dorfman stared fixedly at Gideon.

"I'll tell them," Gideon said. "I'll tell them how brave you are, Melchior." His heart froze at the thought of telling Sarah and Paul and Silas that their husband and father was dead. Because as he saw the wounds in the tinner's chest caused by the heavy shot, all of them gushing blood, he knew the man could not live.

Gideon laid his hand on Dorfman's cheek. The tinner's body convulsed.

Smythe came over. Gideon heard him curse in a strangled voice. Then he vomited.

A hand pulled at Gideon's shoulder. True said harshly: "We need to catch that woman and the man."

Gideon got up on shaky legs. He set his discharged rifle down and got the pistol out of his belt. He looked at the tinner again and saw that he was dead. He told Alonzo to stand guard over Latimer and the Tattered Man, even though Latimer appeared insensible and the Tattered Man lay on his back moaning with his hands gripping his leg where Gideon had shot him. Blood oozed out between the man's fingers.

Gideon and True advanced past the corncrib.

They ran into a wall of smoke that smelled different than the combusted black powder. The wadding from someone's gun or from several guns had set the dry vegetation on fire. Not just in one place, but in three, four, five places. Orange flames rose amid a loud crackling. Tan smoke billowed.

The wind fanned the fires into a blaze as tall as a man. Then as tall as the corncrib. The dry bunchgrass and sweetfern and low pitch pines ignited and flared. The wind sent the fire rolling south.

They heard the cries of the woman and the man hiding in the brush when the flames found them.

Ranaway, the negro, Hown—has a ring of iron on his left foot. Also, Grise, his *wife*, having a *ring and chain on the left leg.*

Chapter 44

⎯⎯❧❧⎯⎯

A LONZO DROVE THE WAGON. OTIS RODE ALONZO'S PAINT GELDING. Benjamin and Thomas doubled up on the Tattered Man's mule. Gideon, True, and Smythe rode their own horses, with Smythe ponying the sorrel gelding with the stiff hind leg, on which sat Amanda Jones. Felix Wiley had chosen to walk, saying that he was unfamiliar with riding horseback. The horses of William Jewell Jarrett and Hack Latimer followed behind the wagon on lead ropes; they had been ridden hard the night before when Jarrett raced to Adamant an hour behind Gideon, told Latimer that the sheriff had found out about their kidnapping operation, and the two hurried back and made ready to depart with the captives.

To Gideon, the bright sunny day seemed almost offensive in view of the terrible price that had been paid.

The bodies of Melchior Dorfman and John Horne lay in the wagon beneath blankets. On the other side of the bed, wrists and ankles chained, sat Hack Latimer and the Tattered Man. Latimer's face was bloody and swollen. The blow from Gideon's gun had broken his nose and likely his cheekbone as well. After Gideon struck him, Latimer had lain unconscious for half an hour, and, after waking, remained mute.

True had cleaned and bandaged the wound in the Tattered Man's thigh caused by the ball from Gideon's rifle, which passed through meat without striking bone or severing an artery. The man might live, Gideon reflected, if putrefaction didn't set in.

While True worked on his leg, the Tattered Man talked. He revealed his name: Gulliver Luck. He told Gideon that Latimer had hired him and Jarrett "to catch darkies for the money that's in it."

They planned to carry their captives to a slave trader of Latimer's acquaintance in Annapolis, Maryland, and sell them. Luck claimed that Latimer had instructed Jarrett to run down Phineas Potter with the wagon on the Halfmoon Valley road after Latimer lured the newspaperman there by telling him the rig was bringing in escaped slaves who needed help. Gideon asked why Latimer wanted Potter dead. "Hack reckoned the paperman was close to figuring out how the coloreds were being snatched," Luck had said. "God's truth, I didn't want no part in killing him. It was Bill run over him with the wagon and knocked him on the head." Luck had shaken his own head and sighed. "And now poor Billy is burned up and dead. Him and Liza both. Their souls absquatulated off this mortal coil."

At the old Brodie place, after the fire had swept past, Gideon and True walked out into the charred brushland and found the bodies. Their limbs were drawn up, the spidery remnants of their hands curled toward their blackened faces, like babies delivered from some smoking hellish womb. Beneath Brodie's corpse lay the keys to the captives' shackles.

Gideon, Alonzo, and Benjamin had taken turns digging a grave. They got the big woman into the hole. They fitted Jarrett in beside her. After they filled in the dirt, Alonzo cast around and found a chunk of pinkish sandstone lying in the weeds and placed it at the head of the grave.

★★★

At McGurk's Store, Gideon addressed Benjamin and Thomas. He pointed west down the road. "Frogville is that way. The Olcotts can bring this mule to the jail the next time they come to town."

Benjamin turned the mule, who brayed, wanting to stay with the group, but finally started walking.

McGurk came out of his store firing questions in his screechy voice. Gideon waved to him but didn't stop. Alonzo aimed the rig toward Adamant and flicked the reins.

By the time the party neared Hammertown, it was late afternoon. Gideon rode beside Otis. "You don't want to go through here in daylight," he said.

Chalmers Smythe said: "I know of a place." He pointed at a narrow track that branched off from the road a few rods farther on. "There's a cabin down that way, with folks that won't turn him in. Otis and me, we can go there now."

"Some people in town can help you get north," said Gideon, thinking of the headmaster and others in the anti-slavery society. "If that's what you want."

Otis dismounted from Alonzo's paint gelding and gave Gideon the reins.

"Goodbye, Otis," True said.

"Goodbye, True."

"You know where we live," Gideon said.

Amanda Jones got down off the sorrel that Smythe had been ponying. "I can walk from here," she said.

Smythe said that he and Otis would take his horse and the sorrel to the cabin so they could leave there in a hurry if need be.

"Where's Wiley?" Gideon asked.

Amanda Jones looked around. She frowned. "Gone, I guess."

★★★

In Hammertown, men and women came out of buildings and stood lining the street. People craned their necks to see. "That's Hack Latimer!" someone yelled. Men hoisted children onto their shoulders, and boys ran along beside the wagon. The horses clopped through the covered bridge and continued uphill toward the Diamond. In Adamant proper, folks came out of dwellings and shops, talking loudly and pointing.

As True rode, she kept an eye out for Gaither Brown, intending to ride up close and spit on him. She didn't see him. But she knew the story of his cowardice would sweep through town like a Barrens wildfire.

At the jail, Gideon and Alonzo locked Latimer and Luck in cells. Gideon came back out to find a crowd. He wondered if anyone had tried to pull the blankets off Dorfman and Horne so they could gawk. True sat there on Jack with her arm across over her chest, holding the detonator in plain view. The bodies had not been disturbed.

Gideon sent a boy to get Dr. Beecham to come treat the jailed men.

He climbed up on the wagon, picked up the reins, and clucked to the bays. The crowd parted. True rode along behind the wagon with Amanda Jones walking beside her.

More people had gathered at the Dorfmans' house. A man stepped up to hold the team. Gideon got down, weary in his body, bleak in his mind. True came and put her arm through his, and together they went to the house. Gideon knocked, and the door swung open. Grief shrouded Sarah Dorfman's face. Her boys were big-eyed and silent.

"I am truly sorry," Gideon said. He knew how the woman must feel, having been stunned himself in the past by sudden violent loss. And Paul and Silas: they would never talk to their father again, learn from him, absorb his wisdom and guidance; they would never feel his arms enfolding them or his strong and confident handclasp. *Lieber Gott*, Gideon thought again. "Melchior was very brave," he said to Mrs. Dorfman and her sons. "So was his friend John Horne."

"He gave his life for us," Amanda Jones said. She went to embrace Sarah Dorfman, who raised her own hands and shoved Amanda backward.

"Get away from me, whore," the tinner's wife said savagely. Then, to some men standing nearby: "Help me get them in the house."

Ran away, Mary, a negro woman and two children; a few days before she went off, *I burnt her with a hot iron*, on the left side of her face, *I tried to make the letter M*.

Chapter 45

⸺⸺◦⸘◦⸺⸺

P EOPLE IN THE STREET PEPPERED GIDEON WITH QUESTIONS, WHICH he fended off or ignored. True thought her husband looked as exhausted and saddened as she had ever seen him.

"I got two good men killed," Gideon said to her. "What a waste."

"It was my fault Dorfman died," True said, her voice choking. "I didn't shoot that woman before she killed him. It was like I suddenly panicked." She swallowed hard, clutched for Gideon. They held each other as the people around them quieted.

Finally they let go. When Gideon hauled himself up on the wagon's seat, it seemed to take every ounce of his strength. He turned the rig around. True got up on Jack.

They took the wagon and horses to the livery. "Let's go home," True said.

"I need to stop at the jail." Gideon knew he should also inform the state's attorney about the gunfight and the arrests. But he did not want to deal with the Cold Fish now. Gideon decided to write a report later and have Alonzo deliver it.

Step by weary step, he and True trudged along.

"I hate what happened," he said.

"I hate it, too," True said. "But if we hadn't gone, those people would have been sold into slavery for the rest of their lives."

They parted at the jail.

Inside, Alonzo told Gideon that the doctor had treated Latimer and Luck. The Belknaps had shown up, inquiring about the fracas in the Barrens. "They want to put it in their paper. I didn't tell them nothing. Not a thing! Except to come back later and talk to you."

Gideon nodded. He felt even wearier and gloomier knowing that he would have to go over the incident again and again.

"Payton's Tavern is sending some food for us and our guests," Alonzo added. "Beefsteaks for us, beans for Hack and that other villain."

"Can you take care of things here?" Gideon asked. "I want to go home."

Alonzo nodded. "Mind if I eat your steak?"

★★★

Gideon came close to falling asleep as he sat forking food into his mouth.

"Do you think Smythe will bring Otis here tonight?" True asked him.

"He'd be better off staying at that cabin."

"I have a bad feeling about that."

"Smythe can be trusted. I'm sure he'll protect him."

The setter, Old Dick, curled up near the fire, suddenly jumped to his feet and started growling.

A knock at the door. True hurried and opened it.

A boy stood on the stoop, a white lad with a grimy face. "I got something to tell the Dutch Sheriff," he said.

"Come in," True said.

Gideon recognized the boy. A fortnight ago, he had met him on the street in Hammertown hauling water: Gideon had asked the young man if he'd seen a colored lad about his own age. The boy had cadged a nickel off him, then laughed and said he would let Gideon know if he happened to lay eyes on a "blackbird" like that.

The boy sauntered over to the table and looked at the food.

"Set yourself down," True said.

The boy sat. He picked up a piece of cornbread in his dirty paws and crammed it in his mouth. "What I have to tell you," he said to Gideon, crumbs falling out of his gob, "is worth a damn sight more than five cents."

True set a loaded plate in front of him, and a knife and fork, and the boy started shoveling food into his mouth.

Gideon said: "What?"

"A dollar," said the boy, munching steadily. "That's what it will cost you."

"A dollar is a lot of money."

"You want to know what happened to that little blackbird, then hand it over."

True went in the bedroom, got out the old sock with the money she had made from selling baskets, extracted several coins, and returned to the kitchen.

The boy swallowed what was in his mouth. He held out his hand to True.

"The last time I gave you money," Gideon said, "you did not have anything to say. Tell me what you know, and I will judge whether it's worth a dollar."

The lad went back to eating.

True laid the coins next to his plate.

The boy put his fork down and pocketed the money.

"They snatched him. The one with the two-hunnert-dollar reward on his head."

"Who snatched him?" Gideon blurted.

"Four men from Hammertown. They bust into Gert Hendershot's cabin and give Chalmers Smythe a good licking and took the boy."

Gideon shot out of his chair. "When?"

" 'Bout an hour ago."

"How do you know this?"

"I seen it. Gert is my ma. They knocked her around some, too. 'Cause she took up with Smythe, and him being colored. I got out and hid behind a tree. I trailed them roughies back to Hammertown and saw what they done with the boy. Then I came here to tell you."

"What did they do with him?"

The boy grinned. "Cost you another dollar to find out."

Gideon kicked the boy off the chair with the flat of his boot, then grabbed his shirt and hauled him to a standing position.

He lifted the lad up on his toes and brought the boy's visage within an inch of his own face. His slashed and battered face.

"All right! They handed him over to the two Virginians. They got paid. They give some of the money to the one that told 'em where he was at—a colored man, used to work at Annie's. Then one of the Southrons tied the boy's hands and put him on a horse behind the other one. A big white horse."

"Where did they go?"

"Crossed the bridge and went south. That's the last I seen of 'em."

Gideon let the boy go. "How is Smythe?"

"Beat up. Missing some teeth. My ma will patch him up."

The boy snatched the last piece of cornbread and darted out the door.

True set about loading her detonator. Gideon had no gun and no time to get one. He told her what he thought they should do.

They chained Old Dick in the yard. Rather than hiking back across town to the livery, they took a shortcut down a steep hill to the main road. They turned south and jogged and walked and jogged until they came to Ike Fye's farm a mile out of town. Gideon quickly explained why they needed two fresh horses and a gun. Fye brought out a pistol, powder, and balls. As Gideon loaded the piece, he told Fye that two of the men who had murdered Phineas Potter were now in custody, and the third killer was dead. Fye nodded and headed off to the barn.

Fye gave Gideon his own riding horse, a bay mare. He handed True the reins of the black gelding Barney, Phineas Potter's horse.

"I want the whole story later," Fye said. "Straight from the horse's mouth. Good luck to you now."

On the road again, Gideon asked True if she could canter.

"Jack does it whenever I cut a switch," she said.

They cantered on straight stretches where the road was good. Ragged clouds made pink by the setting sun rimmed the sky in the east. As the clouds dulled and the land fell into shadow, they slowed the horses to a trot, then a walk. Gideon's whole body ached. He wished he could get off his horse, lie down beside the road, and sleep.

The gelding beneath True moved her up and down in a steady walk.

"This could be a long ride," Gideon said.

"Yes."

The road went through farmland. It climbed toward a gap in the ridge where a wall of trees marked the edge of the forest cloaking the Seven Mountains.

Something pale emerged from the gap.

"Stop," True said.

She peered ahead, her heart pounding. Then realized it was not a glimmering apparition approaching them on the road. It was a white horse, with a rider on its back.

She drew her detonator from the saddlebag.

Gideon got out his pistol.

Ranaway, Sam, he was *shot* a short time since, through the hand, and has *several shots in his left arm and side.*

Chapter 46

⟨∘⟩

TAZEWELL WALLER SAT ON THE WHITE STALLION BOAZ. THE STALlion halted twenty feet from Gideon and True. It danced a little and sidestepped, revealing Otis Johnson seated behind Waller. Otis held a pistol in both hands, its hammer cocked, its muzzle shoved into Waller's back.

Three horse lengths behind, Franklin Blaine stopped his dark bay. Blaine also held a cocked pistol in his hand.

"I'm glad to see you, Sheriff," Waller said. "We have a situation here. I hope you can resolve it."

Gideon held his own pistol in his lap. He wondered how Otis had managed to get hold of that gun.

"I can kill you," Otis said to Waller. "All I need to do is pull this trigger."

"Don't be hasty, Leo," Waller said.

"Tell me what happened, Otis," Gideon said.

"Some men grabbed me and turned me over to him. I am not going back. If I pull the trigger, the one back there—" he jerked his head toward Blaine—"he says he'll shoot me."

"Sheriff, I appeal to your reason and your sense of justice," Waller said. "I am Leo's lawful owner. I am permitted by federal law to take him home to Red Rose. He will be treated kindly there. He will live a good life among family and friends. Red Rose is a fine home, governed by rules and fairness, a place of prosperity and peace."

"No such thing," Otis said. "I have seen men and women whipped bloody. Made to wear collars like dogs."

"Sheriff, I know that you and your wife harbored Leo in your home," Waller said. "I am prepared to ignore that violation of the law. Which would surely cost you your job were it made known. All I ask is that you explain one thing to Leo: that he must accept life the way it is."

"You asked me to resolve this situation, Mr. Waller," Gideon said. "I will do so. I will arrest you and Mr. Blaine for violating the Pennsylvania Fugitive Slave Act by kidnapping this young man. You will be held in jail and then prosecuted. If you are found guilty, you will serve a long sentence in the penitentiary."

"Hogwash," Waller said.

"Tell Mr. Blaine to put away his weapon and raise his hands," Gideon said.

"That will not happen, sir!" cried Blaine, pointing his pistol at Gideon.

True aimed the detonator at Blaine's heart. It steadied there.

"Everyone stop!" Gideon said. "Don't make a mistake, Blaine. My wife shot a man already today." He let out a long breath. "There is another way forward. Mr. Waller, I don't need to arrest you. But you must accept the fact that you are not taking Otis with you. As sure as the sun has set, and as sure as it will rise again tomorrow, you will not carry him back into slavery.

"All of us, we will ride to Adamant," Gideon continued. "Tomorrow, you will draft a legal document setting Otis free— forever, with no conditions attached. You will give your word that you will not try to catch him again. You will go back to Virginia and never return to Colerain County again."

"No," Waller said.

"Then I pull the trigger," Otis said. "I will count down from five. Five. Four. Three."

"You'd do it?" Waller asked, his voice high and tight. "Murder me in front of the sheriff?"

Gideon glanced quickly at True. She still leveled her detonator at Blaine's heart. Gideon looked down the barrel of Blaine's pistol. Another bloodbath. More horror and death.

"Two. One."

"Wait!" Waller collapsed forward toward the stallion's arching neck. "I will sign," he gasped. "I will give you your freedom."

"I already took it," Otis said.

Merry Ewell, a FREE NEGRO from Virginia, was committed to jail, at Snow Hill, Md., last week, for remaining in the State longer than is allowed by the law of 1831. The fine in his case amounts to $225. Capril Purnell, a negro from Delaware, is now in jail in the same place, for a violation of the same act. His fine amounts to FOUR THOUSAND DOLLARS, and he WILL BE SOLD IN A SHORT TIME.

Chapter 47

TRUE GOT UP EARLY AND STARTED COOKING. SHE TRIED TO WORK quietly to keep from waking Otis, who slept bundled in blankets on the kitchen floor with Old Dick beside him. But the dog's tail-thumping woke the lad. He got up and stretched. He looked at True and smiled.

She smiled back, then went into the bedroom and roused Gideon. "There is much to do," she said.

He got up creaky and sore but with the anticipation that coffee would fix things to a certain extent.

When True checked the cut on his face, she made a quiet sound of satisfaction. "It's not infected."

Breakfast was ham, potatoes, and toasted bread with butter and jam. Nobody said much as they ate. In his mind Gideon kept seeing Melchior Dorfman falling backward after the big woman's gun went off. And John Horne, when Hack Latimer pulled the trigger. After a while, he laid down his fork.

He excused himself and headed for the jail. It was a fine spring day, with birds calling madly from the trees and clouds scudding across a blue sky on a fresh breeze. He went into Gaither Brown's leather shop, and when Brown looked up from his work, Gideon said, "You no longer work as a deputy in this county. Not while I am the sheriff." Before Brown could reply, Gideon left.

At the jail he looked in on Latimer and Luck in their cells. Seeing Gideon, Luck lifted his bandaged leg with both hands, swung it off the edge of his cot, and sat up straight. "I hope I see you well, Sheriff." He bared his broken brown teeth in a smile. "That nick in your face looks to be healing good. Bill Jarrett give you that. I stopped him from hooking out your eyeball. You remember?"

"Yes. And I remember you talking about killing me in three or four different ways." Luck was in his stocking feet. "The boots we took from you? We will show them to the shoemaker. I think he will tell us they were made for Phineas Potter. And I think you had a lot more to do with his murder than you told me yesterday."

Luck's smile faded.

Gideon would keep up the pressure. If Fish agreed to reduce the charges against Luck—perhaps limiting them to robbery and kidnapping—he was almost certain that Luck would testify against Latimer for arranging the murder of Phineas Potter. He doubted Fish would bring charges against Latimer for killing John Horne.

And then there was Annie Picard. Amanda Jones was staying with a family who had agreed to house and feed her. Gideon planned to take a statement from her on how Madame Picard had betrayed her and Felix Wiley to the kidnappers. Picard's strongman Pierre must have been involved. Gideon reckoned it was Latimer and Pierre who had choked and beaten him and thrown him into the creek that night in Hammertown, although it was unlikely they would be prosecuted for that act.

Latimer lay on his cot staring up at the ceiling.

"How are you feeling?" Gideon asked him.

The man mumbled something like "Not so good." His face was hugely swollen and blotched with yellow and purple and black.

"Why did you do it?" Gideon asked. "Why did you kill Potter and kidnap those people?"

Latimer said weakly: "A man . . . is entitled to make of himself what he can."

Gideon shook his head and left.

***

At home, he handed Otis the paper Waller had signed and gotten notarized at the courthouse. "Keep this safe."

They needed to return the two horses borrowed from Ike Fye. Gideon had brought them, saddled, from the livery stable. "You should go with us," he told Otis.

"Ride up double behind me," True said. They rode the horses at a walk, taking in the sight of the hills cloaked in new pale green, almost luminescent against the blue sky.

At the farm, Gideon introduced Otis to Fye.

After shaking hands, Otis stood and looked out at the grass fields with horses of different colors, the long mountain ridges carrying beyond. He remembered lying in bed in the attic room of the fancy stone house in Adamant, scared and bored, trying to imagine something good with him in it, and the scene that had come to his mind, that had cheered him and given him courage, was much like the one now before him.

He turned to Fye. "Sir, I am good with horses. Been around them all my life. I can ride them and train them. Even doctor them. Gideon says you need help on this place. I could do that."

"Live here? Work here?"

"For a while, anyway."

Fye got a thoughtful look on his face. After a moment, he smiled. "When would you want to start?"

"How about now?"

Acknowledgments

⸺⸺⸻

B EFORE WRITING *LAY THIS BODY DOWN*, I READ MANY BOOKS AND
articles about slavery, politics, and culture in pre–Civil War
America. The following works were especially helpful:

The Abolitionist Imagination, Andrew Delbanco, Harvard University Press, 2012.

The Fires of Jubilee: Nat Turner's Fierce Rebellion, Stephen B. Oates,
Harper & Row, 1975.

*Four Hundred Souls: A Community History of African America,
1619–2019*, edited by Ibram X. Kendi and Keisha N. Blain, One
World, 2021.

*Freedom at Risk: The Kidnapping of Free Blacks in America, 1780–
1865*, Carol Wilson, University Press of Kentucky, 1994.

Slavery and the Underground Railroad in South Central Pennsylvania,
Cooper H. Wingert, The History Press, 2016.

*Stolen: Five Free Boys Kidnapped into Slavery and Their Astonishing
Odyssey Home*, Richard Bell, Simon & Schuster, 2019.

*The War Before the War: Fugitive Slaves and the Struggle for America's
Soul from the Revolution to the Civil War*, Andrew Delbanco, Penguin
Press, 2018.

The advertisements and notices for fugitives from slavery that
begin each chapter come from Freedom on the Move, a database
supported by Cornell University; from *American Slavery as It Is*, by
Theodore Dwight Weld, published in 1839 by the American Anti-
Slavery Society; and from articles and images found online. Some of

the descriptions have been edited for brevity. All are haunting. Many are stunning in their casual depiction of torture and extreme cruelty.

I received important feedback on the novel from my wife, the author Nancy Marie Brown. I was also helped by Barbara Franco, Cathy Miles Grant, Lamont Newton, Alice Ryan, and Mark Winston. I'm thankful for their reading the manuscript and offering their reactions.

I also thank my agent, Natalia Aponte. My excellent editor at Skyhorse/Arcade, Lilly Golden, helped shape the story and was a source of astute advice and ongoing support.

Thanks to Claire Van Vliet, who created the handsome map of Colerain County, and to Erin Seaward-Hiatt for her compelling cover design for this and two earlier Gideon Stoltz mysteries.

Excerpt from
A Stranger Here Below

And if on earth we meet no more,
O may we meet on Canaan's shore

One

———◊◊◊———

GIDEON STOLTZ STOOD IN THE DARKNESS, SHOTGUN IN HIS HANDS. His breath clouded in the chill air. He didn't see light in any of the windows in Judge Biddle's house. Had the judge overslept?

Yesterday, on the way home from hunting grouse, they'd passed a pond where ducks were coming in. The judge had stopped the wagon and, in the evening light, they had sat side by side on the hard bench seat and watched the ducks fly over, heard the rapid *whick-whick-whick* of their wings, then splashes as one, and another, and another lit on the water and began quacking.

Gideon had suggested they come back first thing the next morning. He was the county sheriff; young for that job. He respectfully pointed out to his friend and mentor, Judge Hiram Biddle, that the pond was no more than a quarter hour's walk from town. They wouldn't need the wagon. Tramp there, get in a quick hunt, and be back in time for the day to begin.

Finally, the judge had nodded.

Now Gideon stood fidgeting in the dark outside the judge's house. In his mind's eye he could already see the ducks floating on the water, bright as jewels. He and Judge Biddle would creep up on the pond. At first light they would rise up together on the brushy bank. Startled, the ducks would lift off. He imagined the brilliant streams of water trailing from their bellies as their wings grabbed the air, mallards with emerald heads and sprigs with long pointed tails and wood ducks with ruby eyes and speckled breasts. How many would they get? He could practically taste roast duck already.

He waited for what he figured was another five minutes. Clearly the judge wasn't out of bed, and his housekeeper, Mrs. Leathers, hadn't arrived yet.

Five more minutes passed. Still no sign of activity from within: no sudden glow as a lamp was lit, no muffled footfalls, no creaking of stairs.

He walked around back to where the judge kept Old Nick. The red setter danced at the end of his chain and whimpered and licked Gideon's hand. When Gideon returned to the front of the house, the dog started barking. Surely that would rouse the judge.

Nothing.

He tried the door. Unlocked. He knew it was a presumptuous thing to do, but he let himself in anyway. He closed the door behind him and stood in the entry. All he could hear was the ticking of the big walnut-cased clock in the judge's study. Gideon knew how the house was laid out: the judge had invited him there for drinks and conversation. They were friends, improbable as that sometimes seemed, the young sheriff from away and the senior jurist who'd had a long and distinguished career in Colerain County. Friends united by their love of sport, the admirable hunt, the gentlemanly art the judge called "shooting-flying."

He called out: "Judge Biddle?"

Nothing.

He leaned his shotgun in a corner, felt his way down the hall, and turned left into the kitchen. Well, they'd be late, but maybe the ducks would still be on the pond. He put his hand on the stove, felt a remnant warmth. A lamp sat on the table. He opened the stove's door. He picked up the poker and prodded around inside the firebox until he saw an orange glow. He got a splint from the tin box on the mantel, held it to the ember, and blew on it gently. He smelled brimstone as the splint flared. He carried it to the lamp, lifted the globe, and held the flame to the wick.

"Judge Biddle?" he called again.

Dead silence. And now he began to worry.

He told himself that Hiram Biddle must still be asleep in bed. The fact that his calling had gotten no response didn't necessarily mean there was a problem. The judge was old. A bit hard of hearing. And no doubt worn out from slogging through the brush all yesterday. Or maybe he was ill—maybe he'd been stricken with an attack of some sort, maybe even expired in his bed. Gideon shook his head and tried to banish that thought.

Holding the lamp in front of him, he went down the hall. He looked into the dining room. Chairs were neatly positioned on both sides of the drop leaf table. He checked the parlor. No one there. The door to the judge's study was half-open. He pushed it the rest of the way.

His nostrils flared at the acrid smell of combusted gunpowder. The tang of blood, like wet hay gone sour, hung in the air. Cutting through those scents, the stench of *dreck*.

Judge Biddle sat sprawled in a chair. He didn't move. In the center of the judge's chest a fist-sized hole punched through his vest. At the edges of the hole the green woolen cloth was charred black.

Gideon groaned. He almost dropped the lamp but managed to set it on the table with a clatter, the flame leaping wildly. He felt a weird prickling sensation gather in the center of his back, then spread out across his shoulders. It almost took his breath away. He knew the feeling, remembered it from the past.

Judge Biddle's eyes were half-open. His head lolled back. His cheeks and forehead were chalk white, his nose pinched and greenish. Blood had pooled in his mouth, run down the side of his neck, and dried there. The chair in which he sat faced the table. The judge's shotgun lay on the table, its buttstock braced against the wall, its twin muzzles aimed at the judge in his chair.

Lieber Gott.

Gideon felt his spine stiffen. Looking at the judge, he no longer saw the body of his friend. Instead he saw something that had dwelt in the back of his mind for years, crouching there like some fearsome ungovernable beast, always ready to spring forth.

"*Memmi*," he whispered.

He saw her plain as day. Lying on the floor, her skirt rucked up around her waist. Her one leg, bruised, wedged against the *brodehonk*. Right there in the *kich* where she always was, where she cooked their meals, where she baked those pies—he liked shoo-fly the best, the gooey kind with plenty of *molosich*—all the goodies she knew he loved, cookies and cobblers, cakes and pies. They smelled like she did, warm and good. Now what he smelled was blood and *dreck*. The air in the kitchen had seemed to be blinking. It pulsed with yellow and purple light. The world had held still for a moment; then it had shuddered into motion again, a new and terrifying place.

He shook his head, forced a deep breath, and made himself return to the here and now. *This is not my mother. But it is bad.* Yesus Chrishtus, *it's bad. Judge Biddle. Dead! Killed by his own hand.*

He heard a rustling and jerked his head around. He came back solidly to the present when he found himself staring into the face of Alma Leathers, Judge Biddle's housekeeper. She stood in the doorway of the judge's study, in the elegant house on Franklin Street, in the town of Adamant, Pennsylvania, in the year 1835. And Gideon was not a ten-year-old boy any longer, but a man of twenty-two.

Mrs. Leathers had hold of the doorjamb. Slowly she slid down it until she was kneeling on the floor, her legs hidden beneath voluminous skirts. She pulled her eyes away from the judge and fixed them on Gideon's. Their gray irises were ringed with white.

"No," she said. She looked at him, seeming to beseech him—as if he could somehow turn the clock back and make things right again.

So many times he had wished he could do that for his *memmi*.

"I waited around for a while and then let myself in," he stammered. "We were going out hunting. Ducks. A big flock of them on a pond. We saw them last night."

"No!" she said again.

He helped her to her feet. The room was growing light from the day coming on. The tall clock in the corner ticked loudly, implacably, ticking away the seconds, ticking away life.

"Go out to the kitchen," he told Mrs. Leathers. "Start the fire. Make some coffee. I will take care of things here."

She turned and walked woodenly down the hallway.

He looked back at the judge, his friend and hunting partner, the man he most admired in the town, slumped in the chair, dead.

He tried to unkink his shoulders and draw air into his lungs. He looked around the room. A poker lay on the floor beside the judge's chair. No overturned furniture, no belongings strewn about, nothing suggesting that an assault or a robbery—or a murder—had taken place.

Next to the judge's shotgun lay a paper with writing on it, held down by a book. He set the book aside, picked up the sheet, and read: a date, some legal verbiage about this being the last will and testament of Hiram Biddle, and superseding all others, and being of sound mind—*How could anyone of sound mind have done this?* His brain barely registered the words until he saw his own name.

I leave my setter, Old Nick, to Gideon Stoltz, Sheriff of the County of Colerain, Commonwealth of Pennsylvania. I leave my Manton shotgun, including gun slip, case, and contents thereof, to Gideon Stoltz the same. I leave the spring wagon, my shooting brake, to Gideon Stoltz, also the bay horse Jack, along with harness and tack. The remainder of my estate, house and grounds, carriage, furniture, household goods, and personal belongings, shall be sold at auction and the proceeds used for the upkeep and betterment of the County Home for the Poor and Indigent.

Instructions for a coffin, funeral, headstone. The judge's signature at the bottom of the page. Nothing else. No reason given why Judge Biddle had killed himself.

Gideon read through the will again. It seemed carefully written and logically ordered—although it must have issued from a deeply troubled mind.

A mind he thought he knew. A keen mind that dispensed a balanced justice in court. A mind that planned their hunts with an almost military precision. He remembered the judge just yesterday saying in his even, matter-of-fact tone: "The wind has now turned into the north. Let us hunt up the steep gully and give Old Nick the advantage of having the scent in his nose." Gideon wished they were there now, on the piece of ground the judge called Seek No Further on account of an apple tree of that variety growing near the cellar hole of a failed homestead, beneath which there always seemed to be a grouse. He wished they could wade into the brush following the setter. A breeze combing the maples, their leaves fluttering red-white-red-white, the tang of fallen apples, the toasted-bread scent of frost.

Instead he smelled blood and *dreck* and the musty air of a cold room.

He said to himself: *You have tasks. Now do them.*

But what could he do beyond saying a prayer, informing the state's attorney of this dreadful event, and seeing to it that Hiram Biddle's body went gentle into the ground?